The truth was t
little too cozy.

Between the children, whom he liked, and the mother-in-law, who had a right to be suspicious, Sam was definitely out of his element.

The beautiful Lucia Swallow, with all that silky black hair and laughing eyes and a body that a goddess would envy, had tempted him. Loneliness had made him stupid. Boredom had made him reckless.

Lucia needed a man like Jerry Thompson, a guy with roots. Sam had walked past Jerry's house on his way to buy the flowers. It was an impressive home, easily the grandest in town. Sam shuddered at the thought of living in a home like that. He'd spent much of his childhood dreaming of escaping the house with the wide staircase and the gleaming floors.

He'd been crazy to invite himself to go with Lucia to the concert, but he didn't know how to get out of it without lying to her.

Dear Reader,

Merry Christmas to all of you! I love writing Christmas stories, especially with children in them. I am in Texas this December, with a little boy who loves dump trucks and bulldozers. It's good to see toys under the tree again.

Last fall, after spending three months without television, the first show I watched in a Montana motel room was something I'd never seen before: *River Monsters,* on the Animal Planet channel. I have never pretended to be the least bit outdoorsy, but there was something about the combination of myth, mystery, dangerous locations and fishing for "the big one" that entranced me. I was, if you'll forgive the expression, hooked. The show's host, handsome and articulate adventurer Jeremy Wade, had his own appeal, so I gave *The Husband Project's* hero some of Mr. Wade's adventurous attributes.

I so hope you love the townspeople of Willing, Montana, as much as I do. I've spent so many months with them and want them all to live happily ever after. I'd love to hear from you and promise to answer any and all emails. Thank you so much for spending time in Willing with me.

Love,

Kristine Rolofson

kristinerolofson@hotmail.com
www.kristinerolofson.wordpress.com
www.welcometowillingmontana.wordpress.com

HARLEQUIN HEARTWARMING

Kristine Rolofson

The Husband Project

⊷ Willing to Wed ⊷

HARLEQUIN® HEARTWARMING™

If you purchased this book without a cover you should be aware that this book is stolen property. It was reported as "unsold and destroyed" to the publisher, and neither the author nor the publisher has received any payment for this "stripped book."

Recycling programs
for this product may
not exist in your area.

ISBN-13: 978-0-373-36652-1

THE HUSBAND PROJECT

Copyright © 2013 by Kristine Rolofson

All rights reserved. Except for use in any review, the reproduction or utilization of this work in whole or in part in any form by any electronic, mechanical or other means, now known or hereafter invented, including xerography, photocopying and recording, or in any information storage or retrieval system, is forbidden without the written permission of the publisher, Harlequin Enterprises Limited, 225 Duncan Mill Road, Don Mills, Ontario, Canada M3B 3K9.

This is a work of fiction. Names, characters, places and incidents are either the product of the author's imagination or are used fictitiously, and any resemblance to actual persons, living or dead, business establishments, events or locales is entirely coincidental.

This edition published by arrangement with Harlequin Books S.A.

For questions and comments about the quality of this book, please contact us at CustomerService@Harlequin.com.

® and TM are trademarks of Harlequin Enterprises Limited or its corporate affiliates. Trademarks indicated with ® are registered in the United States Patent and Trademark Office, the Canadian Trade Marks Office and in other countries.

Printed in U.S.A.

KRISTINE ROLOFSON

Author of more than forty novels for Harlequin,
Kristine Rolofson (along with her husband of forty-two
years) divides her time between Rhode Island, Idaho
and Texas, where her handsome and brilliant grandson
entertains her with drum solos. When not writing, she
quilts, bakes peach pies, plays the fiddle and sings in a
country blues band. She collects vintage cowboy boots
and will not tell you how many are in her closet.

To Glen, who watched endless hours of *River Monsters* with me and did everything he could to be quiet while I wrote this book.

CHAPTER ONE

S<small>AM</small> H<small>OVE</small> <small>TOLD</small> three people where he was going.

His agent was thrilled at the news. Surely in a place without temptations Sam would finish writing his book at last. The manuscript was long overdue and, according to Robert, was certain to be well received. At least by fellow anglers and zoologists.

His doctor took note of the location. Willing, Montana? Where the heck was that? He then reminded Sam to call if he had any questions and wished him luck. He also asked Sam to autograph a photo for his kids.

His best friend and cameraman— Well, who knew what he thought, since he'd been much harder to contact directly. Russ was in the Amazon again. Sam had left a message in Belize with Russ's latest unstable girlfriend. Russ preferred women "on the edge," he'd once explained. Sam kept his opinions to himself. Women—"on the edge" or otherwise—were either a luxury or an irritation that Sam couldn't afford.

Not that it mattered to a man with a damaged heart and three cracked ribs.

A surprisingly easy flight dropped him and his two battered leather bags in Billings, where he'd arranged, via the internet, for transportation to Willing. Finding a way to make getting to Willing work hadn't been easy, but Sam had tracked down someone online who knew someone who knew someone. Samuel Barlow Hove was accustomed to getting wherever he wanted to go. In fact, he'd made a living out of it.

A tall young man standing next to a black Cadillac SUV the size of a tank waved at him. He'd parked along the curb and seemed oblivious to the swirling snow.

"Mr. Hove?"

"Theo Porterman?"

"Yes, sir," the young man replied, and walked swiftly over to shake Sam's hand. He looked about twenty-five, with a large square face, an easy smile and hands like a wrestler's. Theo happened to be an auto mechanic who lived in Willing and he supplemented his income by chauffeuring when a trip happened to coincide with picking up auto parts.

"You visiting someone in town, Mr. Hove?" Theo, wearing a flannel shirt, thick vest and jeans, hefted Sam's two bags into the backseat, then settled himself behind the wheel. He kept his leather gloves on. "Cold day," he said, adjusting the heater knobs.

"Sam. And no, I'm working," he replied, climbing awkwardly into the passenger seat. He'd known Montana would be cold, but the wind and the snow surprised him. He was grateful for his new wool shirt and down jacket, not to mention the waterproof boots, all compliments of Cabela's online catalog.

He shivered and made a mental note to order more wool socks. The landlord had promised internet service, along with other amenities.

"So you're working in Willing? You must be from California." Theo headed west on the interstate and turned on the windshield wipers to bat away the splats of snow hitting the glass.

"Why is that?"

"We've had some Hollywood people

visiting here lately." Theo turned the defroster knob.

"No, I'm from—" He hesitated, thinking over his reply. He leased a room in Florida when he wasn't working in the Amazon and had avoided his home state of New York for almost twenty years. "I've recently been working in South America."

"Really? I've never been there. What do you do?"

"I work on documentaries. And I'm a writer," he admitted. "Sometimes."

"Like now?"

"Yeah. Like now." Sam looked out the window and saw nothing green. Just gray and white and flat, which was pretty much what he'd expected. How long had it been since he'd seen snow? And why had he thought he wanted to live in it for the next three months? He ignored the renewed aching in his side and attempted to make conversation. "I hear Willing is a pretty small town."

"You've never been there?"

"Not yet."

"Huh?"

Clearly, that baffled the driver, so Sam tried to explain.

"A guy I met told me about it. I needed a quiet place to write for a few months. Someplace the opposite of a jungle."

"It's quiet in Willing all right. Most of the time. You can't tell now," Theo said, fiddling with the defroster. "But there's no town prettier in the spring or summer or fall. Too bad you won't be here longer so you could see for yourself."

"I guess I'll just have to take your word for it," Sam said. "I'll be out of here before April."

"You're staying at Meg's?"

"Meg's?"

"She has some cabins for rent at the Willing Café," Theo explained. "They're small, but okay for one person long-term, I imagine."

"Uh, no. I don't think so." He pulled a worn notebook from his jacket pocket and thumbed through it until he found the address. "I'm renting a house from Willing Properties. Two eighty Janet Street. An executive rental."

"An executive rental," Theo echoed.

"Didn't know we had any of those in Willing. What exactly is that, if you don't mind my asking?"

Sam shrugged, then wished he hadn't. It had caused his ribs to ache. He made himself cough to get more air in his lungs and ease the discomfort. "It's better than a hotel room, more like an apartment. Short-term. At least, that's my understanding." He checked his notes. "Jerry Thompson is the agent."

Theo thought that over for a long minute. "You're renting Mrs. Kelly's house," he said at last. "She died last summer."

"Oh?" Sam tucked the notebook in his front jacket pocket and winced.

"Peacefully," Theo added, giving Sam a sideways glance. "In the hospital."

Sam supposed Theo didn't want him to be upset about staying in a home where the former occupant had died. He wasn't about to explain he was wincing from the pain of his cracked ribs, not because someone had passed away in his future home.

"Was she a friend of yours?" Sam inquired.

"Well…she and my grandmother went to school together. Her husband had a '56 Ford

Thunderbird hardtop convertible," Theo mused. "Fiesta-red. A real beauty. It's still in her garage. I'd love to get my hands on that one."

"I'll bet," Sam said, knowing little about cars but wanting to be congenial.

"Jerry hasn't figured out what he wants to do with it." Theo glanced over at Sam. "Did he say you could drive it?"

"No." Nothing had been said about a car. Sam assumed he could walk wherever he needed to go. Or hire Theo. "Do you know Jerry well?"

"Oh, yeah. He's the mayor. You'll meet him soon enough. Ambitious guy. He's buying up the town."

"Really." This was Sam's attempt to make conversation without really conversing. "Why?"

Now Theo shrugged. "He's from California. And I guess he likes buying houses. Jerry figures that Willing is going to make a comeback and real estate prices will rise again."

Sam knew nothing about real estate prices and didn't want to, but he couldn't sit there in silence. He shifted in the big comfortable seat and prepared to ignore the ache settling deep in his chest. "Is there any fishing around there?"

"In Willing?" At Sam's nod, he shook his head. "There are some decent-sized fish in the Judith, but not too many people want to work that hard to catch a trout. Access is tough."

Ah, thought Sam, adjusting his seat belt so he could breathe a little easier. Good news.

"You doin' okay? Got enough heat?"

"Fine, thanks. It's been a long day. I had a bit of health trouble a few weeks ago and I'm still not over it."

Theo shot him a worried look. "You don't look too good."

"I'll be okay. It's getting better."

"There's a real good clinic in Lewistown. We'll be going through there if you need to get checked out."

"I just need a bed and some rest," Sam said. "But thanks for the offer."

"No problem. My cousin Hip is an EMT. You can always call him if you need anything. We live right around the corner at Main and Joyce, two blocks down from the Kelly place."

"I gather Willing's not a big town?"

"Heck, no. We've got a bar, a restaurant, a couple of B and Bs, a hot dog shack and the usual grade school, church, community center, library—well, sort of—and a couple of stores." He grinned. "I hope you're not looking for excitement."

"Just the opposite," Sam assured him.

"We had some television folks here a few weeks ago, though. That had everybody stirred up for a while. We hoped something would come of it, but Jerry says these things take time."

"What kind of things?" Sam stared out the window, hoping to see something other than gray, snow-covered ground and whirling snowflakes, but Interstate 90 disappointed him once again. He leaned his head back against the leather seat and closed his eyes.

"Just an idea Jerry had to generate a little publicity."

Sam heard the click of a radio button, then the muted sounds of guitars and fiddles accompanying a sweet-voiced female singer.

"Do you mind the radio?"

"Not at all." He didn't open his eyes.

"I like that song. She was on *American Idol* last year," Theo said. "Did you watch it?"

"No."

"It's a pretty good show, but my wife says it's not as good as it used to be."

And that was the last thing Sam heard until Theo stopped for coffee and a transmission in a place called Big Timber.

"Do not let him in here," Meg ordered. Her customary jeans, T-shirt and apron had been replaced with a deep blue wool dress and vintage gold necklace, and she had a familiar trapped expression on her face. Meg owned the local café and was happier in work clothes. She was also unaccustomed to being the center of attention.

"He only wants a couple of pictures," Lucia promised. She waved to Mike, the owner of the town's paper, and gave him a thumbs-up while the future bride continued to grumble.

"I don't want my face splashed on the front page of the paper next week." Meg frowned at Mike and the smile on his round face dimmed. Lucia felt sorry for him. Clearly he'd hoped to stay and party with the women. But that wasn't going to happen. There were few women-only events in this town of mostly single men, and the women in town protected their privacy at all costs. He held on to the cupcake he'd just plucked from a three-tiered cake plate, though.

"You're news. Your bridal shower is news. It'll probably end up on Jerry's blog, too." Lucia couldn't hide her amusement. Meg's romance with her high school sweetheart had finally worked out. The two of them were perfect for each other, and everyone in town knew it. Everyone in town had watched it happen, so it was only fitting that any prewedding celebration be detailed on the front page of the local newspaper.

"I don't want to be news."

Lucia laughed. "Meg, anything and everything that goes on in this town is news, and you know it."

"Everyone looks really happy."

"It's not every day we get to celebrate a wedding," Lucia pointed out. "We're going to make the most of it."

"I'm glad. Thank you," Meg said, sniffling uncharacteristically. "I really like my party."

"You are *not* going to cry," Lucia ordered. "Aurora will have a fit if she thinks I've gone all sentimental and made you cry. She's worked really hard to get the bar ready for this." Lucia thought the room looked elegant. Even the stuffed grizzly in the corner wore a cummerbund and a black bowtie. A red silk rose was wired into one large paw, making the town mascot look absolutely gentlemanly.

That had been Aurora's idea, and Lucia had found just the right supplies at a thrift shop in Billings. She and Aurora, her co-hostess, had originally planned to hold the shower at the community center, but they'd had to change the venue to Aurora's bar, the Dahl, because of a conflict with the senior citizens' Christmas potluck later that evening. Lucia suspected that Aurora had planned to have the party at her bar all along. The Dahl, one of the original town buildings from the late 1800s, was almost unrecognizable at the moment, its pine tables covered in white linen and decorated with flowers. Candles lined the bar itself, along with red roses in bud vases.

Lucia assumed every woman in town was

in attendance. What had begun as a ladies' night to celebrate Meg's engagement while Owen was away had turned into a full-blown bridal shower, despite the continuing silence of the future bride and groom about their wedding plans. In winter, even in December with Christmas approaching, no one needed an excuse to party.

Aurora, enigmatic and always glamorous, sauntered over, refilled Meg's glass and set the half-empty pitcher of margaritas on the table. "This is a blast. I knew something was happening that night after the town meeting when you and Owen kept pretending you weren't looking at each other. Your handsome future husband is our local success story, lady."

"He's a *hero*," Lucia added, though Meg looked horrified.

"Oh, please," Meg groaned. "You're both being ridiculous."

"Us?" Lucia feigned innocence by widening her eyes and keeping a straight face. "I'm the town widow and Aurora is the surly bartender. We know of what we speak."

"Darn right," Aurora agreed, tossing her platinum hair over her shoulders. Lucia envied the color, which she had decided was real. The woman looked like a supermodel, even when wearing a faded T-shirt, jeans and Western boots. "No one can stop talking about your engagement. Owen performed a miracle getting you to agree to marry him. Proposing right there in the parking lot by the café, with everyone watching out the windows. You were the talk of the town."

"Th-that was two weeks ago," Meg sputtered, but Lucia saw the way her best friend's eyes softened when she remembered the moment. A large antique ring with sapphires and diamonds sparkled in the candlelight as Meg held up her hand seemingly to stop their teasing.

"Parking lots can be very romantic," Lucia said. She took a careful sip of her margarita. "We both understand that. No one's blaming you for weakening and finally saying yes to the poor man. And think of that honeymoon you're going to have."

Meg, bless her, blushed. "Stop," she whispered.

"I wish you'd hurry up and set a date," Lucia said. "I want to start planning the wedding cake. Do you want real flowers or frosting flowers?"

"Frosting."

"Colors?"

"I haven't a clue," Meg answered, looking pained. "You're the baker. What do you think? I'm not sure Owen would go for anything too pink."

"Some of that depends on the time of year," Aurora said, plopping a wedding veil on Meg's head. She fiddled with the headband and fluffed the white tulle. "Red and white for Valentine's Day would work. It's a bit of a cliché, but Lucia could make it modern."

"I could. Or if you prefer spring, I could do April violets," Lucia murmured. "With yellow daffodils. Or daisies."

"Pretty," Aurora said, arranging the tulle so that it expanded like a cloud around Meg's shoulder-length brown hair.

"A veil? Really?" Meg's eyes narrowed. "How much have you two had to drink?"

"Very little," Lucia assured her. "But I've been baking cupcakes since four o'clock this morning and I'm wobbly."

"The veil was your mother's idea. I guess

it's some kind of family heirloom. I'll go get your wedding photographer," Aurora said. "This talk of baking may make me break out in hives."

Lucia laughed. Meg's expression was anything but amused, though. "I worry about you," she said. "You've been baking cupcakes at four in the morning for weeks."

"It's just for the holidays," Lucia said, wondering how much longer she could keep up the pace. Early-morning baking, dealing with the boys, frosting and decorating dozens of cupcakes for the noon deliveries. Then picking up the boys at school, laundry, cooking and all the things that went into mothering. She loved it all—well, except for the laundry—but at this time of year she was wearing down fast. However, all the baking was adding to her special savings account in the hope of a March break trip to Orlando. "This is my busiest season, especially for pies. After the holidays I won't have much to do until Valentine's Day. So what about February for the wedding?"

"Maybe, but the baby is due that month and Shelly doesn't want to miss the wedding."

"Well, I'm not going anywhere at all until I know when you're getting married."

"You'll be my matron of honor, right?"

"Absolutely." Lucia was happy for Meg. Over-the-moon happy. She remembered those months before she'd married Tony, when the world had seemed made just for them, when every look or touch or kiss was magic and life was filled with endless years of possibilities.

"I can help you with the baking, remember," Meg said. "My kitchen is your kitchen."

"Thanks, but—" Lucia was about to remind her friend that her kitchen actually belonged to Al, a cook who preferred to be master of all he surveyed, when Aurora hauled Mike over to join them at the bar.

"I told Mike he can take one picture of you, one picture of the ring and one picture of the dessert table, but that's it," Aurora said. "And if he complained I'd have Loralee deal with him."

Mike nodded his agreement, his mouth full of dessert. He wiped his fingers on a crumpled paper napkin before lifting his camera.

"That's downright mean." Lucia liked

Meg's mother, but the woman was famous for her multiple marriages and colorful observations, not to mention her flirting skills. Men in her presence were alternately charmed and terrified. She was as different from Lucia's mother-in-law, Marie, as a woman could be.

"That's the way it is," Aurora said with a shrug. "It's a tough world."

Lucia moved out of camera range and surveyed the chattering crowd of hungry women. Mama Marie was fussing over the pile of gifts on the pool table, which had been covered with a huge white-and-silver tablecloth. Marie was just under five feet tall, and almost as wide as she was high. A descendant of Italian immigrants who settled in Boston, she had her roots in pasta, meatballs and "gravy," commonly known in Montana as spaghetti sauce. Her graying hair was cut short and the only makeup she wore was pink lip gloss. She was the most maternal person Lucia knew.

Mike posed Meg behind the stack of presents, took a closeup of the engagement ring and the cupcake stand, then looked longingly at the food table before being hustled out the door by the ever-vigilant Aurora.

Lucia knew that Aurora, thirtyish, mysterious and very self-sufficient, had a lot of experience ushering men out that particular door. She didn't suffer fools, drunks or boors lightly. Since she ran the only bar in town, the men played—for the most part—by her rules. Her customers minded their manners, their language and their alcohol consumption.

Meg, still wearing her veil, carried a paper plate piled high with meatballs and pasta salad over to Lucia. She nodded toward Loralee. "My mother just told me I needed to use more mascara. She seems to be having a good time."

"As always." Loralee, wearing silver boots, black jeans, a white sweater and glittery headband, was knocking back what looked like a blue martini and chatting with Patsy, the local hairdresser.

"She's talking about coming back here when Shelly's baby is born or maybe not even leaving at all."

"Is that a good thing or a bad thing?" Her broken wrist encased in plaster, Shelly moved carefully around the buffet table and chatted sweetly with Mrs. Parcell, an older woman who, along with her husband and grandson, ranched outside of town. The newest resident in town, the former runaway teen's long blond hair was pulled back into a ponytail, and she sported an overlarge pink sweatshirt that covered her growing baby bump. Lucia guessed the sweatshirt belonged to Loralee, the now-surrogate grandmother who had unceremoniously taken the girl under her wing.

"Has Shelly said what she's planning to do?"

"Face reality," Meg said. "At least, that's what she told us."

"What exactly is reality?"

"Raising a baby alone. Giving the child up for adoption. I don't know."

"We'll all help her," Lucia said. "Whatever she decides."

"It won't be easy."

"No," Lucia said, knowing full well how hard it was to raise children on one's own. "It won't be easy. Whatever happens, she's better off with your mother to keep an eye on her."

"Yes, which is amazing, since I'm the one who's always had to keep an eye on my mother." Meg smiled ruefully. "Do you think Loralee is finally growing up?"

"Well, she hasn't been married in years," Lucia pointed out. "That's progress."

"You're right. I should be grateful." Meg perched on a bar stool and surveyed the party.

Mama Marie hurried over. "You'd probably better start opening presents," she told Meg. "You've got a lot of them, and it's gonna take a while."

"I can't believe this," Meg sighed. "A party and presents."

"That's what happens when you get engaged," Mama Marie pointed out. "At last."

"You didn't have to add the *at last,*" Meg grumbled.

Lucia laughed.

"I'd like to make a toast!" Aurora lifted a glass of champagne. "Quiet, ladies! We also have several announcements."

The crowd's chatter died down, but excitement stayed in the air. Lucia met Mama Marie's smile with one of her own. Loralee, standing beside her, winked.

"First of all," Aurora began, "we're here to congratulate Meg for having the good sense to wait for Owen MacGregor to return to town."

"It only took sixteen years," someone hollered. Lucia thought it was Patsy, but she couldn't be sure.

"Whatever," Aurora said, waving her elegant hand. "It finally happened, so let's raise our glasses and wish the couple well. And then? Presents!"

Cheers filled the room as the women clinked glasses.

"Speech!" called Loralee.

"No speech," her daughter said.

"Just a little one," Lucia said, pushing Meg forward so she could see the crowd of friends gathered to wish her well.

"Okay." Meg cleared her throat and smiled at her neighbors. "Thank you, everyone. And thanks especially to Lucia and Aurora for putting this together." She raised her left hand and wiggled her fingers. "You've seen the ring?"

Another round of cheers.

"I wore this secretly for two weeks when I was a teenager," she said. "Some of you have heard the story, I know. And I just want to say I'm really happy to have it back." She laughed when several of the older women fist-pumped the air. "So thank you for coming. It means a lot to me."

"Open the presents!" This came from Shelly, who looked ready to burst from excitement. At more than six months along she looked ready to burst, period.

Now it was Lucia's turn to blink back tears. She remembered the sweet discovery of having created a life and feeling the baby move inside her for the first time.

Shelly had inadvertently created a baby with a man who turned out to be married, a man with the morals of a stray, unneutered dog, and her young life had immediately changed and shifted in ways she never could have imagined.

It was a tough thing to learn. Lucia herself had been smacked in the face with the reality that nothing was forever. You never knew what lurked around the corner.

She'd been tiptoeing around corners ever since.

"HEADING HOME?" The man in the seat next to him turned away from the window and

adjusted his seat belt. They were about to take off from a dirt runway in Nicaragua.

"Not exactly." Sam needed to pick up some things in Miami, then head to Los Angeles for production meetings. "Are you?"

"I'm getting closer," he said, seeming happy with the idea of being on his way. He appeared about Sam's age but had a military look, with his clipped dark hair. "You know what the opposite of the Amazon is?"

"Alaska?"

"Montana," the man had said quite seriously, as though it were a well-established fact. He'd glanced out the window as the plane vaulted into the sky. Beneath them lay thousands of acres of green foliage, brown water and vague dirt roads twisting into the jungle.

"Montana," Sam repeated. He'd never been there. "Any special place in Montana?"

"Willing," the man replied immediately.

"Excuse me?"

"Willing. The center of Montana." He'd flipped through the pages of a tattered airline magazine until he found a map of the United States. "There," he said, tapping his

index finger on the page. "That's the best place in the world."

Sam believed him. The stranger was earnest, his expression one of intense longing.

"And that's home?"

"Yeah," he said, flipping the magazine shut and stuffing it into the seat back pocket to join a wad of out-of-date reading material. "Always."

"We're here," someone said. "Welcome to Willing."

Sam dragged himself out of the memory and realized he must have dozed off. He blinked, then focused his eyes, and realized Theo was driving down what Sam assumed was the main street in town. It was growing dark and the snow was still falling, so there wasn't much to see. Theo turned right at a flashing red light and crawled down the dimly lit street.

"I'll give you the tour," he said. "You've got the library on the right, but it's closed now," Theo said. "The town council's hoping to get some volunteers to keep it going. That log building? It's the community center." The street curved at a ninety degree angle, with a battered building with neon beer signs sitting in the elbow.

"That's the Dahl," his guide explained. "The one and only bar. You'll meet just about everyone in town in there sooner or later." Theo slowed and almost stopped in the middle of the street. "Looks like the party's breaking up. My wife was going to the bridal shower this afternoon."

Sam closed his eyes again. He had three months to learn what the town looked like.

The Escalade slowly escalated and turned a corner onto a narrow residential street. "I'm here on this block, right on the corner," Theo said. "You're the last house on the left, next block up. You're actually closer to the main road north, but we just made a big *U* through town so you could get your bearings."

"Thanks." Sam didn't mean it, but Theo seemed like a decent, well-meaning guy. One block later Theo parked the car. Sam peered out the window at a two-story white bungalow, floral curtains barely visible through the snowflakes.

"Here you are," Theo announced.

"Thanks." Sam unbuckled his seat belt

and took two one-hundred-dollar bills from an inside pocket of his jacket. "I appreciate the ride."

"That's more than—"

"We're good," Sam declared, while struggling to open the car door without passing out from the effort of twisting his body to the right.

"Do you have a key or was Jerry going to leave the house unlocked?" Theo asked.

"Leave it unlocked," Sam said. "He told me he might be out of town."

"Yeah, that could be. Is this all you have?" He lifted Sam's duffel bags from the backseat.

"Yeah, thanks." The cold air cleared his aching head at the same time as the wind whipped across his face and pelted him with snow.

"You travel light."

"Always," Sam said.

"Makes it easy to get out of town fast?" Theo joked, hanging on to the bags and tromping up the recently shoveled cement walk and three cement steps. He stopped at the front door.

"That's the idea," Sam said, keeping his

voice light. "Except I won't get far without a car."

"Call me if you need to go into Lewistown—or anywhere else, for that matter. I'm the local taxi." Theo opened the door and set the duffel bags inside. He didn't enter, though, explaining that he didn't want to track snow into the house.

"It's not real warm here. I guess Jerry left the electric heat on just enough so the pipes wouldn't freeze," he said. "There's a wood-stove, though. You know how to get a fire going? Oh. Food. I guess I should have asked you if you needed to stop for groceries. The café will be open until eight if you want dinner. Head north, and turn right at the main road. It's across the street."

"Thanks. I'll be okay. Jerry said he'd have someone get the house ready for me."

"Probably Lucia," Theo said, looking eager to get back in his car and head home. "Lucia Swallow." He pointed to a bright yellow house next door. "Makes the best pies in town."

That sounded promising. A little old pie-baking woman next door would be a plus.

Sam thanked Theo again and shut the door

behind him, leaving the merciless wind to batter the windows.

He stood on ancient brown carpet and surveyed the living room. He didn't know how old Mrs. Kelly was when she died, but from the furniture he'd guess about a hundred and ten. The room ran the width of the house. The wall directly opposite the door was lined with bookshelves stuffed with ceramic animals and glass vases. To his right stood a dark dining room table with six ornate chairs; to his left lay a red velvet couch that looked old enough for Queen Victoria to have fainted on it. A wood stove occupied one corner and an empty wood box sat next to it.

Sam ignored the snow on his boots and made his way around the dining room chairs to a long, narrow kitchen. All the appliances he needed were there, and the room was spotless. A small Formica table sat in front of a picture window that faced what he assumed was the backyard, though the area was hard to make out in the storm. A woodshed backed up to a fence and a row of evergreens, but if there was a path, he didn't see it. He completed his tour of the main floor, noting the back door, a hallway that led to a set of stairs, a bathroom and a large bedroom that opened onto the living room. He had no reason to explore the upstairs, not tonight.

All in all the place was perfect, though the downstairs bedroom looked as if its owner had been way too fond of purple. Purple bedspread, purple throw pillows and purple shag rug.

He'd manage. The house was luxurious for a guy who usually lived in a tent. In addition to a real bed he had an indoor bathroom. A picture of a vase of violets dangled from a hook on the wall over the toilet. Purple hand towels hung on a rod beneath the framed print.

The house still had a lived-in quality. It was as though poor Mrs. Kelly had just walked out of her house one day and never returned. The mayor must have bought the place "as is," except for a brand-new bar of soap in a dish next to the sink.

Sam returned to the kitchen and opened cupboards until he found the drinking glasses. He removed his jacket, tossed it on the back of a chair and pulled a bottle of prescription pain pills from his shirt pocket.

He'd had to keep them close. Not that he liked taking them. But traveling had been the hell his doctor had predicted.

In fact, now he couldn't bend over.

He'd have to go to bed with his boots on.

Once again, nothing new.

He shivered, chilled to his bones, and after a brief struggle managed to get his jacket back on. He'd do one more thing before he collapsed into the purple bed, and that would be to examine the woodstove and get a fire going. He'd seen a thermostat on the wall between the kitchen and living room, so he could turn up the heat easily enough, but he didn't like to depend on electricity. Especially not in a storm.

Besides, he liked carrying wood and building fires. He allowed himself a small ironic smile. He'd wanted cold weather, had dreamt of icicles the last time he was on the Rio Purus.

Acknowledgment of his sheer stupidity replaced whatever reason he'd chosen Montana for a winter retreat. He'd let a brief conversation with a stranger lead him to renting a cold house in a cold town in the middle of cold nowhere.

He usually had more sense, he realized.

No, that was wrong.

He was a man who took chances, who didn't look before he leaped and jumped into murky rivers without knowing what waited for him.

Compared with the jungle, this town would be a piece of cake.

CHAPTER TWO

"MOM! HELP!"

"Mrs. Swallow?"

"Mommy!"

Lucia heard the screams coming from her backyard as soon as she opened the car door. It took her six seconds to run, slipping on fresh snow piling up on old snow, from the driveway through the space between her house and the Kelly house. Sure enough, there was a body in the backyard. Lucia's heart seemed to stop for a moment, until she realized her three children and their babysitter, Kim, were not hurt. They looked at her and called for her, but their voices held more excitement than horror.

Her first thought: someone had fallen. The witch next door? No, the body was large, man-sized. Had Kim's grandfather had a heart attack? The old man sometimes stopped in to check on his granddaughters, twin volleyball stars.

Tony, age four and the image of his father, ran as fast as he could toward Lucia. "Mom, we caught a thief! We caught a thief!"

"A robber," her oldest son, Davey, insisted, calling from the back of the small yard. "I hit a robber!"

"He doesn't dress like a robber," was the first thing Lucia said as she hurried over, because the man lifting his face from the snow wore a new jacket and expensive hiking boots. "What happened? Did you call Hip?"

"I was just about to," Kim said. "We were checking for a pulse. He has one. It's a little rapid, but within range." She held up her phone. "I just looked it up."

Lucia leaned closer. "Can you tell us where you're hurt?"

"I don't think he's a robber at all. He's a nameless victim of inclement weather," her babysitter declared, her cell phone clutched in her ungloved hands. "That's my theory and I'm sticking to it."

The so-called robber groaned and rolled over onto his side. Thank goodness he wasn't dead. Finding a dead thief in the backyard would not keep one in the holiday spirit. Finding some poor man frozen to death less than twenty feet from her warm kitchen would be positively tragic.

Boo growled, warning the man not to leap up and attack the children.

"Boo," Lucia said, hoping the dog would listen to her. "It's okay." When he looked to her and wagged his tail, she knew the animal was enjoying the drama as much as her babysitter was. He turned back to the man in the snow and whined.

"Help," the stranger groaned. "Get…them… away from me."

"He was stealing our wood," Davey said. "I was getting wood, like you told me to, and there was a guy stealin' it!"

"Stealing our wood!" Matty cried, jumping up and down in the snow. His hat was missing and his ears were red. "The man was stealing our wood!"

"He's not dead. See? I told you he had a pulse," Kim said as she took pictures with her cell phone.

"Kim, stop that," Lucia ordered, but she knew it was useless. Within seconds at least half the senior class of Willing High would know there was a strange man in her back- yard and by tomorrow morning his pho- tograph would be on the front page of the *Willing Gazette*'s Facebook page. "Don't Twitter it, either."

"Too late," she said, stuffing her phone into her pocket. "Already sent. It's a done deal, Mrs. Swallow. Sorry. But I'm glad he's not dead. Really." She pulled her phone out of her pocket and studied it for a few sec- onds. "My grandpa wants to know if you called the sheriff."

"Tell him I'll get back to him."

"Okay." Kim's thumbs flew over the key- board. "I'll tell him to 'stand down.'"

"Down!" echoed little Tony, holding Lu- cia's hand as he bounced up and down like his older brother. "Down, down, down!"

"Shh," Lucia said. "All of you, be quiet and let me find out who he is."

She knelt over the stranger in the snow, looked into pain-filled blue eyes and saw a very angry, very unfamiliar, very hand- some man. He didn't seem dangerous. Just intensely aggravated and somewhat humili- ated, the way men get when they're not in control. "Can you tell me who you are? Are you hurt? We're going to call for help."

"Don't. Need. Help. Ribs," he rasped. "Cracked."

She turned to her son. "You broke his ribs?"

Davey stared at her, his eyes large. "Not on purpose. He was stealing our wood," he whispered. "*No one* steals wood. Except bad people."

"Not. Stealing." The man moaned. "Renting. House."

"From Jerry? Claire's house?"

"Kelly," he said. "The woman who died." He tried to take another breath, but winced. "Purple."

Kim muttered, thumbs once again punching her phone. "How do you spell delirious?"

Lucia ignored the question and focused again on the man. There was no blood, no obvious broken bones, but that didn't mean he was okay. "I think you need to go to the hospital."

He struggled to sit up. "I just…got out of one. So, no. The answer…is no."

"You might want to think about it," she said. "You look a little out of it."

"Long…day," he said.

"Okay," she told him, deciding to save the discussion for later, after they were all out of the snow. "Just hold on for a sec and I'll get you back inside before we all freeze to death out here." She straightened and faced her boys. "Davey, take your brothers home. Now."

"But—"

"Now."

He knew she meant it, so he reached for Tony's hand and led him across the snow-covered yard. Her youngest child continued to bounce despite the snow that should have slowed him down.

Matty hesitated. "Can I stay?"

"No, sweetheart. Your ears are cold. Go on, and call Boo with you."

The dog had planted his rear end in the snow and had taken it upon himself to guard the new neighbor, someone he obviously saw as a potential threat to his temporary family. He'd been staying with Lucia while Owen, the future bridegroom, was out of town. It was like having another child, Lucia thought, watching the dog's ears flick when he heard his name.

"Boo," Lucia said. "Go with the kids."

The dog looked disappointed. He may have even sighed. But he stood and shook off the snow before trotting obediently after Matt.

"We're gonna have cookies," the boy promised. "A whole lot of 'em, and they have red sprinkles on top. Green, too."

Boo knew what cookies were. He wagged his tail a couple of times and broke into a run, racing Matty to the back door.

"Can you stand?"

"Eventually."

She turned to her teenaged babysitter. "You get on one side, I'll get on the other."

She looked back down at the man. He was about forty, broad-shouldered—and more than a little handsome, she noted anew. "So you're renting Mrs. Kelly's house?"

"Yeah." He managed to nod as he lifted himself up on one elbow. "Get me up. The wood stove," he panted. "Needs wood."

"Sure." She motioned to Kim to help her. Together they managed to hoist the man to his feet. Split logs lay in the snow at their feet, and Lucia bent to collect them, until she realized he couldn't walk without help. She'd come back for the logs later.

"I'm really sorry about this," she said, dusting snow off the front of his jacket. "Put your arm around me. You don't want to fall again."

"I didn't...want to fall the first time."

At least he was breathing a little more normally. He was taller than she'd thought, at least a foot taller than her. His close-cropped dark hair was flecked with gray and wet with snow, which also clung to the front of his jeans. He shivered and crossed his arms in front of his chest.

"I can help—"

"I'm fine," he interrupted, but he sounded more tired than angry now. "I can walk. What I can't do is...fend off little boys... and a dog. In a foot of snow."

He tromped carefully toward Mrs. Kelly's back door, Lucia and Kim following him until Lucia told Kim to go back to the kids. "I'll be home in a few minutes."

"No hurry. I'm gonna go put the pics on Facebook."

Wonderful. "My mother-in-law will phone

me as soon as you do, so tell her I'll call her back after I defrost the neighbor."

"Cool."

She followed the nonrobber into his house, where he made it clear she wasn't welcome. He sank onto one of the two kitchen chairs and stared at his wet boots. Lucia paused inside the door and kicked her suede boots off. She walked gingerly around the little mounds of snow the stranger had tracked in and turned up the thermostat on the wall next to the refrigerator. "It's cold in here. You were trying to get a fire going?"

"I wasn't stealing wood." He gestured out the window to the shed.

"Of course you were. You just didn't know," she said, hoping to comfort him.

"That's not my shed?"

"Nope."

He sighed, a deep heartfelt sound that was almost comical.

"I can see where you'd think it was," she offered cheerfully. "The yards kinda blend. I'm going to build a fire so you have a little more heat in here. Go take a shower. Can you manage that? You need to warm up."

"I don't know you. I'm Sam Hove."

"I'm Lucia Swallow. Your next-door neighbor. Your—"

"The pie lady?"

"Yes."

"You smell like rum, your kids run wild and your dog attacked me."

He looked so disappointed. Obviously she was not what he'd expected. If she hadn't been so amused, her feelings would have been hurt.

"I smell like rum because I was at a bridal shower and there was punch. A really delicious punch." She didn't explain that she'd spilled some on herself while washing the punch bowl, or that she'd been too tired to have more than a token sip during the toast to Meg's marital bliss. "My kids are boys. I try not to let them run wild, but they do… run. And the dog? Is not mine, but he's not wild, either. I'm dog sitting for the groom."

"Groom?"

"Who's marrying the woman whose bridal shower it was, but he's out of town. Now, go take a shower and I'll make a fire." She didn't say she'd return with some lasagna and garlic bread leftover from last night's dinner. He looked as though he could use something to eat.

"I can't," he said after a long moment.

"Why not?" She was as patient as she'd be with little Tony, who often stared at his feet and said "I can't" in a pitiful voice.

"I can't get my boots off." He smiled, the barest of smiles on his tanned face. Her heart did a tiny—very tiny—flip.

"Ah, those cracked ribs." She drew a chair up opposite him. "Come on, give me your foot."

He hesitated, eyeing her as if she might be playing a joke on him.

"I'm a mother," she said. "I do this kind of thing all the time."

"Not to me," he muttered, but raised his leg and rested the heel on her leg. In a matter of seconds she'd untied the snow-drenched knot, released the frozen laces and pulled his new boot off. She did the same for the other boot. "You were going to wear these until your ribs healed?"

"I didn't think that part through."

"Obviously." She held the boots by two fingers. "I'll put these by the stove so they'll dry out."

"You don't—"

"It's okay," she assured him. "I thought *you'd* be a lot older."

"I feel about ninety."

"Jerry said you were some kind of professor. Retired. I pictured a frail, fragile elderly gentleman who liked soup and drank Earl Grey tea."

"I thought pie ladies were old. Great-grandmothers wearing aprons."

"Then I guess we're *both* disappointed," she assured him.

DAVEY SWALLOW NEVER meant to kill anyone, but for a few minutes outside in the snow he was awfully afraid he'd done it anyway. He and Matt had taken Boo outside to play in the snow after convincing Kim that their mother wouldn't mind. Mom didn't care if they made snowballs and built a snow fort as long as they didn't leave the yard. Davey knew he was in charge of Matt and Matt knew it, too, though sometimes he griped. Most of the time Matt just followed him around and that was okay.

Sort of.

Except that Matty talked too much. Tony

used to be quiet, but lately he'd started talking, too. Except he was only four and didn't know any different. Davey thought that the world would be better if people didn't talk so much. There were seven girls and four boys in his third-grade class and the seven girls never shut up. They talked about books and horses and television and video games and their older sisters. They talked about their dogs and their kittens and their favorite colors and when their mothers would let them get a cell phone.

They talked about homework. They talked about each other. They talked about the boys.

One time Davey wore ear plugs, but Mrs. Kramer caught him and made him take them out. She made him stay after school and asked him a lot of questions about whether he was happy or having a hard time or being bullied or having trouble at home.

He'd tried to tell her he liked being quiet. He told her he liked The Quiet, as if it was a place he could escape to: The Quiet, like The Beach. The Desert. The Mountains.

She wrote a note to his mom suggesting he have his ears checked.

When he told his mom about The Quiet,

she'd listened very carefully. He liked that about his mom. She listened harder than anyone he knew. He bet his dad liked to talk to her. Sometimes, if he concentrated real hard, he could hear his dad's voice. When he was in bed at night, he'd pretend he could hear the murmurs of his mom and dad talking. He'd remember his mother laughing a little bit, his father teasing her, the noise of the television or the water splashing in the sink as the dishes were washed.

He liked *those* sounds.

But now he was stuck with listening to Tony and Matt fight over who had the best Matchbox car while Tony's favorite television show blared in the background. Kim's thumbs were flying over her cell phone, which impressed Davey no end. At this rate he'd be twenty before he ever got his own phone.

And who was the man in the snow?

"I didn't mean to knock him down," he told Kim. "Boo kinda bumped me and I kinda bumped the man."

"I know," Kim assured him. "You're not exactly the violent type."

"What type am I?"

She glanced up from her phone and gave him the once-over. "You're a cute, geeky boy, but geeky in a good way, you know?"

Davey guessed that was okay. "He said he broke his ribs."

"Nah," she said. "I think he was just being dramatic. He looked like the type."

"You think this'll count against me?"

Kim tilted her head and considered the question. She knew all about the third grade project, knew that Davey wanted to win the prize. "You have the rules somewhere?"

"Yeah."

"Let me see."

Davey pulled out his notebook and removed a carefully folded sheet of blue paper from the inside pocket of the binder. He unfolded it and handed it to Kim. "I don't think it'll count against me, but I'm not sure."

Kim read it carefully, moving her lips a little as she did. She shook her head. "There's nothing here about penalties." She handed it back to him. "Just a warning that you can't, well, arrange things so you can get a point."

"Yeah. I didn't get that part."

Kim thought for a second. "It would be like making a big mess in the kitchen, without anyone knowing you did it. Then you clean it up, like you're surprised there's a mess. That doesn't qualify as a Random Act of Kindness."

"It has to be random," he said, trying out the word on his tongue. "Random Acts of Kindness."

"Yep." She grinned. "Like when you see I don't have a cookie and you know I like the ones with the red sprinkles and you sneak one in front of me when I'm not looking."

Davey grinned back. "You talk a lot, but that's okay."

He gave her two, both with red sugar sprinkles, the biggest ones he could find in the plastic box.

SHE WAS BEAUTIFUL, but that was the least of his problems. He'd been around beautiful, black-haired women before, though this one was exquisite. Petite and delicate, with that waterfall of silky hair and greenish eyes that twinkled with good humor. The problem was his feeling that she was pure steel. Her sons had not argued with her when she'd told them to go home. The hellions had done what they were told, however reluctant they were to leave her with a firewood thief. He looked forward to meeting her husband. He pictured a soft-spoken giant who took orders well and behaved himself.

He'd never felt so helpless in his adult life.

She wasn't getting the message to leave him alone. In fact, she'd ordered him to have a hot shower—after checking to make sure there was hot water, a slip-proof mat in the bathtub and fresh towels—and she'd carried his two duffel bags into the bathroom. She'd even unzipped them to save him the trouble of bending over to do it.

When she'd left the bathroom, he'd managed to kick out a clean pair of sweat pants and a long sleeved T-shirt.

"Are you okay?" she called from the hall. He locked the bathroom door because he wouldn't put it past this woman to walk in and make sure he'd washed behind his ears.

"Yes, but you don't—"

"Good."

He'd heard nothing after that, so he carefully stripped off his clothes and, with some dexterous toe action, removed his thick wool socks. He adjusted the water, eased his cold body under the shower spray and realized the pain pill had eased some of the ache in his chest. Hallelujah.

He was going to survive this day after all. He retrieved the new bar of soap he'd noticed earlier and, after scrubbing himself with a faded purple washcloth, stood underneath the hot stream of water for at least ten minutes before carefully stepping onto the bath mat that Lucia Swallow had put in place. Both bath towels had violets embroidered on the edges. He rubbed his hair with one towel and wrapped another around his waist.

And he spotted the electric heater imbedded in the wall. *Thank you, Mrs. Kelly,* he thought, pushing the buttons until a blast of hot air hit him in the knees. He stood there for long, blissful minutes as the heat fanned his legs and warmed his feet.

"Mr. Hove?"

Damn. He drew a deep breath, then regretted the action when a now-familiar pain caught him in the right side of his chest. "Yes?"

"Just checking," she said through the door, her voice as cheerful as a nurse's. "You're okay?"

"Fine."

"No dizzy spells or anything like that?"

"No," he declared, gingerly pulling the shirt over his head. "I thought you'd left."

In fact, he'd hoped like hell she had. He stood half-naked in a purple bathroom. There was no sound from the other side of the door, so he hoped she'd finally taken the hint and gone home to her kids and her cowed, silent, pathetic husband. Sam finished putting his pants on, but decided not to struggle with socks. He unlocked the bathroom door and stepped out into the hall.

He smelled tomato sauce. Oregano. Coffee.

He inched down the hall and around the corner to the kitchen where Lucia Swallow stood in front of a microwave oven. Inside the oven a dinner plate rotated and sizzled, its wax paper tent flapping.

"I built a fire," she said without turning around. She opened the microwave door and poked at the wax paper topping the food, then closed the door and turned the microwave back on. "It might take a while for the house to warm up, but the woodstove's big and it should be fine for the night if you turn it down before you go to bed."

"You carried wood?"

She turned and smiled at him. "How else would I fix the fire?"

"You didn't have to do that."

"My kids knocked you down." Her smile had disappeared.

"Your kids didn't break my ribs."

"So who did?"

"It was an accident." She stared at him, waiting for more of an explanation. He felt about ten years old. "At work. I was hit by an Arapaima."

"A what?"

"A fish."

She frowned. "A fish broke your ribs?"

"A very large fish. And it cracked my ribs, not broke them. Three of them. Hurts like he—heck."

"I'm sure it does." A little furrow sprang between those delicate wing-shaped eyebrows.

"I'm actually doing fine. Healing according to schedule."

"Even after falling in the snow?"

"Yeah. Even after that." He didn't feel any worse now than he had a couple of hours ago. In fact, after the hot shower and donning warm clothes, he felt better than he had in days. "The pain pill has kicked in."

The microwave stopped groaning and pinged. Yes, he definitely smelled oregano and garlic.

"I assume you're hungry?"

"Uh, yeah."

"Sit."

He sat. She placed silverware and a napkin in front of him, then uncovered a plate piled high with lasagna and meatballs.

"You're kidding me."

"What? You don't like Italian food?"

"It's not that. It's…the best thing I've seen in weeks." Since a plate of *pasticho* in Brazil, but he'd been in too much pain to really enjoy that meal.

"I made coffee."

"How did you do all this so fast?"

"I'm a mother. I'm efficient. I had Kim— the babysitter—bring over a plate of leftovers." She shot him a quick smile. "And you take very, very long showers."

He picked up his fork and tasted heaven, Italian style. Meanwhile Lucia Swallow shrugged on her jacket, which she'd hung by the back door, wound a striped scarf around her neck, tugged on her thick suede boots and pointed to a piece of paper stuck by a flower-shaped magnet to the refrigerator. "Jerry left you a list of contacts, including someone who'll deliver firewood."

He nodded, his mouth full of pasta.

"You're welcome to our wood until you get your own. I'll have the boys stack some by the back door for the morning."

He swallowed and attempted to thank her, but before he could get the words out, she was gone.

Thank goodness.

"Wait a minute, say that once more?"

"He told me I smelled like alcohol and my kids were hellions." Lucia laughed again just thinking about it. Curled up on her couch with three children, a dog and four bowls of popcorn, she was ready to talk over the afternoon with Meg. Her best friend had had little free time for phone calls lately, so this was a luxury.

"And you said?"

"Well, I told him I'd been to a bridal shower."

"Seriously, Lucia, you are too nice." It

didn't sound like a compliment, and since Lucia had heard that description of herself before, she didn't take it as one.

"I know. I should have lost my temper and hit him with a piece of red fir. I was rude to him, though."

"Lucia, sweetie, you couldn't be rude if you tried."

"Wait until you meet him. He's hurt, so I get the 'injured male' frustration, but he won't exactly fit in around here. I mean, he's got major attitude happening." She moved a popcorn bowl away from Boo's sneaky nose.

"What does he look like? How old is he? Did he really look sick?"

"He's handsome, late thirties, early forties, maybe. And he really did look as if he was in pain. I felt bad about that. You should have seen him, a body in the snow, with the kids jumping around and Kim taking pictures with her phone." Now Lucia's boys were entranced with a movie about a reindeer, one of their very favorites. The kids seemed like little angels, but she knew better.

"Handsome," Meg repeated. "I knew I should have come home with you."

"My life needs some excitement. I wonder how he got here?"

"Have Mike interview him for the new arrivals section."

"There is no new arrivals section," Lucia pointed out.

"He could make one up, just so we'd know who this guy is. Remember a couple of years ago? The man with the snowmobile?"

"The one who was hiding from the mob?"

"He had no credit history. And he wasn't very friendly."

Lucia lowered her voice. "I don't want some mobster hiding out next door, but this guy doesn't even seem like *he* knows what he's doing here."

"Jerry will know. He gets back tomorrow. I'm going to email him now. Have you done a Google search on the guy?"

"I will later. I'm going to frost another batch of cookies as soon as I hang up."

"Can I come over?"

"Of course—if you want to watch *Rudolph* again."

"Maybe not." She paused. "I loved my party."

"I know."

"I loved all my gifts, even the frog sponge holder. *Especially* the frog sponge holder. I don't know how you find things like that."

Lucia climbed off the couch and retrieved the empty popcorn bowls. "It takes talent to be tacky."

"It's a real gift," Meg agreed. "You're a thrift shop queen."

"No, I'm a boozed-up bad mother with a vicious dog."

Meg's howl of laughter rang through the phone loud and clear. "If he only knew."

"I do feel bad about the kids knocking him down."

"They're too little to knock anyone down. I don't believe it."

"Well, the snow was slippery. Davey said the man lost his balance, and Boo didn't help."

"Stay away from him," Meg said. "At least until Owen gets back and can check him out."

"I left a message with Jerry," Lucia admitted. "I asked if he'd done a background check on the guy."

"I'm going to do a Google search on him. If I find anything I'll call you back."

"You're not coming over?" Lucia tried not to sound disappointed, but winter nights were long and she'd looked forward to the company.

"There's another foot of snow on the ground," Meg said. "I think I'll stay home, look at bridal magazines and admire my gifts."

"Pick out a cake," Lucia said. "I need design ideas."

The next time the phone rang, Lucia was washing cupcake pans. She dried her hands and checked the caller ID. "Hi, Mama."

"Who is this man in the snow?" Marie didn't waste time with pleasantries.

"What man?" When in trouble, feign innocence. Her kids had taught her that.

"On Facebook. I'm friends with Kim."

"You've friended everyone in town."

"It's nice. All my friends in Rhode Island do it. It's how we keep in touch."

"The man in the snow is renting Mrs. Kelly's house," Lucia explained.

"She was a nice woman," Mama went on. "But no family. I always thought that was strange—not that I would say anything. But she was good to the boys, letting them come over and eat candy—not that I approve of too much candy. But it was good of her to be kind to them."

"She was a lovely person," Lucia agreed.

"Unlike the witch on the other side of you."

"Mama!"

"Even her cat didn't want to live with her. First her husband leaves and then the cat."

"I think she's a very unhappy person." Lucia didn't know why she was defending the woman. There wasn't a meaner person in town than Paula Beckett. No one knew if she was seventy or ninety; she'd moved to Willing years before Lucia and Tony had bought their house. They'd attempted to befriend her, but she'd told them to stay on their side of the fence and not to have any wild parties, wild dogs or wild children. Lucia, holding her first adorable infant, had been shocked into silence at such rudeness. Her husband, a dangerous glint in his eye, had replied, "Yes, ma'am, and I'll expect you'll do the same."

"I won't waste any prayers on her," Mama sniffed.

It was the ultimate rejection.

"The party was wonderful," Lucia said,

attempting to distract her mother-in-law from worrying about the neighbors. "Meg was thrilled."

"She's a good girl. And that Owen? A good man. He reminds me of Tony, big and strong."

"He does a little." Although her husband had been five-ten, a burly wrestler type and solid muscle. Owen, a rancher now, was taller. More basketball player than wrestler. And Sam Hove? Six-two, at least, and definitely in shape. She suspected he had spent a lot of time outdoors. His skin was tanned, his large hands calloused and scarred.

A boxer, she thought. He had hands like a fighter. What had he said about being hit by a fish?

"Stay away from that man, and keep the boys away until we find out more about him."

Lucia promised and ended the call. Good thing she hadn't told Mama about making the poor man take a shower.

CHAPTER THREE

CONTRARY TO THE MESSAGES he was receiving on Twitter, the posts on Facebook and the texts on his cell phone, Jerry Thompson was not harboring an escaped criminal inside his rental property.

Jerry fumed as he drove down Main Street late Saturday night. The lengths his constituents would go to avoid minding their own business never ceased to amaze him. He wasn't in the habit of renting homes to questionable tenants, and he was as committed to keeping peace in his town as the county sheriff. So why was he getting those messages? What had happened to privacy? To benefit of the doubt? To the right to do business?

And what happened to the guy who was supposed to plow out his driveway?

Two words, George Martin had typed. Witness Protection.

Myth, he'd texted back. He'd heard that old story twenty times since he'd moved here. A mobster with a big mouth sent by the Feds to Willing to hide out until some supposed trial. But the guy had been too aggressive about his privacy and tried to run over a neighbor with his snowmobile. He'd disappeared after a brief court date in Lewistown and was never seen again. That was back when Gary Petersen still worked at the co-op and had sworn the stranger had no credit record and must have been living here under an assumed name.

Psychopath? Background? another text said.

All okay, had been his response. When had Meg Ripley turned into such a worrier?

Who is Hove? Aurora had sent that.

Writer! had been his reply. She wouldn't believe him anyway.

Mean to Mrs. Swallow, Kim Petersen, one of Gary's twin granddaughters, texted. With pictures of the guy in the snow surrounded by firewood.

Jerry replied with a Don't worry text and knew he'd have more messages on his home phone. Marie Swallow had most likely called him ten times.

So his renter, if not dead of hypothermia or a victim of Neighborhood Watch, had gone from being a perfectly sane travel writer—if writers of any kind could be considered perfectly sane—to a psychopath thief with a possible head injury. He hoped the guy wouldn't sue him.

Jerry was no stranger to drama and excitement, having activated the desire to gain publicity for Willing by attracting reality television to the town. More drama and excitement were coming. The last thing he needed were distractions, especially now that the bachelors were ready for dating and, he'd just learned yesterday in Los Angeles that Sweetheart Productions was primed for making a TV show.

He had to park in the street. It was dark, close to midnight and really, really cold. Bone-chilling and windy. The snow had stopped falling, but what looked like two feet of it lay piled up in front of his house, a huge Victorian that faced the small public park and boasted the only stained-glass windows in town. Built by a prospector who'd left

South Dakota a rich man, the house had been intended for a fiancée who'd died of influenza before arriving in Willing for the wedding. Jerry bought it from its fourth owners, a gay couple from Oregon who loved the house but not the winters. Jerry loved everything about the beautifully restored home except that he lived there by himself.

He grabbed his suitcase and his laptop case, trudged across the lawn, up three wide steps and stopped in front of his door. A few minutes later he was inside, his boots kicked off onto a thick mat, his coat hung on one of the hooks placed near the door. He switched on a light, boosted the thermostat and welcomed himself home with two sips of single malt Scotch and a peanut butter sandwich.

Tomorrow he'd have to come up with some way to introduce his renter to the general population, which meant a breakfast at Meg's. Sam Hove was a bit of a mystery. He'd said he was a writer who required a quiet place to work. He'd listed his occupation as a producer and director of travel films. How the heck could that be remotely suspicious? Jerry was looking forward to meeting the guy and hearing some interesting stories. Come to think of it, Sam Hove might be an attractive bachelor for the show. He could add a little international class that was missing in Willing.

No, bad idea. He'd likely overshadow the local men, and the show was all about Montana men looking for love. Sam Hove wasn't looking for anything but big fish to catch and weird animals to film.

Mike could do an interview with him. That was easy enough to arrange. The rumors would stop, the holidays would keep everyone occupied, and then Jerry could go back to the really important matter of saving the town.

SAM DIDN'T HAVE the slightest idea where he was. He thought about opening his eyes, but even that small movement seemed like too much work. He thought he'd simply lie there in the queen-size bed and enjoy the warm blankets weighing him down. He was warm *and* out of the weather, two very good things.

Sam knew enough not to move. The ache banding his chest was a constant reminder to be careful. His head throbbed and his nose was cold.

Nose cold? Ah. Montana. The old lady's house with the woodstove.

The wild kids. The barking dog.

The annoyingly beautiful neighbor.

Lasagna.

It was all coming back to him. The food was the only positive memory, though. Little Mrs. Swallow made a lasagna to remember. She'd also built a fire to heat his house, which he realized he should now do something about. He opened his eyes and, looking at the watch he'd worn to bed, saw that it was a few minutes after nine. In the morning.

Twenty minutes later he'd managed to add some logs, coax the fire into a roar and start a pot of coffee. There was, as Lucia Swallow had said, coffee in the freezer. He wrapped a lavender blanket around him and gazed out the kitchen window while he waited for the coffee to be ready. He'd never seen snow like this. He'd grown up in Florida, lived in England for a while, spent most of his time in South America. He knew monsoons, but blizzards? Not so much. He wanted to buy snowshoes and explore, but he'd have to heal first.

He was supposed to stay inside and work. Let his ribs knit. Plan the next project. Sam looked at the snow piled high in the backyard and realized someone had shoveled a path to the woodshed. But it wasn't his woodshed and it wasn't his wood.

Somehow the knock on the front door didn't surprise him. Neither did the man standing on the porch. He was of medium height, tanned and wore a big smile, as if he and Sam were old friends.

"Jerry Thompson?" Sam guessed, opening the door to let him in.

"Yeah. Good morning." He shook Sam's hand and grinned. "Welcome to Willing. It's great to finally meet you in person."

He stopped on the plastic mat just inside the door after closing it.

Sam took a step back. "Come on in."

"I won't stay long." He glanced down at his snow-packed boots. "Don't want to track all over the carpet."

"I just made coffee," Sam said. "And I haven't had any yet."

"I don't want to intrude." But he was already bending over to remove his boots, so Sam assumed the guy was staying. "I just wanted to see if you needed anything, had any questions, any problems with the house."

"I'm going to need firewood, according to the woman next door. I don't think she wants me to keep using hers." He opened two cabinets before finding coffee mugs. He'd expected floral tea cups, but he found serviceable white mugs instead.

"Lucia? She won't mind till you get your own." Jerry followed him into the kitchen. "I heard you met."

"Yesterday." He didn't elaborate. He poured two cups of coffee and handed one to Jerry. "I hope you like your coffee black. I don't have any food yet."

"No problem. You saw the note I left? You can call Hip for wood. He's also our resident artist and EMT."

"Theo's cousin?"

"Yep."

"I'll phone him this morning. You want to take your coat off?"

"Well, sure," Jerry said, turning back to the living room. "I stopped by to see if you wanted to have breakfast. If not this morning, then any morning when you're up to it. You could meet some of the folks here in town."

"I'm not really here to—"

"People in Willing always like to welcome someone new," he said. "Most of the time."

Sam eyed the old couch and decided not to chance it, but Jerry set his coffee on the glass table, tossed his thick blue parka on the couch and made himself comfortable amid the fringed pillows. Sam eased himself into the recliner and hoped he'd be able to get out of it without screaming in pain.

"How do you like the place?"

An interesting question. "It's, uh, fine. Did Mrs. Kelly have any family?"

"No, not a soul. I bought the house from the estate. She left everything to the Methodist Church and they sold it to me. Lock, stock and barrel." He looked around the living room with some satisfaction. "Totally furnished, which is what you requested. I had Shelly—she lives in one of the cabins at the café, you'll see them when you eat there—clean out the clothes and personal items, but we left the rest to keep it homey. The church took the canned goods for the food bank." He glanced at his mug. "Except the coffee, I guess. It lasts forever in the freezer. You can hire Shelly to clean and do errands, if you want. She's reasonable and can use the money."

Sam liked the sound of that. "Can I hire her to get some food for me?"

"Probably not. She broke her arm a few weeks back and I don't know if she's driving. I'll give you her number. There's a little market, more of a convenience store—Thompson's, no relation—on Main Street across from the library. They do real estate, too, if you decide you want to buy something. Anyway, the market doesn't deliver, but you can walk there. How are you doing? I thought you had a broken arm."

"Cracked ribs," Sam said, figuring his injuries would get him out of interacting with people. He wanted to do nothing more than write the damn book and feel sorry for himself. "And a bit of trouble with my heart. I was— Well, never mind." He didn't want to go into the details. He felt stupid enough as it was.

"No car? Or you can't drive?"

"Both, for now."

"I heard you had a little trouble yesterday." The redheaded mayor took another sip of the coffee and grinned at him. "Stealing wood from Lucia."

"Ah," Sam said. "She's already complained?"

Jerry laughed and shook his head. "Twitter. You saw the babysitter? Thumbs like a machine, according to her grandfather."

Sam's head began to throb. "I mistook the shed for mine."

"The photo of you in the snow was grim, but now that I know you're okay—"

"Photo?"

"Told you," Jerry said. "The kid's technologically advanced. But I guess they all are these days. Sorry." He reached into his pocket, which was buzzing, and retrieved a cell phone. "Hello?"

Sam drank the rest of his coffee as fast as he could without burning the inside of his mouth. He needed the caffeine. He also needed food. Lots of food. Enough food to last him until the first of April, when he could leave this place and go back to his day job.

"It's fine," Jerry was reassuring someone.

"He's okay, a perfectly nice guy. I'm here with him right now."

So the incident yesterday had been blabbed all over town. Typical, of course. Sam had lived in villages along the Amazon and knew how fast news traveled.

"Tell you what," Jerry said, radiating good cheer and agreeableness. "He and I are going to have breakfast." He paused to listen. "Where else? You can meet him then." Another pause. "Well, okay, next week then." Pause. "Yeah, that's Thursday at seven. You got the email."

Sam heard Jerry say "Fine" and "No problem" a few more times before Jerry clicked his phone shut and apologized. "Sorry. Member of the town council."

"It's okay," Sam said. "I imagine you're a busy man."

"I just returned from L.A., as a matter of fact." He set his coffee mug on the mahogany coffee table. "I don't suppose you've heard about our town project."

"Uh, no." Sam's headache intensified, as did the ache in his chest. He really, really didn't want to hear about the town project, whatever it was. Had he seen half a loaf of bread in the freezer? Was there any lasagna left? "Where did you say the market was, Jerry?"

"Two blocks away, around the corner on Main. But it's closed on Sundays in the winter."

"Damn."

"What do you need?"

"Food, of any kind. I'll call Theo and see if—"

"Hold on a sec." He opened the phone and hit a number. A few seconds later he said, "Hey, Luce. It's me, Jerry." Pause. "Great. I'll have a meeting Thursday to update everyone— Yeah, I'm home." Pause, with a glance at Sam. "Thanks for doing that. Hey, you're going into Lewistown today, right?" Pause. "What time?"

Luce? It didn't take a genius to understand that Jerry was talking to the black-haired neighbor.

"Can you pick up some groceries for my renter while you're there?" Pause. "Just the basics, I guess. He can give you a list."

Sam caught Jerry's eye and shook his head. Oh, man, he didn't want to give her a list. He didn't want her to do him any more favors. He didn't want to be in her debt any more than he was, despite the fact that her kids and her dog cost him a painful night.

Okay, *he'd* slipped first, at the beginning of the attack. And he'd hit his own head on the wood when he fell. And he'd yelled, although more out of frustration with his own weakness than in pain. He'd been rude, which wasn't how he usually conducted himself.

He was sure she was a very nice person— he knew she was, because she'd built up the fire and brought him dinner even after he'd yelled at her children. He expected her husband to knock on the rear door and tell him to back off. He would definitely apologize. Grovel, even. Because he would be living here for three months and maybe she'd make lasagna again.

"What do you want? Eggs? Meat? Milk? Bread? What?" Jerry asked.

"I don't want to put her to any trouble."

Jerry ignored him and spoke into the phone. "He doesn't want to put you out. Just get him the basics, enough for a couple of days. I'll drive him into Lewistown later in the week if he's up to it. Okay?" Pause. "Thanks."

He flicked the phone shut once again, tucked it into his pocket and picked up his coffee mug. "There, you're all set."

Sam realized he'd had no input in this. Frustrating. "I didn't want to bother her," he reiterated.

"No bother," Jerry said. "She goes into town every Sunday to take her mother-in-law to church. They were just leaving. If she couldn't do it, I'd drive over there myself. Can't have my new tenant starving to death."

"I don't want Mrs. Swallow running errands for me."

"Mrs. Swallow is her mother-in-law. You're talking about Lucia, the goddess of baking."

"The what?" First the "pie lady," now a goddess. An interesting neighbor, all right.

"She went to school for it with Meg, who owns the café. Between the two of them, no one in this town goes hungry."

Good news, Sam thought. "How far away is this café?"

"One block east and two blocks south. You can almost smell the bacon from your front porch." Jerry leaned forward. "You're looking a little rough there, pal. Are you sure you're okay? Getting some food in you would help, but are you really up for a walk? I can get you something and bring it back here."

"Food would be good, if the café's not too far away. I could use the exercise." He looked down at his sweat pants and socks. He could probably lace up his boots if he did it real fast. "Let me get some clothes on."

"Good. Pardon the cliché, but we'll kill two birds with one stone." Jerry sipped his coffee and leaned back on the sofa as though he planned to spend the day there.

"What do you mean?" Sam paused in front of the bedroom door.

"You need to meet some of your neighbors and show them you're normal, just a regular guy who's not going to cause any trouble."

"Why would I cause trouble?"

"For starters, your coming here is suspect. I mean, who moves to Willing in the winter?"

Sam shrugged. He wasn't going to explain about the man he'd met on the flight to Miami. He'd sound like an idiot.

"Second," the mayor cheerfully continued, "you've been searched for on the internet. People like the writer, adventurer, documentary-maker thing, but they don't completely trust it. It could be a cover."

"A cover for what?"

"Who knows? Criminal activity, insanity, government plots." Now it was Jerry's turn to shrug. "Hey, I'm just the landlord here. You seemed okay to me or I wouldn't have rented the house to you."

Sam doubted that. They'd traded emails and had one brief phone conversation. The check for three months' rent had been cashed. Sam turned back to the bedroom, where the purple violets on the wallpaper greeted him.

"But the biggest thing," Jerry said, slurping coffee, "is who you're living next to."

The violets would have to wait another minute. Sam gingerly turned around again. "What does Lucia have to do with it?"

Jerry cradled his coffee and looked very, very serious. "She's a widow. She's a good person. She doesn't date. And her pie crust will make you weep."

"A widow?" The beautiful Lucia Sparrow,

who baked like a goddess and could handle a woodstove and three boys, was single? What was wrong with the men in this town?

"Yep. So don't mess with her unless your intentions are honorable."

"My intentions?" He chuckled. "My intentions are…nonexistent. What are you, her father?" He couldn't help laughing at his landlord again.

"Hey, this is no joke. If anything happens to Lucia because of me…" He picked up his jacket and gave Sam a warning look. "I'd never win another election."

"I'll be on my best behavior," Sam promised. "For your sake."

JERRY DEBATED BETWEEN a booth or a stool at the counter, since the old guys weren't in their regular spots. Being Sunday, the café wasn't filled with regulars the way it was on a weekday. Well, Sam would meet the old guys soon enough.

"Could we sit at the counter?" Sam asked, seeming to read Jerry's mind. "Easier to get on and off."

"The ribs are bad, huh?"

"They're taking longer to heal than I want."

Jerry introduced him to Shelly, who wore a battered cast on her arm and had her blond hair pulled back into a ponytail. Her belly appeared to have tripled in size since the accident, yet she seemed to still enjoy working for Meg. She certainly seemed thrilled to see him and his guest.

"How are you feeling?"

"I'm really good," she said, holding the coffee carafe in her good hand. "I get the cast off in two and a half more weeks." She twinkled at Sam. "Coffee?"

"Please," Sam said, sounding a little out of breath, though they'd walked slowly on the shoveled sidewalks.

"Shelly, I'd like you to meet Sam Hove. He's new in town."

"I know. Everyone's talking about you. I saw some of your videos on YouTube last night. Awesome stuff."

"Thanks."

"Those rivers looked spooky," she said, shuddering momentarily as she placed two coffee mugs in front of them. "I'm glad I don't live in those places."

Al hurried out of the kitchen to shake Sam's hand and introduce himself. "Man, I saw that show on the giant catfish a couple of years ago. I'll never cook catfish again."

"Catfish?" There were people who watched shows about catfish? Well, then, viewers were going to love a show about Willing, Montana.

"CAN I DO IT?"

Lucia, busy organizing groceries on her kitchen counter, glanced at her oldest son. "Not alone. But you can come with me." Or the four of them could walk over together. The boys could wait outside, carry wood and give Boo some time to run off some energy in the yard.

"I want to do it by myself."

"Sorry, pal," she said, but not about to explain the reason that mothers didn't let their little boys go to strangers' houses.

"Why not?"

"We don't know anything about Mr. Hove," she said, rearranging the supplies she'd purchased for her new neighbor. "Except what we read on the internet."

"Yeah, we do. He's famous."

"Remember? You can't believe everything you read on the internet."

Davey sighed. He'd heard that a hundred times. "But *Grandma* said he was famous."

"Well…maybe a little famous." Marie had printed out a biography off Wikipedia and a spotless people search report she'd actually paid money for. As she'd said, it didn't hurt to be careful. But Lucia thought the man lived an exciting life. He'd produced documentaries for various cable channels that specialized in adventure shows on jungles and strange fish. They'd discussed him all the way to Lewistown, the three boys asking questions no one could answer. She'd finally distracted the kids when they were in the fish section of the supermarket. There, questions about where frozen shrimp originated had replaced questions about the mysterious neighbor.

"Maybe he could come to school. You know, talk about the jungle and stuff."

"Maybe."

"Can I ask him?"

"Maybe. When he feels better." Lucia doubted that would be anytime soon. The man couldn't even take his own boots off. Now that had been an interesting little moment yesterday. She wouldn't even tell Meg about it because of how silly it would sound: "I untied his boots—the most intimate moment I've had with a man since the night before my husband went to war."

"Mom," her son said. *"Mom."*

"What?"

"You're not listening."

"I apologize. I was thinking about dinner," she fibbed. She was thinking about Sam Hove's blue eyes. "There," she said, giving herself a mental shake. "I guess I have everything he'll require for a few days. Maybe even a week."

"I need more points," Davey, still angling to do the job himself, said. Lucia admired his competitive spirit but wondered if this Random Acts of Kindness project was something he worried about too much. Davey was her quiet son, the philosopher of the trio.

"You could shovel Mrs. Beckett's steps."

"She'll just yell at me."

Yes, she probably would. "You're right. She's not worth the points."

"I think she likes being mean," he said, but Lucia could see him considering whether being yelled at was worth a point or two on the Kindness scoreboard.

"Some people do," she agreed. Her eight-year-old was wrestling with big concepts now. She wanted to hug him, reassure him that people were good and kind and life was fair and the world was his oyster and all that, but the truth was a little harsh: mean people existed and weren't worth the do-good-things points.

Davey pondered that for a long moment, while Lucia dug through her purse for the grocery receipt. She'd kept Sam's food separate from hers. It wasn't the first time she'd delivered food next door: Mrs. Kelly had become more dependent on help that last year she'd lived in town. Lucia had agreed to Jerry's request to pick up supplies for the new neighbor—after all, the man was practically an invalid, and she was going to the store anyway—but once in the middle of the IGA with three lively boys and a horde of intense Sunday shoppers, she'd wished she'd refused.

She was such a sucker. Someone sick? Lucia made chicken soup. Someone need a ride? Lucia was going to Lewistown anyway. Want a shoulder to cry on, help with a television show, a piece of pie, a cake for a bake sale?

Groceries for the new neighbor with cracked ribs?

She wondered if her phone number was on the entire town's speed dial. She wondered how many Kindness points she'd racked up the past seven years. Probably enough to win a great big trophy.

"What's the prize?" she asked her son, snapping out of her reverie.

Davey's face lit up. "It's a secret," he breathed. "No one knows."

Which meant, Lucia suspected, that the teacher hadn't come up with anything yet. "Hmm," she said. "That's interesting. What do you want it to be?"

"Money," was his immediate answer.

"Money? For what?"

"What about Mr. Hove? Is he mean?" Davey asked, ignoring Lucia's question and switching the conversation back to the topic of mean people.

"Maybe, maybe not." She thought Sam Hove was grumpy, but he'd been hurt and humiliated. Mr. Big Adventure Man had most likely not landed facedown in the snow before. Soon there could be a lot of activity for a sleepy winter town. There would be young women who would need sugar carbs to keep up their spirits. Women who might fall in love with a few of the local bachelors and stay in town. There would be publicity, too, once the show aired. People would flock to Willing and, as Jerry said, long to be part of small-town America. They would start businesses, shop in local stores, bring in their friends, attract tourism and pay taxes. They would eat, of course.

What a lovely fantasy.

Lucia loved this town. But even so, she'd thought about moving south to Lewistown, where she could expand her business. Even Billings or Bozeman was an option.

Except she wanted to stay here. She wanted to be here when Meg had children and she wanted her sons to have "Uncle Owen" to emulate. She wasn't looking for a husband or a boyfriend or even someone to date occasionally. Or was she? Would she like to find a kind, quiet, solid man to be part of her life? Yet who would want to take on three boys? Who would understand that her boys always came first?

No, she was better on her own. It was less complicated.

The man next door was the perfect example of the kind of man to avoid. Not that he'd be attracted to a rum-soaked widow with wild kids.

"Mom! What's so funny?"

She looked down at her oldest son. "Something someone said yesterday. It made me laugh."

HE HEARD THEM COMING, the children, the woman, the yipping dog. There was a flurry of activity at his back door and then the sound of knocking. He didn't realize how much he looked forward to the company.

He opened the door, heard himself say, "Come in," and sound sincere.

He saw the woman's surprise, before she dropped her eyes and ushered her sons inside, told them to stay on the rug and not track snow on the floor.

There was a bit of commotion with the grocery bags and the boots and the boys telling the dog to wait outside. The dog protested, but sat down and stared at the door until it closed.

"Will he be okay?" the oldest boy asked his mother. "What if he runs away?"

"Go out with him," she said. "To make sure."

He gave Sam a pleading look. "I'm sorry we made you fall in the snow."

"I'm sorry that I yelled at you," Sam replied seriously.

"You didn't really yell," the boy pointed out. "You looked like you wanted to yell a lot more, but you didn't, that was all. You looked pretty mad, though."

"Mad at myself," Sam explained. "For being hurt in the first place." The dog barked, insulted to be left outside in the gray afternoon cold and his boys where he couldn't see them. "You can let him in," he said, "if you're sure he won't pee in the house."

"He won't." The boy shot him a look of gratitude and eased past his mother to open the door.

"That's really not—" Lucia said, frowning. "We're not going to be here more than a few minutes."

The dog rushed inside, but skidded to a stop when he saw Sam. He let out a growl, yet wagged his tail at the same time. The tallest boy grabbed his collar and kept him on the rug.

"It's okay," Sam reassured the animal.

"Boo! Quit that." Boo stopped growling and decided to whine instead.

"Boo? Is that really his name?"

Boo wagged his tail and smiled at Sam. He glanced around the kitchen as if hoping to smell something good to snack on.

"Yes. He's going home this week. He belongs to a friend of ours who lives outside of town," Lucia said, taking the grocery sacks from the two biggest boys and setting them on the counter. She had kicked off her boots again, but Sam saw that the boys stayed on the rug. They watched him as if he was going to do something interesting. The middle one set a gallon of milk on the rug.

"The bridegroom," Sam said. "I remember."

"Yes." She started pulling things out of one of the plastic bags. "Jerry told me to get what I thought you'd need. Multigrain bread, two dozen eggs, a pound of bacon." Another bag. "Canned beans, flour, sugar, salt, baking soda, baking powder, cinnamon…and, oh, black pepper and chili powder."

"Great," he managed, easing over to examine the stuff covering the counter.

"Next," she stated, "protein. A pound of ground sirloin, two rib eye steaks, a package of pork chops and a roasting chicken. Whatever you don't plan to eat in the next two days, you can freeze."

"Okay."

She moved on to the fourth bag, which she unloaded with frightening efficiency. Lucia Swallow knew what she was doing when it came to food. "Vegetables," she announced. "Frozen. And the same with fruit, although I splurged on bananas because they were on sale."

"Anything else?"

"Cheese," she said, opening another bag. "Half-and-half, another bag of coffee and some green tea. Mayonnaise, mustard, ketchup. I also bought a bag of Oreos, because the boys insisted you would like them."

"We like them," the littlest boy echoed. "We like them a lot."

The middle child giggled. The oldest shushed him. Lucia paid no attention because she lifted a cooked turkey breast from the last bag. "This is still warm," she explained. "They do them on a rotisserie at the store. You can get a couple of meals out of it, plus a sandwich or two."

"Thanks for all this," he said, which sounded weak. "I owe you."

"You're welcome. I didn't buy any fish— nothing was on sale. But since you're a fisherman, you probably know what you like and you're used to fresh."

"I can skip the fish, thanks."

"Good." She brushed past him to start loading up the refrigerator. She smelled like vanilla and cinnamon. Apple pie, that was it. Had she been baking? He thought of apple pie and his mouth watered.

"Here," he said, grabbing the bag of frozen food. "I'll do that."

She saw him wince, and took the bag from him. "Maybe you should sit down."

He glanced over at the wide-eyed children standing there on the rug watching their mother give him orders. Boo stayed on the rug, though his front paws edged onto the floor a few inches. Yesterday Sam was in pain, and she was a bossy neighbor whose kids had tossed him into the snow. Today she was a widow who had done his grocery shopping. He felt like a real jerk.

"Maybe I should have some Oreos. What do you think? Want to join me?"

"That's not—" Lucia began, but Sam ignored her. He had some fences to mend here.

"You'll have to tell me your names first. I'm Sam."

"Mr. Hove," Lucia corrected, giving Sam a look that said her children were expected to show respect to their elders. Sam let that one go and turned to the oldest boy.

"I'm sorry I don't remember your name."

The oldest, the one who looked as though he took everything in and kept his conclusions to himself, said, "Davey. I'm in third grade."

His younger brothers were suddenly speechless, so Davey pointed to the middle one, a slender version of his mother, with black hair and a sweet smile. "That's Matt and this is Tony, the baby."

"I'm not a baby," the little boy protested. He was short and stocky, with curly dark brown hair and big brown eyes. "I go to preschool."

"Of course you're not a baby," his mother

assured him, but the laughter in her voice didn't convince anyone. He was her baby, Sam knew, and the kid would have to live with that for the rest of his life.

"I think you should have cookies with me," he told the boys. "You must be hungry after shopping in town."

There was a flurry as jackets and mittens were tossed to the floor. Even the dog trotted over and licked his knee.

Lucia protested, then relented. "Okay, but just one cookie each. Take off your boots," she said to the boys. "Mr. Hove doesn't need snow on the floor."

Sam doubted snow could hurt the old vinyl floor. He wouldn't want to guess what color it had been a hundred years ago when it was installed. Gray? Green? "It doesn't matter," he said. "Really."

"Um, have you ever lived in snow country before?"

"No."

"Well, we take our boots off at the door," she explained. "Everyone does."

"Oh." Now he was an outsider again. Well, hell. "How much do I owe you?"

She fished around her jacket pocket and pulled out a folded receipt. "It's all here."

"I really appreciate the help." Sam took the bill, set it on the counter and ripped open the Oreos. He put the bag in the middle of the table and asked Davey to bring the milk over.

"You're still hurt?" the boy inquired, padding over in his sock feet.

"The doctor said it could take a few weeks." He drew three glasses from the cupboard and brought them over to the table. "Can you pour?"

"Yeah." Davey unscrewed the cap and filled the glasses, barely splashing any milk on the table. The kid had had some practice. "Mom said you hit a fish."

"More like the fish hit me."

"Weird," said the boy, pushing glasses of milk in front of his wide-eyed brothers.

"Yeah. That's what I thought, too." He turned to Lucia. "Do you want milk? Or coffee? I can make some."

"No, thank you."

"You can see I'm trying to apologize for yesterday," he said.

"All right," she replied, staying on the rug

as if cemented there. "You really weren't that terrible, you know."

"Apologize because you took our wood?" Davey asked, half an Oreo in his mouth.

"Please don't talk with your mouth full," Lucia said, which sounded more automatic than annoyed.

"Well, that, too." He paused, gave the mother what he hoped was a sheepish smile. "Because I was rude about falling down. And a jerk when you tried to help me."

"Mom said you acted like a brat," the littlest boy announced. The other boys giggled.

"Tony!" She flushed. "I didn't think he'd repeat it," she said, shooting Sam an apologetic look of her own. "I should know better."

She was stunning, and he doubted she was aware of it. "I'll mind my manners from now on," he promised. "Let me get my wallet and pay you for the food."

He left her standing on the rug, the boys at the table, cookie crumbs falling for the dog to lick off the floor, while he carefully walked to the bedroom to retrieve his wallet from the top of Mrs. Kelly's oak dresser.

The pain was creeping up on him again; he'd grown to expect the worst late in the day.

He paid Lucia for the groceries, thanked her again.

"We'd better go," she said, hurrying the children out the door. "It's a school night."

The oldest boy paused. "Thank you for the cookies," he said seriously.

"You're welcome. Thanks again for the food."

And then they were gone and the house was empty.

Sam wasn't used to being alone. He'd lived in villages—well, visited villages—and traveled with a film crew. He was rarely alone, unless he was between trips. And even then he was busy with projects and coworkers. He didn't especially care for being isolated, which would account for his manuscript not being finished.

What he did like was being in motion, traveling, energetically confronting each day and the unknown that lay ahead.

Living in a strange country for a few months was a piece of cake, but living alone in a purple house would be another thing altogether.

Well, he'd made up with the neighbors. He'd shown his face at the local eatery with the jovial mayor, where he'd left a big tip for the pregnant waitress and complimented the cook on the pancakes.

Now he had to knuckle down and write a book.

CHAPTER FOUR

"GONNA BE a mean winter," the gaunt elderly gentleman said. Sam didn't know who the man was talking to until the guy turned his stool toward Sam as Sam carefully lowered himself onto a stool at the end of the counter.

"It's cold out there today," Sam said. He'd walked to the café slowly and by himself this morning, taking his time, making sure he wouldn't slip and career into a snow bank. The large room was warm and noisy, surprisingly busy at 7:12 on a Monday morning. The place smelled like bacon, coffee and cinnamon, a good combination on a dark winter morning. He'd ignored the array of food in his refrigerator and told himself he'd make chili or something later on. He needed some air. And he sure as anything needed a little company.

"I can feel it coming," the man continued. "Something mean."

"Really?" Sam didn't discount the opinions of elders. He'd met enough of them in villages along the Amazon and believed that without their help and advice he'd be dead. "What makes you think that?"

"It's cold in a mean way. It just has that feel, you know?"

Sam contemplated what "the feel" meant, but nodded as if he knew what the man was talking about. "Well, I hope you're right. I haven't been around snow for years, so it would be fine with me."

"You're the fellow renting Claire's house, aren't you?"

"Yes." He set down his coffee mug and stuck out his hand. "Sam Hove."

The man took it. His hand was the size of a banana leaf. "George Oster. Glad to meet you. I've heard all about you."

Sam didn't know what to say to that, so he kept his mouth shut and waited for the man to explain. He didn't have to wait long.

"You really got hurt by a fish?"

"I did." Caught on camera, too, which was the only useful thing to come of the event. The footage had been impressive. "The fish was a beauty. Ninety pounds of pure muscle."

"There aren't any big fish around here," George said. "I hate to disappoint you, but that's the truth. Don't let anybody tell you different."

"I'm not here to fish," Sam assured him.

"Well, that's good, because if you were you'd be disappointed."

"That's what I hear."

A pretty brown-haired woman hurried over to him. She wore jeans, a red T-shirt and a red-checked apron, and her brown eyes sparkled with good humor. He was dazzled for a moment when she smiled, and then when she set coffee in front of him, he was dazzled again by the sapphires and diamonds in her engagement ring.

"Hi," she said, sounding breathless. "I'm Meg Ripley."

"She owns the place," George said.

Sam shook her hand. "Sam Hove. It's nice to meet you and to have a place to eat. Now I know I'm not going to starve this winter."

"I heard you were in yesterday. I'm sorry I missed you." She set a container of half-and-half in front of him.

"Your mayor and I had a great breakfast."

George snorted and shook his head. "He didn't waste any time. He want you to be on the show?"

"Show?"

Meg chuckled, produced a coffee mug and filled it from the nearby carafe. She put it in front of Sam before he could ask for it. "See, George? I told you Jerry wasn't recruiting any bachelors from out of town."

"Thanks," he said, sliding the mug closer. "Theo Porterman told me there was something going on," Sam said. "A television show?"

"Publicity stunt," George grumbled, and another elderly gentleman next to him lifted his coffee cup and said, "You got that right."

"Harmless, I guess, as long as it doesn't raise taxes," George grumbled.

Meg and Sam exchanged a smile.

"We've been getting ready, just in case," Meg explained. "Jerry was in L.A. last week for meetings, but he hasn't said what happened."

"He didn't tell me anything," Sam said.

"Did he ask you if you were single?"

"No." Sam couldn't remember if he'd volunteered that information or not. He'd always been single and he always would be. End of story.

"Huh." Meg tipped her head, her forehead furrowing. "That's odd."

"Why? Does he, uh, go around asking people that?" He took a sip of very strong, very good coffee. "It's not like it's anyone's business."

George snorted. "Like that's ever stopped him!"

"He has enough people for the show," Meg mused. "He wouldn't mess with the numbers." She eyed Sam. "I hear you've met Lucia."

"She brought me some food. Nice lady."

"Extremely nice lady." There was warning in the comment.

He sighed. "I'm not a serial killer, a psycho, an escaped convict or anything weird. I write. I fish. I travel. I am not married, never have been. I don't con widows out of their pensions or have a prison record. I've never been arrested—except one time, for fishing too close to the Laotian border." He pulled in a shallow breath. It hurt. "I had malaria once."

"Malaria?" George stared at him, fascinated. "My older brother got that in the war."

Someone else muttered, "Jeez."

Sam ignored them and looked at Meg. "Am I still allowed to live next to Lucia for three months? That's how long I've paid my rent for," he added, letting his aggravation show. "Three months."

"I read about that arrest. They thought you were a spy. You look younger on the internet," George pointed out.

"Yeah, well, I'll bet you do, too." He plucked the plastic-coated menu from its holder next to the salt and pepper shakers while George cackled. "I think I'll have the blueberry pancakes again, with scrambled eggs on the side. And sausage, please."

"Mountain Man Special," George informed him. "That's what it's called. And you get orange juice."

Meg winced. "Should I say I'm sorry? I'm a little protective."

"That's okay," Sam said, suddenly tired and painfully out of breath. "The world is a dangerous place."

"You should know," George said and lifted his mug for a refill.

DAVEY WAITED UNTIL Matt went upstairs to brush his teeth before taking three green-sprinkled sugar cookies from the plastic container on the counter. Mom had packed his and Matty's lunches already, so she would want to know why he wanted more. But she was upstairs helping Tony dress and he was squealing about something dumb because he was mad every morning that he wasn't old enough to go to regular school. Davey had the kitchen all to himself.

Except for Boo, who always stayed close to where the food was. The dog had finished licking the toast crumbs off the floor, found a couple of wayward Cheerios and now stared at Davey with the concentration of a hungry wolf.

"These aren't for you," Davey whispered. He slid the cookies into a little plastic sandwich bag and carefully zipped it shut. "They're not for me, either."

Boo's intense expression didn't change, not even when Davey fumbled through his backpack to find the stickers Becca Miller had traded him for half a fudge brownie last week. He'd planned to give the glittery star stickers to Tony for Christmas, but this was more important. He stuck one in the center of the plastic bag, which made it look really good.

Like a gift.

Like a *Kindess*.

He heard Matty's footsteps coming down the stairs, shoved the bag in his jacket pocket, shrugged the jacket on and then worked on his boots. "I'm taking Boo out!" he yelled, knowing his mom would hear him, even though she was upstairs. His mom could hear anything.

"Okay!"

Matty stomped into the kitchen. "Can I go?"

"No." He and Boo were out the door before anyone could say a word.

One more point for David Swallow comin' up.

SAM SPENT A comfortable hour and a half in the midst of the local population, who believed in going out for breakfast, no matter what the weather or how bad the roads. He was officially "the man who was hit by a fish," which he doubted anyone actually believed. He shared travel stories with a retired teacher—John, if he remembered correctly—and listened to a number of fish tales about Alaskan salmon. He ate four fat sausage links, demolished a stack of blueberry pancakes topped with real butter and drank enough coffee to wash it all down. A couple of guys thought they might have seen one of his documentaries. There was some discussion about searching on Netflix, which led to some bickering about wasting money on satellite TV and the price of gasoline. Sam wasn't sure how those two things were related, but everyone agreed taxes were too high.

He stood when the pain started, perched back on the stool when it eased off. Then it didn't ease off at all, which meant he must have looked bad enough for Meg to ask if he needed a ride home.

"You've gone white," she said.

And then six different men who resembled retired ranchers offered to drive him the two and a half blocks to Janet Street.

George's friend Ben Fargus, who was obviously a regular customer, pulled out his car keys and laid some bills next to his empty coffee cup. "Come on. I'll drive you.

Wouldn't want a moose coming along and knocking you over."

Sam wasn't sure if that was a joke or not, so he didn't laugh. "I appreciate it."

"Maybe we'll see you again tomorrow," Meg of the sparkly ring said. "You'll have to meet Owen, my fiancé."

It clicked. "You're the bride? Lucia's friend who's getting married."

She wiggled her left hand. "You noticed."

"Congratulations."

"Thank you." She chuckled and leaned closer, her voice low. "Did you really think she was a bad mother?"

Sam winced and hoped she was just teasing him. "It was a rough day. That's all I can say."

"Whoa," George said, giving him a hard stare. "Did that fish crack you in the head, too?"

"It was the pain pills," Sam said. "And the dog. And the kid knocked me into the— Never mind."

"I heard all about it. There's going to be a photo in the paper on Wednesday."

"Photo? Of what?"

"You in the snow," Meg said. "Remember the teenager?" He nodded. "Cell phone."

"Oh, yeah. Jerry told me about that. Said the kid is a real wizard with texting."

"Jeez," someone said. "You're kind of accident prone, aren't you?"

"I apologized to the boys with Oreos," he assured Meg. "And they forgave me. Honest." He paid his bill, left a healthy tip, managed to put his jacket on without screaming like a baby. "Thanks for breakfast."

"You don't want to get on Meg's bad side," Ben warned, holding the door open for him. The cold slapped him in the face. "She'll ban you from the café and you'll end up at home all by yourself eating shredded wheat."

"Has that ever happened to you?" He hurried to put on his gloves, thermal lined and waterproof, before instant frostbite set in.

Ben shuddered. "Had a few close calls when she said I talked too much and her ears needed a rest," he said. "But Meg's been a lot more cheerful since she got that ring."

"Women are like that," Sam said. He took shallow breaths, hoping to ease the pain in his rib cage. "Not that I've ever been married, but I've noticed they tend to like dia-monds."

"Huh," the old man grunted. He pointed to a blue Ford pickup. "It's unlocked."

It took a couple of careful moves to ease himself into the truck. He ignored the seat belt, figuring the painful contortions out-weighed the risk of Ben sliding off the road. The roads had been plowed, the sidewalks shoveled, which looked like business as usual for central Montana.

"Ah," Ben said, pulling up in front of the first house. "Claire and her husband, Arthur, were good friends. I spent a lot of time in that house playing cards."

"You're welcome to come in," Sam said, his hand on the door handle. The house looked empty, despite the smoke coming out of the chimney. He hadn't left any lights on and he knew it wouldn't be as warm as the café. It certainly wouldn't smell like bacon and cinnamon rolls.

"Another time, maybe," the old man said. "I've got to get home to the dogs."

"Thanks for the ride, Ben." Sam eased himself out of the truck and shut the door.

The driver's-side window rolled down, and Ben leaned out.

"Anytime." He gave Sam a hard stare. "Be careful, son. You don't look too good."

The window rolled up, the car jerked away from the curb, and the old man headed west to the center of town.

Sam didn't feel all that great, either, but getting out had been worth it. He would spend the rest of the day resting, maybe pulling his notes out, his new laptop unpacked. Jerry had kept Mrs. Kelly's internet connection, phone and cable television account intact; the amenities were included in the rent. Sam would check his email, read the news, do a little research, all from the comfort of the recliner.

Instead of going up the front steps, he trudged through the side yard to the back door. Theo's cousin was supposed to have delivered and stacked a load of split wood, complete with tarp, to the back door, but he hadn't arrived yet. Instead, there sat ten neatly placed chunks of firewood, topped with a bag of…cookies.

His neighbor, the lovely Lucia Swallow, had struck again.

He didn't know what to do about that. He should walk over and thank her, but his chest hurt so badly now that all he wanted to do was sit in Mrs. Kelly's easy chair and take a pain pill.

He didn't want to encourage Lucia Swallow.

There had been a spark, just a small one, the first time they'd met. He'd been ready to pass out when she'd untied his boots, but he'd noticed the smile hidden behind that long hair when she bent to work on the laces.

Oh, man. He wasn't marriage material, wasn't the kind of man who got involved in women with children and homes and sparkling engagement rings.

He would have to watch his step. Domestic women could be more dangerous than red-bellied piranhas.

EARLY TUESDAY MORNING Hip Porterman, a lanky, quiet man who looked a little like Abraham Lincoln, arrived with a load of firewood. Theo drove the truck, parked it in front of the house, waved and walked away.

Sam asked to him to stack thirty or so pieces in Lucia's shed, thanked him, paid him and put in another order for next week when Hip said he was available again. Hip lived around the corner, he said. And Theo would come by later to get the truck.

That afternoon Sam found a small casserole—frozen chicken pot pie, he guessed—on top of his woodpile. This one was tied with red and green ribbon.

He baked it that night, savoring every homemade bite while he wondered how to thank her. Gratitude without involvement, he decided. He would tell her he was feeling better, which wasn't exactly a lie because he'd learned how to be careful with the way he handled the wood and loaded the stove to avoid extra pain.

He suspected Lucia was looking for a husband, and from what he'd seen so far at the café there wasn't a lot to choose from.

On Wednesday he walked through light snow to that eatery, where he exchanged weather stories with George and Ben. They talked about snowstorms; he told them about a lightning strike on the Amazon back in 2007. His thick rubber-soled boots had saved him from electrocution.

He was informed that as much as they appreciated a good story, neither man thought Sam was too smart going out in a dugout canoe in between storms.

Sam gave up his stool to John Ferguson, who arrived at his usual time (so the men explained to him), and moved over to a nearby table. Leaning back against the chair seat seemed comfortable enough, if anything could be considered comfortable.

The weather was discussed further, as was Janet Ferguson's physical therapy and the price of wheat. Sam let the conversation drift over him and relaxed into the comfortable warmth of the restaurant. He was tempted to close his eyes and take a quick nap, but George and Martin started to bicker about politics, and their voices grew loud.

Shelly, the pregnant waitress, showed Sam the Willing newspaper. He'd made the second page, with a photo of his body in the snow, but his face wasn't visible. The headline read, Fishy Thief? with a paragraph detailing his name and occupation. Someone at the paper had a sense of humor.

On the front page a large headline read, Mayor Returns, Meetings Held, with a black-and-white photo of Jerry posing near the Hollywood Sign. Another article had a photo of Meg Ripley posing behind a stack of wrapped presents. Willing Wedding At Last? queried a column detailing the bridal shower given by Lucia Swallow and Aurora Jones at the Dahl.

"They haven't set a date," Shelly said, refilling his coffee. "But it will be soon."

"It seems to be a big deal," he said. The photograph of Meg was bigger than that of the mayor.

"Oh, yeah, it is." She absently caressed her blooming, apron-covered belly. "Meg went to Billings to pick him—her fiancé—up at the airport and then they were going to shop for furniture. I think she looked at wedding dresses, too, before Owen's plane got in."

"When's the baby due?"

"February twenty-second," she said. "It's a girl."

"Congratulations."

"Well…thanks. Can I get you anything else?"

"Just the check. I'd better get going." Today he really needed to start work. He had a rough outline of the stories he wanted to tell, one story per chapter, but he hadn't done more than organize his notes and unfold a couple of dozen maps.

"You might want to wait a sec," his waitress said, her gaze on the front door. "He sure appears excited."

"Who?" He turned to see for himself. Jerry, his face flushed from the cold and a black stocking cap covering his red hair, hurried into the restaurant as if chased by a wild animal.

A few heads turned in his direction, and the beaming man opened his arms as though to envelop the room in an embrace and loudly announced, "I— We—just got the official call! It's a go!"

"Oh, wow," Shelly breathed. "Meg's gonna love this. It's so cool."

"What?" Sam asked, but the waitress scurried off to the register and picked up the phone.

"It wasn't official until this morning," Jerry told the handful of people, who looked interested. Two young cowboys in a corner booth high-fived each other. "I've already scheduled a town meeting for tomorrow night, hoping I'd have news, since last week's meetings went so well and—"

"When are the women coming?" someone hollered.

"Ah," Sam said, turning to Shelly. "The television show?"

"City women and Western men," she said. "You haven't heard about it?"

"Just bits and pieces. I don't watch much television."

"It's a new dating show. The local guys have been getting ready for weeks. They've worked really hard." With that she hurried off to refill more mugs and take more orders. It was a busy morning in Willing and Sam enjoyed sitting back and watching the activity. He realized he was settling into a comfortable routine, with mornings at the restaurant and the rest of the day stoking the fire, working and napping in the recliner, catching a little news on TV and eating an occasional turkey sandwich. He ordered more socks and a couple of thick wool sweaters from Cabela's and spent most of his time as close to the woodstove as he could get without setting his clothes on fire.

"Thursday night," Jerry was saying. "You'll have all your questions answered then. Seven o'clock." He paused at Sam's table. "Mind if I join you?"

"Of course not."

"I need a neutral place," Jerry explained, pulling out a chair and settling himself in it. He removed his hat, shrugged off his jacket and waved at Shelly for coffee. "I have to eat without answering a lot of questions."

"Well, shoot." Sam smiled. "I had a few for you."

"You're not a voter, so I don't have to care if I answer them or not." He grinned. "Unless you decide to stick around, make me an offer on the house you're renting?"

"Not a chance. I've never been so cold in my life."

"You didn't get wood from the Portermans? I thought—"

"I did, and I keep the stove full. It's just… winter, I guess." He looked out the window at a heavy gray sky; snow was forecast for tonight. "I'm not used to it."

"Living alone sucks," Jerry said. Shelly set coffee in front of him. He thanked her, then said, "The usual."

"One on one?" she asked.

"Yep." He took a sip of coffee and sighed.

"One pancake and one fried egg," he explained to Sam. "I'm cutting back."

"There must be a woman," Sam said.

"Oh, yeah, there is, and I'm not getting anywhere."

"Someone local?" For a second Sam thought of Lucia. Those eyes could make a man do just about anything, whether he wanted to or not.

"No. A producer in L.A. Tracy. She'll be here right after the holidays."

"Is this a longtime thing?"

"We had something going for a while, then she broke it off and I moved here. Now I'm trying to get it back on. So far so good." He frowned. "I think. She runs hot and cold."

"Long distance is tough."

"Yeah." He took another sip of coffee. "We've got a lot in common, though. Except for me being here and her being in L.A."

"Maybe you can work it out," Sam said, not believing the words for a minute. Luckily Jerry's breakfast arrived and the topic of conversation switched to the mayor's dating disasters since he'd arrived in town.

"Last time we counted," he said, pouring "lite" syrup on his pancake, "there were maybe seven single women under the age of forty in this town. I went out with almost every one of them. But they're hard women to pin down," he confided. "Independent, which I like. Opinionated," he said. "Which is also good."

"Why do you say maybe seven?"

"Well, Meg's off the list. Joanie Parker is on and off with someone, Aurora doesn't date at all, and neither does Lucia. That leaves Patsy Parrish—the hairdresser—and Iris, who owns one of the B and Bs. Plus Maxine, who lives out of town." He waved toward Shelly. "Naturally, we don't count teenagers, especially the ones wearing maternity jeans."

"That's it?"

"Yep." He ate the egg in four bites. "In a town of forty-eight eligible single men. So you can see why a dating show is pure genius."

"Who's Aurora?"

"Aurora Jones. She owns the Dahl. She might be your type. No one knows much about her, but the bar has been around for as long as the town has. I have never asked her out, by the way." He shuddered. "She's a beautiful woman, but she has a mean streak. I admit to being frightened."

Sam didn't particularly care for mean or frightening women, but he promised himself a beer at the Dahl when he was feeling more energetic and brave. "What about Lucia?"

"I invited her out to dinner. Offered to pay for the babysitter, even. She said no and baked me a peach pie."

"Nice of her."

"I would have rather had the date," Jerry admitted. "But the pie was really good." He finished up the pancake and wiped his mouth with a napkin. "Mike's going to call you to set up an interview for the paper. Do you have a website?"

"No."

"Okay, well, tell him about the book, then. Give him a photo of you with some big fish from somewhere."

Sam finished his coffee. The ache was beginning to set in. "I think I've been searched for on Google a lot."

"A little more info won't hurt," Jerry said. "I still can't believe how many calls I got. Marie Swallow was the worst and Gary Petersen wanted to phone the sheriff."

Sam stifled a laugh. He'd never been considered dangerous before. "I've been on my best behavior," he assured Jerry, and he struggled to his feet. "Time to go to work," he said. "Congratulations on the show."

"You need a ride home?"

"No, thanks. The sidewalks are clear and it's not snowing. I can make it." He'd already paid for his breakfast, so he donned his jacket, hat and gloves and assumed he wouldn't freeze to death while walking the two and a half blocks home.

Jerry, on his third refill of coffee, told him to call if he needed anything. Shelly waved, as did some of the men at the counter. George warned him about ice, said the temperature was going to drop. Sam shivered, assuming the man knew what he was talking about.

Sam kept his head down against the wind and walked home. When he arrived, he headed to the back door and the woodpile. Two red-frosted cupcakes sat on a paper plate, the whole thing wrapped in plastic and topped with a silver stick-on bow.

Lucia Swallow was either a very generous or a very determined woman.

"How DID YOU get all these points?" Lucia examined Davey's Random Acts of Kindness chart and noted the number of checkmarks this week. Her son had ramped up his competitive streak lately.

Davey shrugged and jammed his schoolwork into his Seattle Seahawks backpack. It was bedtime at last. And tomorrow was the last day of school before vacation, and Christmas was only a week away. Lucia had one more weekend of baking and then she could take some time off, thank goodness. Boo was going home tomorrow, which would be disappointing for the boys, but Lucia suspected Boo would be visiting again, when Meg and Owen went away on a honeymoon.

"I'm not sure I'm supposed to tell," he said, looking a little worried.

"I think you can tell me," Lucia said. "I have to sign the sheet saying you did it."

"I think you're supposed to believe me. Like the honor system."

"Honey, I know you wouldn't cheat," she said, looking down at those clear, brown eyes. Her oldest son's heart was huge, but he kept his feelings hidden under a layer of quiet. She worried about that, about how he preferred to be alone with a book or sitting with her in the kitchen instead of watching television with his younger brothers. There's nothing wrong with being quiet, Mama Maria insisted. He's a thinker, like his grandfather was. The strong, silent type, like in the movies. "I'm just curious, that's all," Lucia told Davey.

"I wouldn't cheat, not ever," he insisted. "I'm getting some really good points doing some really good kindness things."

"Like what?"

"I helped Tony get the toothpaste on his toothbrush."

"Okay." She waited.

"I carried wood for Mr. Hove."

"Very neighborly of you."

"Well," he said, biting his lower lip, "he's old and he's hurt."

Old? Lucia struggled to keep a straight face. Sam Hove was anything but old.

"And I, uh, gave Heather Madsen a pen. She lost hers so I put it in her desk, like a surprise."

"I'm sure she was happy about that." Heather's father had been out of work for months.

Heather's mother had left last summer, so theirs was a sad situation in many ways.

"Heather cried and kicked Becca when Becca laughed."

Becca was a little witch sometimes, Lucia thought.

"Becca got really mad," her son continued. "She was really screaming. Heather got in trouble for kicking."

Lucia could picture it. As much as she'd wanted a daughter, there were many times when she was relieved she wouldn't have to deal with all the girly drama she heard about from other mothers. She glanced over the Random Acts of Kindness chart. "You don't have to list what you did?"

"No. I mean, you can if you can remember, but you don't hafta write a whole lot. Mrs. Kramer said she'd ask us, in private, if she got confused."

He sighed. "I did other things, too, but I really don't want to go into it."

"Wow," she said. "You sound just like your father."

"How?"

"I really don't want to go into it," she repeated, lowering her voice an octave. "That means I'm supposed to mind my own business."

Davey's face brightened. "Cool."

"Am I supposed to sign this tonight?" She held up the paper.

"No, not yet." He took the paper and carefully folded it in fourths, then slid it into the Velcro pocket on the front of the backpack. "I've got more to do over vacation."

"Davey?"

He looked up at her, a little wary, if not a little guilty. Was she missing something here?

"It's nice you're doing this," she said. "Really nice."

Davey shrugged. "There's a prize," he reminded her.

"Well, it's not all about the prize," she replied. "Remember that."

CHAPTER FIVE

THE FROZEN CASSEROLE DISH, meatballs nestled on a bed of pasta, pushed Sam over the edge from content to euphoric. He lifted the dish from its perch on top of the woodpile by the back door, heated it up in the microwave and gobbled it down for lunch on Thursday.

Lucia Swallow had done it again.

So, the woman was either a saint or in desperate need of a husband. Sam figured it was about fifty-fifty either way, but it was time to say something. Like "Thank-you" or "Can I pay you to cook for me?"

Neither one was a particularly terrible response, especially the latter. From what he'd heard, Lucia had a thriving baking business in Lewistown and supplied pies to the café. In fact, he'd had a piece of apple pie after breakfast this morning. Tomorrow he might have two.

He could just call her on the phone and

thank her, but that seemed ridiculous when she lived twenty feet away. He needed to knock on her door and say thank-you in person. But he should bring something; he couldn't go over there empty-handed, especially not after the meatballs.

Time to pop a pain pill and stagger downtown.

"SWEETHEART, HE'LL COME BACK. I promise." Lucia held her sobbing four-year-old in her arms while Matty wept on her shoulder and Davey hugged the dog as if the animal were dying. Poor Boo wriggled out of the stranglehold and wagged his tail. He whined in Davey's face as if to say, Hey, what's your problem, dude?

All five of them were sitting on the kitchen floor, while seven pie plates lined with crust sat on the stainless-steel counter. Two pumpkin pies sat cooling on racks. Four more pies were in the ovens and the smell of apples and cinnamon filled the air. Tonight's dinner, a thick chili, sat simmering in her largest slow cooker.

"You can visit him at the ranch," Lucia said, patting her baby's back. "And he'll stay with us again when Owen and Meg go away on trips."

Tony shuddered. "Really?"

"Cross my heart." She twisted to kiss Matty's cheek. "Okay? Are we going to survive this?"

"No," Matty said. "I'm really sad. I want a dog."

"Me, too," Tony sniffed. "That's all I want for Christmas. A dog just like Boo."

She knew that was coming, had prepared for it. "Santa is not going to bring a dog this Christmas. Maybe in a few years, when you're all older."

"No dog is gonna be like Boo," Davey declared. "He's a really good dog."

"Yes, he is," Lucia said, releasing her children and climbing to her feet. She thought the worst was over, at least until Owen showed up to collect his one-of-a-kind dog. The tears would flow again, but she could put everyone to bed to sleep off the misery.

She gave Boo a pat on the head. "You are welcome here anytime," she told him, and went to the sink to wash her hands. Tony threw himself facedown on the floor, Matty threw his arms around her thigh and Davey answered the knock on the back door.

Lucia turned, expecting to see Owen. Instead, Sam Hove stepped inside and stood obediently on the rug by the door. His gloved hands carried a tissue-wrapped bouquet of red and white carnations, which he held out to her as Boo barked and wagged his tail. The younger boys' sobs turned down a notch, but the boys continued to whimper, tears running down their cheeks. Davey appeared stunned to see the neighbor in his house.

"These are for you. Obviously. It was all they had," Sam said, looking embarrassed. "I was hoping for something more, uh, exotic."

She crossed the room in four strides and accepted the bouquet. There were candy canes and baby's breath mixed with the carnations. "They're lovely. Thank you."

She thought for one mad moment that she had invited him to dinner and forgotten. No, she would have remembered. She would have put on earrings and a clean sweater. A V-neck sweater, maybe red and festive.

With her black brushed denim leggings and heeled ebony boots.

She would have brushed her hair. Instead she was in her oldest jeans, striped red socks and long-sleeved T-shirt that had once advertised a northwest huckleberry festival.

"Uh, have I caught you at a bad time?" He was staring at the two little boys hiccupping all over the dog. They looked as if they'd been beaten. Davey, still at his side, had recovered enough to appear somewhat normal, but had yet to make a sound.

"Boo is going home tonight," she said in her best mother voice. "We're all going to miss him."

His eyebrows rose as he assessed the situation. He turned to Davey. "I'm sorry to hear that. Dogs make good friends."

Davey nodded. "Yeah. I'm gonna get my own dog when I'm older."

"That's definitely something to look forward to," Sam said, turning back to Lucia. "Hey, I guess I should have called—"

"Would you like to come in?" Surely he would refuse to enter this den of tears and mucous.

"Well," he said, glancing toward the pies on the counter. "Just for a minute."

Boo disentangled himself from the boys and trotted over to sniff Sam's gloved hand.

"You don't have to take your boots off." She waved to a wooden chair, one of three tucked around a small round table. "You're injured, so you get a pass."

"I'm getting better at managing the injury. I have a system." He lowered himself onto the chair and regarded her littlest son, who was now whimpering, "I want Boo to stay, I want Boo to *stay*."

"Tony may have to go to bed early," Lucia murmured, turning back to Sam. "So, what's your system? Please don't tell me you're sleeping in those."

Davey edged closer. "I can help," he said. Lucia could see another check mark in the Kindness column. Smart kid.

"That's not—"

"—a bad idea," Lucia finished the sentence for him. "Let Davey help. He's working on a school project."

"But I do this thing with a barbeque fork." Sam pulled a chunk of metal out of his jacket pocket. "See? I found it in one of the drawers with a lot of utensils." He unfolded it and showed her. Meanwhile her three sons were struck silent by the wonder of a folding tool with pointed edges.

"Please, put it away before someone loses an eye." She was only half joking. "Why would Claire have something like that?"

"Mrs. Kelly liked hot dogs," Davey answered, busy unhooking the laces of Sam's left boot. "She liked to cook them over the stove. They were good."

"Thanks for the help," Sam told him. "I've got a few kinks to work out with the fork."

"That's okay."

Matty came closer. "Can I help?"

"No," was Davey's first response, but then he changed his mind and said, "Okay, you take the other one." Lucia anticipated another Kindness point, as in I-let-my-little-brother-help-me. Boo sat next to Tony and licked the tears off the child's face whenever he could get a clear shot at some skin.

"Your house is the same as mine." He glanced around the room, at the wood floor, the stainless-steel counters, the large gas stove top and the modern sinks. "But completely different."

"It's also the same layout as the neighbor on the other side of me," she said. "Three brothers built identical houses on the three lots back in the 1930s. Just like yours—the living room across the front, a bedroom on one side and a kitchen on the other, with a bathroom in the middle. Plus two bedrooms and a bathroom upstairs."

"But you have a real kitchen."

"I do," she said with not a little pride. She loved her kitchen and had designed it herself with her passion for baking in mind. She'd wanted double ovens and an oversized gas cooktop, along with lots and lots of counter space. Her husband had been determined to have it finished before he left and had done a lot of the work himself.

"There," Davey said. "I'll put your boots by the stove."

"Thanks, but—"

"Let him," Lucia said. "It's what we do here."

"I obviously have no idea how to behave in subzero temperatures." He looked at his feet. "I invested in expensive wool socks, thank goodness. That's important no matter where you are."

She smiled. "You can't go wrong with expensive socks." She realized she was still holding the flowers. "I need to put these in water," she said, handing them back to him. "Can you take them for a minute while I find a vase?" She turned to the boys on the floor. "Go upstairs and wash your faces, please. Leave that poor dog alone for a few minutes." They did as they were told, scrambling up the stairs in the hall.

"I thought about candy," Sam said. "But the fancy boxes appeared a little...dusty."

"Thompson's?"

He nodded. "Is there anyplace else?"

"Not now. There used to be a gift and flower shop on First Street, but it closed last year." She pulled a tall crystal vase from an upper cupboard and carried it to the sink to fill with water. "Thompson's will be getting in some fancy candy for Valentine's Day, but otherwise they don't carry it."

She took the flowers from him, their fingers touching for one brief, warm moment, and dismantled the wrapping before tucking the bouquet in the vase. She set it on the table.

"I know it's not much," he said. "I wanted to say thank-you."

"All right," she said. "But you replaced the wood, and it wasn't that big a deal, really."

"The meatballs," he said. "The food. That's been—"

There was a knock on the door before it opened and admitted a gust of cold air and two people to the kitchen. "Hello! We've got food!"

Meg, her cheeks and nose red from the cold, kicked off her boots and greeted the barking dog. Bedlam ensued as Boo raced across the room to Owen, who was sandwiched between the door and Meg. The boys came running down the stairs, Davey from around the corner, and the aroma of oregano and pepperoni wafted through the air.

"We brought pizza," Meg announced. "Whoa, Boo, calm down! Owen, don't drop it. Here, let me take—"

Sam stood and reached past Meg for the stack of pizza boxes that Owen was trying to juggle as he greeted his excited dog.

"Here. Let me have those," he said to Owen.

"Thanks." They sized each other up, while

Meg looked at Lucia, then the flowers on the table.

"Owen," Lucia said. "This is Sam Hove, my new neighbor. Sam, Owen MacGregor, Meg's fiancé and Boo's owner."

"Nice to meet you," Owen said, a pleasant smile on his face that didn't fool Lucia. Sam would be competently assessed within ten minutes.

"Same here," Sam said. "I've heard a lot about you at the café."

They shook hands, and then Meg and Owen removed their jackets, hung them on the oversized hooks by the door and stepped farther into the kitchen. Sam still held the boxes. In fact, he still wore his winter coat.

"Where do you want these?" He eyed the counter, where there wasn't any available space due to the array of pies.

"In the living room," she said. "Right on the dining-room table."

"Okay."

Boo bounced after the smell of pizza, and Owen followed Sam, the pizza, Boo and the three boys into the front room, after giving Lucia a curious glance. Meg wasn't so subtle.

"What's going on?" she whispered, as Lucia opened one of the ovens and peeked inside at a nicely browning pie.

"Not much," Lucia replied. "The apple pies are almost done, and I'm going to make the peach pies, but freeze them instead of baking them."

"Very funny. What's Sam doing here? With carnations?"

"Truthfully? I don't know." She closed the oven door and turned back to Meg.

"He just showed up at your door with flowers?"

"That's right."

"That's weird." Meg frowned. "Or sweet. I can't decide."

"I know."

"Well, it was nice of you to invite him for dinner."

"I didn't," she whispered. "He stopped in a few minutes ago. He's sort of...lonely."

"He's a nice guy," Meg said. "At least, he seems to be. He's been in the café every morning for breakfast and everyone likes him. Even the old guys. *Especially* the old guys, because they've been telling him all their ancient fishing and hunting stories."

"Mama's calmed down after reading about him. I've had calls from Jerry, Iris, Gary and Kim telling me that he's who he says he is—some kind of adventurer in the Amazon—and Mrs. Kramer, Davey's teacher, wants me to ask him to talk to the class about the rain forest."

"So your new neighbor is a *Raiders of the Lost Ark* kind of guy. Lucky you, with a handsome bachelor next door."

"Yep. A man who lives in the jungle is every widow's dream." She laughed.

"And he brought you flowers."

"He takes the loan of firewood very seriously."

"I like him," Meg declared. "Look." She pointed through the doorway to the dining table. The men had opened the pizza boxes and were checking out the contents, while the older kids climbed on chairs and peered into the boxes. "Tony's hanging on his leg and he doesn't even notice."

"Is that Mama's pizza?"

"Of course. She called me an hour ago and told me to bring it to you. I guess she would have driven it over herself, but she said her book club was coming for dinner."

Lucia grabbed a stack of paper plates from a drawer under the counter. "Who's working at the café?"

"Loralee, and Al's brother is cooking. I don't think it will be busy, so they're going to close early if it's too slow." She paused. "Sam resembles Harrison Ford a little. You know, when he was younger."

Lucia eyed Sam, who was listening to something Owen was saying while the boys tried to get their attention by shouting at one another. "Indiana Jones? Maybe. Just a little."

"He has that ruggedness to him. Like he has scars and tattoos all over his body."

"I get that vibe, too." Which was why she intended to keep her distance. Widowed mothers had no business flirting with dangerous men.

"It might be time."

"For what?"

"To start dating."

"I don't think so. Especially not with Indiana Jones out there."

"It's been four years," Meg pointed out. "Not that that is a long time, but you're still young, and according to Jerry there are forty-eight single men in this town."

Lucia shot her a withering stare. "And I'm not interested in any of them. Remember what happened with Joey Peckham. One dance at a birthday party and he thought we were made for each other. It was embarrassing."

"Sam Hove's about ten years older than Joey," Meg noted, keeping her voice low. Lucia peered through the oven windows this time to check her pies. "Unlike Joey, Sam Hove is all grown up."

"And he'll be back in South America or Florida or wherever he goes in three months. I don't need to make a fool of myself."

"It would be okay, you know, to go out once in a while. Just for fun."

"Look who's talking." Lucia couldn't help laughing. "Two months ago you didn't date, either. Before Owen came back to town you hadn't had a date in two years. Besides, dating doesn't sound like fun."

"Don't let Jerry hear you say that." She grinned. "He's counting on dating being a whole *lot* of fun here."

"Sam's more Aurora's type," she said, feeling the tiniest pang of envy for her sophisticated friend. "She could handle the 'love 'em and leave 'em' kind of guy a lot better than I could."

"Maybe," Meg mused, taking the paper plates out of Lucia's hand. "It will be interesting to see."

"Yes," Lucia said, unable to picture Aurora with anything less elegant than a bouquet of luscious, bloodred roses. "It will."

"MY GRANDMA MADE IT," the middle child told him, pointing to the pizza. "She's got boxes and everything."

"I see that." Apparently, he was expected to stay, so he removed his coat and draped it on the couch, one of those comfortable U-shaped pieces of furniture that looked like three couches put together. A small round coffee table covered with paper and crayons sat in the center of it. A woodstove was tucked in a corner, the same corner as his, and a heavily decorated Christmas tree, its white lights twinkling, blocked the front door. The walls were a soft white, the floor the same light wood as the kitchen. A television sat on a bench under a front window, with a pile of plastic toys in front of it. Books lay scattered everywhere. The place looked the way a home should, the kind of home he'd seen when he was a kid.

Meg handed him a plate, Owen grabbed a couple of extra chairs from the kitchen, Lucia tossed a pile of forks and napkins onto the large cloth-covered dining-room table and told him to help himself. Sam, seated between Davey and Meg, did exactly that. Lucia was to his left, at the foot of the table, and across were the two littlest boys. Owen sat at the head of the table and was now in charge of handing out pizza slices as needed. Meanwhile, Lucia served milk to the boys and offered wine, beer and water to the adults. Everyone opted for water. Owen noted he was driving, Meg was too tired for wine and Sam rarely drank alcohol. Boo sprawled near the boys, obviously accustomed to their food falling on the floor.

"My mother-in-law is starting up a pizza business," Lucia explained. "She's practicing."

"This is *practicing?*" Owen slid a piece of pizza onto his plate. "Looks like she knows what she's doing."

Sam agreed. "It's really good. I didn't expect to find pizza like this in Montana."

"She's going to work out of the café on weekends," Meg said. "To see if she wants to do it full-time."

"Now I know what I'll eat on Saturday nights," he said, already making plans. "Do I call the café to order?"

"I think she's going to have her own number, but you can phone the café, too," Meg said. "We haven't worked out the details, but she'll be up and running after Christmas."

"Wait until you meet her," Owen said. "She also makes the meatballs for Meg."

Sam turned to Lucia. "Do you do catering, too?"

"No," she said. "Meg's going to cater the TV show and I'll help her, but I trained as a baker."

"We went to school together," Meg added. "That's where we met."

"Meg told us—my husband and me—about Willing, so we came here after she moved back to town."

"So, Sam, what brought you here?" Unsurprisingly, this question came from Owen. The rancher looked as if he'd be quick to protect the women in his life, and that included his future wife's close friend. "Do you have any family in the area?" Owen inquired.

"No. I grew up in New York," Sam said. "When I'm not working I live in the Florida Keys. But I'm usually working."

"I worked in D.C. for years," Owen said. "I'm glad to be out of the city."

"Yeah, I know what you mean. It's not a place I'd want to go back to," he said, hoping Owen wouldn't ask any more personal questions. He could talk about fish and wildlife all day long, but he didn't like to get personal.

"New York," Davey said, as if trying out the words on his tongue.

"That's really far away," Matty said, and the littlest boy agreed.

Meg wasn't the least bit deterred. "So why Montana?"

"This'll sound a little weird," Sam said, wiping his mouth with his napkin, "but I sat next to a guy on a plane in Nicaragua who came from here. I never forgot the conversation, so when I needed a quiet place to work for the winter, I did a little research and found a house to rent."

"Who was it?" Meg helped herself to another pizza slice. "I've never heard of anyone from around here going to Nicaragua."

"The Fergusons went to Machu Pichu after John retired, but that's in Peru."

"I don't know his name. I figure I'll run into him one of these days, though. I hope so. He might not remember me, but I remember him."

"Was he young or old?"

"My age," Sam told Lucia. "Maybe younger. I got the impression he grew up here."

"Did you know how *cold* Montana is in the winter?" This came from Meg. "I mean, did you know what you were getting into?"

"Didn't have a clue," he admitted. "I knew I couldn't take one more day of hot weather, and I'd already sublet my apartment in Florida before the accident—"

"A fish!" Matty told Owen. "He was hit by a fish! Can you believe it? Isn't that cool?"

Owen laughed. "It must have been a big fish."

Davey told his brother to be quiet, Tony burned his tongue and complained, Boo began to bark for pizza crust and Matty helped himself to another slice. A buzzer went off, and Lucia excused herself from the mayhem and hurried into the kitchen.

"I saw a lot of pies on the counter," Owen said. "Are any of those for us?"

"Nope," Davey said. "I already asked."

"Darn."

"Yeah." Davey glanced sideways at Sam. "Do you like pie?"

"I sure do. I had your mother's pie at Meg's restaurant. It was really good."

"What kind?"

"Apple."

Owen turned to Meg. "Is there any left over? I could stop on my way home."

"We can check," she promised. "Is everyone done? I'll clear off the table."

Everyone had finished, although five pieces still remained in box number three. Pizza crusts had been saved for Boo, who was eating them in the kitchen. The boys helped Meg clear the table.

"I cracked a couple of ribs when I was a kid," Owen said. "I still remember how much it hurt."

"There's not much I can do about it except rest and let the ribs heal."

"Not much else to do around here in the winter except rest," Owen pointed out. "I hear you're writing a book."

Sam told him about it and Owen asked some questions; they were feeling each other out, looking for common ground, deciding if there was potential for friendship or if they should avoid each other unless stuck in a social situation.

Lucia returned to the table with a tray of coffee cups. Meg carried in a platter of thick sugar cookies, the three boys scurrying behind her. The talk moved to the weather forecast (more snow), the holidays (Meg was going to take some time off), Jerry's television show (which was actually going to happen in January) and the wedding (still no firm date). Sam listened to it all and felt surprisingly comfortable with these people he barely knew.

Matty wanted everyone to compliment the Christmas tree and insisted they admire each ornament, whether it was a Hallmark collectible or handmade from construction paper. Tony stated that he was going to sleep under the tree Saturday night.

"We take turns," Davey said. "Matty gets tomorrow night and I'm Sunday. The tree's pretty cool with the lights on."

"I've never heard of sleeping under the tree," Sam said.

"We invented it," was the boy's solemn reply. "With my dad."

"It's a great idea," Sam assured him. "I'll bet it smells good under there."

"Yep."

"You're lucky you have such a great tree," Sam told him. The bottom branches were high enough to form a small cave, just right for a child to crawl into.

Sam hadn't given Christmas a single thought. In Florida there would be a party on the beach with the locals who didn't think about Christmas too much, either. The town would be decorated, the tourists would flock in and there would be ornaments made of shells and decorated with red felt for sale everywhere. He wouldn't do anything different from any other day. When the hoopla was over, he was always relieved. New Year's Eve, when he was in town, had a much better vibe. Yet when it came down to it, that was just another day, also.

"I asked Santa for a really big truck," Tony confided.

"What kind of truck?"

"A dump truck," he said. "A *yellow* dump truck."

"I want a horse," Matty said, gazing at Owen. "Do you still have yours?"

"They're living with someone else right now, but they'll be back in the spring and you can come riding again."

"Thanks," he said. "I like the ranch."

"It'll look a lot better after we get the place fixed up," Owen said. "You'll have to get out and see it before you leave town, Sam. In three months the snow might even be gone."

"Where will you go from here?" This was from Davey, who stared at him with big eyes. "Back to the jungle?"

"I'm planning another trip to South America," he said. "We're going to look for a giant catfish again."

"Will you take a picture of it?"

"I will, and I'll send it to you."

"Will you come back here after?"

"I don't think so," Sam told him. "Once I finish my book I have to go back to work."

"Oh." The child appeared so disappointed that Sam immediately felt like the biggest jerk in the world. "I'd like to go to South America someday. Is it quiet in the jungle?"

"It's noisier than you'd think," he said, "but you have to be very quiet on the rivers, because fish have such good hearing. And they're smart."

"My dad took me fishing when I was four, but we didn't catch anything," he said, a thoughtful expression on his face. "Maybe we were too noisy."

"Could be," Sam said, feeling helpless in the face of a child's matter-of-fact grief.

Lucia cleared her throat. "Who wants a cookie?"

SAM INTENDED TO LEAVE immediately after Meg and Owen, who had Boo on a leash. The dog's tail wagged as he said his good-byes.

Fortunately the boys didn't cry when Boo actually left. They seemed almost stoic as they watched the dog bounce through the open door and onto the back porch, but once the door shut the three children trudged back into the living room and threw themselves on the couch. Tony grabbed a Spider-Man blanket and clutched it to his chest. Matty started to sniffle and Davey eyed Sam with a pleading expression.

"They'll cheer up after Santa arrives," Lucia said, removing the platter of cookies from the table. "Do you want another cookie?"

"I should be heading home." He definitely wanted another cookie. He'd lost fifteen pounds this year, and the accident had turned him gaunt and shaky. He'd decided the only cure was lasagna, meatballs, chicken pot pie and desserts.

He also wanted to stay. Oh, he could go home, turn on the computer, the television, the heat. But he knew for certain now that he wasn't fond of silence. He followed Lucia into the kitchen before he remembered Davey had placed his boots by the stove.

"Please stay for a minute, just to get their minds off the dog," she said. "Maybe you could tell the boys about the jungle. But nothing too scary. Just…educational."

"Educational," he repeated. "But without nightmare potential."

"Exactly. And," she cautioned, "without setting a bad example, you know, of doing dangerous things."

"Anything else?"

"Well," she said, solemnly thinking over the issue, "nothing too bloody or graphic. Matty might throw up. He has a sensitive stomach."

"Maybe I could just read them a bedtime story about bunny rabbits."

She ignored his teasing. "I'll give you all the leftover pizza if you'll keep them occupied for twenty minutes."

"You're bribing me?"

"I believe in bribery," she said. "It's part of the maternal tool kit."

"Well, okay then."

"Seriously, I really do need to get these pies filled and in the freezer."

He glanced at his watch. "It's almost eight o'clock. Do you always work this late?"

"Now's my busy season. And the next batch is going to be frozen, not baked. I'm using my peach preserves from last summer."

He had no idea what she was talking about, but he had no desire to head home to his empty house. And he had a great story about fishing with spiderwebs and kites, which wouldn't give anyone nightmares. He pretended to stall, enjoying gazing at the beautiful woman in the warm kitchen filled with pies.

She smelled like cinnamon and vanilla.

"Sure," he said. He was a hero, taking care of the kids. Saving the pies. Rescuing the woman. "Do you have an aspirin?"

CHAPTER SIX

SHE GAVE HIM a couple of aspirin, of course—she'd forgotten about his injured body. Lucia would have given him anything in the kitchen just to hear a male voice in the living room talking to her boys.

She knew she'd missed that since Tony had died, but she hadn't known how much. There were no grandfathers, no uncles. She and Tony had been only children. Her parents had passed away when she was a child, and her grandmother in Wyoming had raised her. Mama Marie's husband had died shortly after Tony and Lucia's wedding. She remembered a heavyset man with a big laugh and kind eyes. Matty, for whom he was named, resembled him.

The boys were alternately laughing and screaming, but they were having fun. She could hear it in their voices.

She hadn't realized that South America

was so interesting. Tony had mentioned a trip to Venezuela once, but he'd kept his missions secret and she'd known not to ask. An army wife learned early on that there were things her husband couldn't talk about, and her children certainly never knew their father traveled to anywhere but Washington, D.C.

Lucia carefully removed the pie crusts from the refrigerator, then assembled her pies using the peach filling. She topped seven pies with a woven crust brushed with egg white and sprinkled with coarse sugar crystals, then carefully wrapped the pies for freezing.

An hour more and Sam Hove could go home. She looked at the carnations, a cheerful holiday bouquet on her kitchen table. No one had brought her flowers in years. She shouldn't take the gift seriously. Sam was a lonely man, she thought, as she tiptoed to the doorway to the living room, where she could see her children gathered around him as he drew something in Davey's sketch pad. He certainly wasn't used to such a slow pace. Willing in the winter wasn't exactly a hotbed of activity.

"There," he said. "That's the way it looked from the air."

"Can you write the name?" This was Davey, her precise child.

"Sure." Sam printed something at the bottom of the paper. "Sturgeon," he said. "You can look it up. They're huge."

"And you caught one?" Matty yawned. "A huge one."

"Not a huge one," Sam said. "A medium-sized one. And I didn't keep it. I let it go."

"Why?"

"So it could grow," he explained. "We try to catch and release everything. We want to teach people like you about the fish and the animals, but we don't want to kill them while we're doing it."

Well, that was admirable, Lucia thought. She'd pictured Sam living in a house with dozens of stuffed fish mounted on glossy pine-paneled walls.

"Tell us about bait again," Tony said. "That was gross."

"Next time," Sam promised, catching sight of Lucia. "All done with your work?"

"Yes." She looked at her sons, who suddenly pretended they didn't see her. "Bedtime, guys. Say good-night to Sam and head upstairs. I'll be up in a minute."

Davey sighed. "We have to get our pajamas on and brush our teeth," he told Sam. "It's a pain."

"I'm going home to do that, too," Sam said, and yawned to prove it. The boys scrambled off the couch, said goodbye and raced each other through the kitchen and up the stairs.

Sam retrieved his warmed boots from the hearth and followed Lucia into the kitchen. She'd turned off most of the lamps and the room seemed just a little too cozy with only the light over the sink glowing on her soaking mixing bowls.

"Thanks for dinner," he said, taking a seat at the table. He shoved his feet in his boots and tucked the untied laces inside them. "For dessert, too. I hadn't intended to stay so long…"

"Thank you for the flowers. You didn't have to do that. You already returned the wood—which you didn't have to do, either." She heard herself babbling like an idiot. Something about him flustered her. She'd been able to cover up her discomfort by bossing him around like one of the kids, but right now it was showing and she was making no sense.

He stood up and smiled at her, lifted his jacket from the hook where she'd hung it earlier and shrugged it on. "You are a dangerous woman," he said, pulling his gloves from the pockets.

"I am?" Was he flirting with her? And was she so out of practice that she couldn't tell?

"Absolutely, without a doubt, dangerous."

Definitely flirting.

"I almost forgot the pizza," she said, and practically jogged to the refrigerator for the plastic bag with leftovers. "Here you go."

"You make me nervous, too," he said, accepting the bag from her outstretched hand. He took two steps toward her and brushed her cheek with his lips, a brief kiss that could have been described as a polite peck but wasn't.

Oh, it definitely wasn't, because her face felt hot and she knew she was blushing like a thirteen-year-old. Sam undertstood how to make a good exit, because he went right out the door with his future lunch in his gloved hand and not another word to say for himself.

She didn't think he had a flashlight, but her porch light was on and would illuminate his walk across the yard to his own back door. She stood in her kitchen and waited a few minutes until she saw a light go on in his living room. He was back in his own house, his temporary home.

But he'd left her with three tired boys, a vase of carnations and a smile on her face.

"DON'T TOUCH. I mean it." Davey glared at his younger brothers, who watched as he taped Sam's drawing to the wall. He'd placed it carefully above his desk so it would be safe and he could see it from his bed. His room was the smaller of the two bedrooms, but it was his.

You had to be *invited* in, he reminded his brothers daily. They shared the big room on the other side of the second floor and didn't care much about privacy or being quiet. Their window faced Mrs. Beckett's house, but Davey's overlooked Sam's. He couldn't see anything from upstairs, but if a light was on in Sam's living room, he figured he was awake. Probably working on his computer, writing all about his adventures, about being quiet so the fish wouldn't hear you coming with your bait.

"It's not yours," Matty said. "It's all of ours."

"It's on my paper," Davey declared. "That makes it mine. But you can look at it, see?" He pointed to the sturgeon. "Pretty cool."

His younger brother sighed. "I miss Boo."

"Don't think about it," Davey said, a sudden lump blocking his throat. "Think about something else."

"Like what?"

"Like...Christmas."

"And presents?"

"Sure." He looked up at the picture again. The next time they went to Lewistown, he would go to the library there and get a book on Alaska. Sam had told him there were big fish and unusual creatures all over the world, even in Alaska, which, when Davey checked the map taped to the wall above his bed, wasn't *that* far away.

"It's not working," Matty whispered. "My heart still hurts."

"Yeah," his older brother said, letting himself remember his dad's hugs. "But you get used to it."

SAM SPENT SOME productive early morning hours on the internet Friday until he was satisfied he'd accomplished what he needed to.

By the time seven o'clock rolled around, he was ready for pancakes and eggs. Or maybe an omelet, with cheese and sautéed vegetables. And a muffin. Or a piece of pie.

No, no pie. He didn't want to think about pie. Because pie reminded him of Lucia Swallow. And when he thought about Lucia, he thought about the way her lips curved into a smile when she teased him, how her eyes twinkled when she gave him orders, how she smelled like cookies and how her skin was so soft under his lips.

No, he wasn't going to think about pie.

Pie really was dangerous.

Not that anything dangerous had ever stopped him.

Friday mornings must be busy, was his first thought upon arriving at the café. The usual cast of characters occupied the counter stools, while people he'd never seen in the café before occupied most of the tables and booths. Elvis sang "Blue Christmas" from the ceiling speakers, and the noise of conversation came close to drowning out the words of the song.

"Hey, Sam!" Jerry waved at him from across the room and pointed to an empty chair next to him. The large table was otherwise filled with men Sam hadn't met before.

He made his way over to them, carefully avoiding Shelly and a tray of meals about to be served. Meg was busy at the register and didn't notice him, but Lucia was presiding over a collection of homemade baked goods displayed on the center table.

Sam headed over to say hello, but an elderly woman blocked his path by holding up a plate of brownies and asking Lucia a question. Well, he could wait for her to finish selling. He turned away, disappointed, and took the empty seat at the mayor's table.

"Lucia's in charge of the Christmas bake sale," Jerry explained, noticing Sam's interest. "It's the annual fundraiser for the search and rescue team, all volunteers. They need some new equipment."

"Half the restaurant's proceeds today and tomorrow goes to it," one of the men added. "The other half to the food bank."

"The pies are all sold," one of the young men said, frowning at him.

"All of them?" He craned his neck to see the gaily decorated table of food.

"Let me introduce you to some of our bachelors, soon to be television stars," Jerry said. "Joey Peckham, who was here at five-thirty this morning to buy himself a couple of pies." Sam shook his hand, but the kid didn't appear happy to meet him. He was lanky, but his muscled shoulders said he worked out regularly with weights.

"Nice to meet you," Sam told him. He didn't feel that it was, but he couldn't put his finger on why. He shook hands with the others, four men who were on the town council: Les Parcell, a twentysomething cowboy type with a shy smile; Pete Lyons, a rumpled school bus driver who seemed pleased to be on vacation; Mike Breen, a short square-faced reporter from the news-paper; and Gary Peterson, sixtyish and balding, but with a big grin on his face.

"Hank Doughtery is home with a cold," Jerry said. "But you met him Sunday. And Jack Dugan, another member of the council, took off to California with one of the film crew. I'm not sure if he's coming back."

"He fell in love before the show even started," Les explained.

"Which was a real shame," Jerry said. "He was one of our best-looking bachelors. He would have gotten a lot of screen time."

"You still have me," Pete said. "Your Hollywood girlfriend said I had a 'certain charm.'"

Jerry sighed. "Do you realize you've told me that at least ten times?"

"It's worth repeating." He turned to Sam. "The women around here don't give out a lot of compliments."

Sam eyed Jerry. "Is your Hollywood girlfriend going to move to Willing one of these days?"

"Well," Jerry began, "we've been on and off for a few years."

"Mostly off," the oldest man stated, winking at Sam. "But I wish you luck, Jer. She's a beautiful woman."

"Speaking of beautiful women," Joey murmured, gazing at Lucia. She seemed not to notice his attention. Instead, she sold a chocolate cake to a man in an orange hunt-er's vest and thick rubber boots. Two more women arrived and placed their offerings on the table. They all laughed about something and glanced out the window. "I hear you're living next to her, Sam."

"Yes." *And it's none of your business, kid.* Something about Joey's tone didn't set right with Sam.

"And I heard you met my granddaughter," Gary said to Sam. "The day you arrived."

"The girl with the cell phone?" Sam grinned. "She caught me at a bad time."

"I almost called the sheriff." He chuckled. "Thought you were dead when she texted that picture."

"Made a great photo, though," the newspaperman said. "I'd like to do an in-depth article on you after the holidays, if that's possible." Mike drew an index card from his shirt pocket and Sam gave him his cell phone number.

"How long are you staying in town?" the disgruntled pie hoarder wanted to know.

"Until the middle of March. That should give me enough time to finish the project I'm working on."

Shelly delivered breakfast to three of the

men, including the young cowboy, who blushed the moment she arrived at the table. Was he the father of the baby? Sam didn't think so, because the waitress seemed oblivious to the lovestruck expression on his face.

"Hi, Sam," she said. "Are you here for breakfast?"

"I am. I'll have the Mountain Man Special again, thanks."

"And coffee?"

"Please."

"Okay. I'll be right back with the coffee."

"So, this bake sale is a Willing tradition?" he asked the men.

"Meg and Lucia have been doing it for about four years," Jerry replied. "They raise a lot of money. Everyone tends to donate extra money, too." He grinned. "I hope you brought your checkbook with you."

Sam watched as Lucia rearranged a display of cupcakes and chatted with two older women. He wished he'd gotten here earlier. He'd bet those orange stickers on the pies meant they were sold.

Why was he getting so obsessed with food lately? Maybe years of eating fish had caught up with him. Maybe he'd go to Thompson's after breakfast and buy a couple of steaks. And stuff to make a salad. Broccoli, too.

Shelly hurried over with a mug for Sam and a carafe, from which she poured refills for the table.

Jerry frowned. "Are you sure you should be working this hard?"

"What do you mean?"

"I *mean*," he said slowly, "you're really pregnant and you have a broken arm."

"Are you kidding?" She gazed at him as if he were insane. "I get great tips looking like this."

"W-well," he sputtered, "I guess as long as you're not in pain…"

"She's tough," Les said, admiration written all over his face as he watched her hurry away.

"You'll get no argument from— Oh, no, not again!"

"What?" Sam gazed past an elderly man and woman who had stopped to chat with someone at a nearby table and saw Lucia in conversation with a stunning woman with long, light blond hair tumbling down past her shoulders. She wore a red knitted headband and a matching vest, tight jeans and sheepskin boots. She held two plates piled high with what appeared to be cookies, which she set down on the table. The two women laughed together like old friends. "Who *is* that?"

Jerry rolled his eyes. "That, my friend, is Aurora Jones. She owns the Dahl, which I'm guessing you haven't been to yet."

"No. I'm not much of a drinker."

"She's not exactly your friendly neighborhood bartender, either." He sighed. "She hates me."

"That's true," Gary agreed, and Les nodded. Sam noticed that Joey stared longingly at Lucia, and Mike's attention had been captured by two men at the next table over who had pictures of elk.

"Why?"

"It's a zoning issue. She's touchy about it."

"Ah."

"And she can't bake worth a damn." He nodded toward the plates of cookies now exhibited at the front of the table. Lucia held a roll of masking tape and a Sharpie; Sam guessed the women were discussing a price. "Those cookies she brought? They'll be like bricks. Even if they look halfway decent, which they won't be—they'll taste like bricks. Flour bricks."

"True," Gary said again to Sam. "He's not exaggerating. That's probably why she's so skinny. Probably lives on toast and apples."

"Or those frozen dinners," Les said. "Some of them aren't bad."

"I had to buy three plates of her cookies last year because no one else would. It cost me twenty-one bucks, which I didn't mind spending because it was for charity. And I'm all for charity, but I'm telling you, the things were not edible. Not even close. If I'd had a dog, he wouldn't have eaten them, either."

Gary nodded. "Good thing you don't have a dog then."

"Maybe her cooking skills have improved," Sam offered.

"Fat chance."

"No way," Les said. "My grandmother says some people aren't meant to cook and Aurora Jones is one of them."

Gary took a sip of coffee. "Really? Your grandmother said that?"

"They're in the same quilting group. Whenever it's Aurora's turn for refreshments they ask her to bring the tequila."

"Here she comes," Jerry warned them.

"I hope she sews better than she cooks," Gary whispered to Sam.

"She does. I've seen her quilts," Les said. "They're pretty cool."

Joey stopped pining over Lucia for a second to watch Aurora approach. He looked like he wanted to run. So he was, Sam assumed, a coward and a spoiled brat. "I'm gonna get my pies and get out of here," the young man said, scooting away as Aurora shot him a disapproving glare. Sam watched the kid hustle over to the baked-goods table and stand too close to Lucia. She didn't appear overjoyed to see him, but she reached for a box from under the table and began to load pies into it.

"Quit cowering, Jerry," Aurora said. She perched on the chair Joey had just vacated. "You look as if I'm about to audit the town treasury."

"Merry Christmas to you, too, sweetie." He plastered a fake smile on his face. "How's life in the bar?"

She ignored the question and extended a hand to Sam. "I'm Aurora Jones. I'm guessing you're the body in the snow?"

He shook a cool, elegant hand. "Otherwise known as Sam. Sam Hove."

"Yes," she said, blue eyes assessing him. He had the uncomfortable feeling he'd been hooked, hauled out of the river and examined for flaws. "You're here for the winter writing a book. Welcome to Willing."

"Thank you."

Shelly arrived with his breakfast. "Sorry it took so long. We're swamped."

"That's okay," he said, moving his coffee. "I'm in no hurry."

"Well, that's good," the girl said, "because I sure can't move any faster."

"Where's Loralee?" This was from Aurora.

"Christmas shopping," Shelly said. "She's working tonight and all day tomorrow. We're gonna be closed from the twenty-fourth through the twenty-sixth. I'll get a lot of rest then."

"Maybe you should sit down now," Les said, half rising from his chair. "I could pour coffee. You know, help out?"

She patted her belly. "Thanks, Les. I'll keep that in mind."

He sat back down, disappointed, and Shelly scooted off to the cash register.

Aurora sighed and then turned her sights on Jerry again as Sam reached for the salt and pepper and seasoned his eggs. "Tell your pretend girlfriend to stop texting me. I refuse to answer any more questions about Montana breweries."

Jerry glared at her. "Only you, Aurora, would complain about more business."

"I am *not*," she said, "complaining about more business. I've agreed to close the bar for filming any day or night. I've agreed to stock something called Power Mango energy water. I've agreed to almost every demand your idiot part-time girlfriend has come up with, including live music *with a banjo* and allowing a taxidermist to come in and groom the bear."

"Bridegrooms and Bear Grooms," Jerry said. "I like it."

Mike reached for another index card and wrote that down.

"How I wish you weren't such an ass." She stood and pulled her gloves out of her jacket.

"I love you, too," Jerry said. "And I always

will." He made a kissing sound, which Aurora ignored.

"Stop in at the Dahl anytime," she said to Sam. "The first drink is on the house."

He wiped his mouth with a napkin. "Thanks."

"New Year's Eve is traditionally a good party." She studied Jerry. "You might want to consider going to a gym."

"A banjo? Really?" Mike picked up his coffee cup. "I always wanted to learn how to play the banjo."

They watched Aurora wave goodbye to Lucia, stop at the counter to give Meg an envelope and then stroll out the door. She looked like a supermodel on a runway, Sam thought. "Is there something going on between you two?"

Jerry appeared stunned. "She's like the older sister I never had. The one who beat me up every morning before school."

Les seemed confused. "I thought you were an only child."

"I was trying to describe the nature of the relationship, Les. It's not sexual, in other words."

Sam believed him. The mayor would be

completely overmatched in that pairing. That particular woman would run him over with her truck and never feel the bump.

"Oh." Les watched Shelly take a breakfast order from a table of six road workers.

"So," Jerry said, "go for it if you're interested. The silver-haired witch isn't dating anyone that we know of, but then again, she doesn't volunteer much personal information. Just be careful. She's probably caused more pain than that alligator or whatever it was you were filming that was on YouTube."

"Caiman. Black caiman."

"Whatever, that's Aurora."

"She doesn't appear like the jungle type." His gaze drifted to Lucia. She wore a red sweater and feather earrings that swept to her shoulders. She looked exotic, he thought. All female in all the right places.

"Aurora's tougher than Meg," Mike said. "And that's saying something."

"Meg's tough?"

"You didn't know her before Owen put a ring on it," Jerry said. "She's almost sweet now."

"I met Owen last night at Lucia's. He seemed like a decent guy."

Silence greeted that announcement before Mike found his voice. "You were at Lucia's?"

"She's my neighbor, remember? We had pizza."

"Huh." Jerry glanced over at Lucia. "She looks good in red."

Les sighed. "Is it okay to ask a pregnant woman out on a date?"

"No," Jerry said. "Not when you're committed to be on a television show dating women from California in a few weeks."

"I don't want to date women from California," Les moaned.

Sam finished the last of his pancakes, waved to Lucia and said, "Neither do I."

"THIS IS INTERESTING," Meg mused, handing Lucia a cup of coffee laced with cream and sugar. "The shoe being on the other foot and all."

"Don't say a word," she said, and took a sip of the coffee before setting the cup down on the candy cane–print cloth. "And thanks."

"Do you want breakfast?"

"No, thanks. I'll eat later." She fiddled with the arrangement of zucchini breads donated by Janet Ferguson. The donations had been flowing in since six o'clock. She'd left her sleeping boys in the care of her mother-in-law, who had arrived at the house with nine dozen baked anise cookies for the sale and offered an IOU on a pan of lasagna for the silent auction. So far the bidding was up to thirty-five dollars.

"Poor lonely man."

"Stop it." Lucia retied a red bow on the anise cookie platter. "And he's not that lonely. Aurora was over there a little while ago."

"I know. I asked her to check him out. That woman has some kind of spooky radar when it comes to people, especially men." She leaned over and wrote her name on the sheet of paper for the lasagna and moved the bid to fifty dollars.

"You know, I thought Jerry had rented the house to a white-haired professor. I pictured Albert Einstein, with lots of books and thick glasses."

"She gave me a thumbs-up before she left."

Lucia glanced toward Owen, who was deep in conversation with Jerry, Les and Mike. She couldn't help wondering what was so interesting. "She could stick a gold star on his forehead and that still wouldn't mean I'm interested."

"Oh, you're interested, all right," Meg drawled. "But that's not the issue."

"The issue," Lucia repeated, crossing her arms in front of her chest. "What exactly is the issue?"

Meg laughed. "Albert can't stop looking at you."

And sure enough, he strolled over as soon as Meg was called back to the kitchen.

"Good morning," Sam said, a pleased smile on his face.

"Hi."

"You didn't tell me there was a bake sale," he chided. "I would have been here earlier to snag a pie."

"I'll save you one the next time I bake," she heard herself promise. She sounded like such a prim old lady, baking pies, working at the bake sale, greeting everyone in town by name.

"Do you take orders?" She watched him peruse the array of offerings. He was so darn good-looking. The dark blue sweater emphasized his silver-blue eyes. He was tanned, unusual for anyone in this town at this time of year, definitely a man who spent time in the sun all year round.

"Not right now." She rearranged Aurora's cookie plates, knowing they wouldn't sell to anyone who recognized the bartender's offerings. "I'm on vacation."

"Good," he said, flashing a pleased smile. "Are you free for dinner tonight?"

"Dinner?" At first she thought he was asking her to cook a meal for him. "Tonight?"

"I can cook fish," he said. "And steak. Your choice."

"I'm not free," she said quickly.

"All right. Short notice, I understand." He seemed sincerely disappointed, which made her feel a little sad for him.

"I don't date," she said.

"Not ever?"

"No. I have the boys and my business and my friends." She shrugged. "That's enough."

"I can understand that," Sam said. "You're a busy woman. I get it."

"I am." So why did she feel disappointed? "Please don't take it personally."

"You've crushed my enormous ego."

"You'll most likely survive."

"Let me ask you, though, as long as we're on the subject. What do people do around here?"

She thought about that for a moment. "There's a movie at the community center every Saturday night. Sponsored by the Senior Citizens."

He winced.

"There's caroling Sunday afternoon, starting and ending at the Dahl. Hot rum punch will be served."

"Caroling outside?"

"That's the general idea. But there is hot chocolate and rum punch afterward."

"So no one freezes to death."

"Hopefully." He looked appalled at the prospect of people roaming around town in this weather.

"There's a holiday concert at the church Saturday night," she continued, "and a kids crafts—"

"Would you like to go to that? The concert. With me."

"I don't—"

"You don't date," he finished for her. "I get that. But it's not fun going to these things by myself."

"I'm taking the boys. And my mother-in-law."

"Does that mean I can tag along?"

"You are that desperate?"

"I am," he admitted. "I'm not used to sitting in front of a computer for hours every day. This could be a long winter."

"If you'd like to go with us, you're certainly welcome to. Drop by my place at six-thirty and we'll take my car." The invitation was only polite, she decided. Neighborly, even. She would have done the same if Sam had been the elderly professor.

"Tomorrow night," he said. "Six-thirty."

"If you don't come to your senses first," she said. He picked up the pen next to the silent auction sheet.

"What's this?"

"Bidding for a lasagna."

"Yours?" He appeared impressed.

"My mother-in-law's," she said. "She donates one every year. Made to order, whenever you want it. In an eleven-by-thirteen-inch pan."

Sam bent over the table and wrote his name and an offer.

She peeked, reading upside down. "Three hundred dollars?"

"It's for charity, right?"

"The record is one fifty."

"Do you think I'll be outbid?"

She shook her head. "I doubt it, but you have until tomorrow at noon to keep bidding, so you can always check to make sure you're still in the lead."

"I'll do that," he said. He hesitated before walking away. She assumed he was heading home. "Thanks for last night."

"Anytime," she quipped, again out of politeness.

"You don't really mean that." His eyes twinkled. She was certain her face was flushed, making her wish she could run outside into the cold air and take a couple of deep breaths.

"No," Lucia told him. "I really don't."

CHAPTER SEVEN

DAVEY SPENT TEN MINUTES rummaging through the chest freezer. He'd sneaked down to the basement, a dark and menacing place with spiders, while his grandmother cooked pancakes upstairs.

He discarded big square pans of macaroni and cheese as options—his mother labeled everything neatly with black marker and tape—and quarts of chili. He debated over the chicken pot pies, since he'd already delivered one of those to Sam. There were no more small plastic boxes with Grandma's meatballs, though. Unless he could get into Grandma's freezer the next time they were over at her house, Sam wasn't going to get meatballs again anytime soon.

And the meatballs were the best. Davey thought he should get bonus points for giving those to a neighbor who was hurt and didn't have a car.

Uh-huh. Something to talk to Mrs. Kramer about when school started again.

He carefully moved frozen pies to one side and sifted through bags of berries and vegetables.

"You're gonna fall in."

Davey almost toppled off the stool he was using to reach inside. "Matty, jeez, don't sneak up on me!"

"What are you doing?" His brother, the snoop, looked down into the freezer. "Mom's gonna be mad."

"She asked me to get something for her," Davey lied.

"No, she didn't. You're lying."

"I'm telling the truth," Davey insisted, but he wasn't a good liar and everyone in the family knew it. His voice wobbled when he tried to get away with anything. "Go away."

"No."

Davey wondered if letting his little brother stay would be a Kindness and an extra point. Probably not, but Matty would blab about it all day long if he didn't get his way.

"So what are you gonna get?" Matty peered into the freezer and poked at a bag of strawberries.

"Where's Grandma?"

"Upstairs with Tony. He spilled the syrup all over his pajamas."

"Good."

Matty's eyebrows rose.

"I'm doing a Kindness," Davey confided. "But it's gotta be a secret."

"Okay," his brother whispered. "Is it for Mom?"

"No." Davey eyed a brick of meat loaf and considered it, then put it off to one side where he could find it again. He was careful moving the pies, because his mother didn't like it when the wiggly edges of the crusts broke. He didn't dare bring Sam a pie, because Mom counted them.

She counted them a *lot*.

But then again, he thought, she could always make more.

"Is it for Grandma?"

"No."

"Who's gonna get the Kindness, then?"

Davey sighed. "I told you, it's a secret. That's the rule."

"Oh." He watched his older brother sift through the vegetables. "What's that?"

"Lentil stew," Davey read, making a face.

"I can't give him that." He tossed the container back into the freezer. Stacks of uncooked chicken and various white-wrapped packages from the butcher filled the rest of the freezer.

He'd have to go with the macaroni and cheese, which was pretty good stuff, because Mom put bacon on top. Sam would like it, but Davey wished he could have found something else. Still, a point was a point.

And there was a prize. It better be a really good one.

THE NOISE BEGAN after ten. Sam, stationed at the dining table and facing the front window, saw a truck pull up in front of Lucia's house. The headlights stayed on for a few minutes, illuminating the empty street. He heard music, something loud and twangy with a strong bass beat, as the driver's door opened and closed. The music stopped and the lights went off.

Curious, Sam went to the window at the other end of the living room and saw a man in a heavy coat wobble up the front walk to Lucia's house.

"Lucia, my love! Lucia!"

Lucia, my love? The voice sounded young. Lucia's front porch light went on.

"Lucia, sweetheart! Give a guy a break!"

Whoever he was, he sounded drunk. What was going on here?

Sam went around the corner to the bedroom, where one of his windows overlooked the side of Lucia's house. The guy was still yelling, but fortunately Lucia hadn't opened the door to the idiot.

"I'm not too young," he wailed. And then he began to sing something about love and memories and dancing. It was not a good sound. And he was going to scare the kids if he kept this up.

If they weren't already awake. The thought of this drunk, whoever it was, bothering that family really set Sam off. He didn't like drunks and he didn't like drunks bothering women and kids. So Sam tromped into the kitchen, stuck his feet in his boots, threw on his jacket, grabbed his gloves and headed through the kitchen to the front door.

He switched on his porch light and stepped outside.

"Hey!"

The guy didn't seem to hear him. Sam saw

Lucia in her living-room window. A light went on upstairs.

"Hey, you!" Ignoring the cold and the ache in his chest, Sam hurried down the steps and trudged across the yard to Lucia's porch. "What do you think you're doing?"

Joey Peckham, the surly young man he'd met at the restaurant this morning, snarled down at him. "None of your bidge-ness," he blathered. He turned back to the door and banged on it with both fists. "Come on, Luce, let me in!"

Lucia opened the door and held up her portable phone. "I'm calling the sheriff, Joey. Go home."

"No, just let me—"

Sam was up the stairs in three bounds. He grabbed the collar of the man's jacket and pulled him away from the door. "Get out of here," he ordered, keeping his voice low.

"You can't—"

"Yes, I can," he said, hauling him off the porch and down the stairs.

"Don't hurt him," Lucia cautioned. "He's just a kid."

"He doesn't look like a kid to me," Sam

sputtered. He looked like a man out of control hassling a woman late at night.

Joey started singing again, some nonsense about a river and a truck and wine, so Sam told him to shut up.

"Sam." Lucia stood in the door, halfway out onto the porch. "It's okay. Joey's just, well, Joey. He'll leave." She looked over at the drunken kid. "Right, Joey? You're going home now, before the sheriff comes? Can I call someone to pick you up? It might be a good idea to call a friend, don't you think?"

"Sheez mine," Joey growled, glaring at Sam. "You're nobody, just some old fisherman. What're you doin' here, anyway?" He swayed alarmingly. "Why don't you go back to the ribber?"

"Ribber?" Sam blinked. That was when Joey took a swing at him and hit him in the face. It wasn't much of a blow, considering Joey's hands were encased in heavy gloves, but Sam wasn't amused. He hit him back, planted a solid punch on his nose and knocked him backward into the side of the truck. While a cursing Joey slumped to the ridge of frozen snow between the sidewalk and the road, Sam went around to the driver's side, opened the door and removed the keys from the ignition.

"You boke my noth, man."

The truck reeked of beer and whiskey, a bad combination in any season. Sam debated tossing this guy in his own truck and leaving him outside until he sobered up, but he doubted he was physically capable of it. Give him a couple of more months, though, and this guy on the ground would be tossed in the truck like a sack of fish bait.

"Shut up and don't move." Sam was out of patience with the whole situation. Not that he'd had any patience to begin with. "You took a swing at me. You're drunk. And you're scaring Lucia."

He returned to the front door, where Lucia stood wearing a fluffy blue robe that covered her to her ankles. Flannel ruffles peeked above the collar. She blinked back tears and still held the phone. "You hit him!"

"He swung first."

"Did you *hurt* him?"

"He's okay," Sam said, a bit defensive. "He's sitting by the truck now. He's pretty drunk."

Lucia peered past him into the darkness

to where Joey's truck stood against the curb. "I can't believe you actually hit him. He's harmless."

"Not exactly," Sam countered, relieved that the guy had worn gloves. Joey's punch had had some heft behind it. "You could be a little more appreciative," he suggested. "What would you have done if he'd pushed his way inside the house?"

She had no answer for that, Sam noticed.

"I called the sheriff," Lucia said. "He's on his way, but it might take a little while."

"Exactly."

"I hate to see Joey get in trouble, but he can't do things like this."

"You know him pretty well?"

"It's not what you're thinking," she said, sounding offended. "He's had a, um, crush on me for a few months now. But he's never done anything like this before."

"For the record," Sam said, "I wasn't thinking anything about you and Peckham. I assume you'd have more sense." He looked back at the snowbank where Joey sat muttering. "I don't think he's your type."

"Mom?" Davey eased past his mother to look at Sam. "What's going on?"

She squeezed his shoulder. "Get away from the door. It's cold."

"But what's going *on?*"

"Someone's had too much to drink," Sam answered. "We can't let him drive home so we've called the sheriff."

"The noise woke me up. I was scared."

"Me, too," Lucia said. "But there's nothing to worry about. Go back to bed."

"No," the boy said. "He's still making noise. Who is it?"

Sure enough, Joey had launched into another verse of whatever song he thought he was singing, off key and nasal.

"Joey Peckham," his mother replied.

"Oh." Davey frowned. "I don't know him, do I?"

"No," Lucia said. "Sam, you must be freezing out there. Come on in."

He shook his head and kept his hands jammed in his pockets. "I'm going to keep an eye on Peckham and wait for the sheriff."

"He shouldn't be driving. What if he gets in his truck and leaves? We can't let him do that."

"I took the keys. Does he live around here?"

"I'm not sure. Somewhere out of town, I think."

"Look, go back to bed." He glanced down at Davey. "You, too. I'll handle this."

"Can I watch?"

"Watch what?"

"The sheriff and everything."

Lucia eyed Sam, her eyebrows raised. He shrugged.

"He's going to stay up anyway," he said. "At least he can see it's all taken care of."

She sighed. "Okay, Davey. You can watch. But from the window," she said. "And just until the sheriff gets here."

Davey grinned and hurried away from the door to the window near the dining-room table. For some odd reason he turned on the switch to light the Christmas tree, making the room appear inappropriately welcoming.

Lucia's phone rang. "Maybe that's the sheriff. Hello?" She listened a moment, her face flushing. "I've already called," she said after a long moment, and then she ended the call. "That was my neighbor. She's furious. She wanted me to know that she phoned the sheriff to report drunks and strange men in and out of my house all night long."

"I'll go talk to her."

"Don't bother. She'd probably have you arrested for stepping on her property."

"That bad?"

"Yes, that bad."

"Shut the door. Lock it, if that makes you feel better. I'll let you know when this has been dealt with."

"Did he hit you?"

"He got in one shot. Not a very good one." Sam didn't add that it gave him a good excuse to hit the guy. Anyone who would scare a woman by getting drunk, coming to her house and waking her children deserved more than a punch in the nose. Though it was a good start.

It had certainly made Sam feel better. He'd grown up with drunks and had no tolerance for that kind of bad behavior. The drunken singing continued, which reassured Sam that the guy hadn't frozen to death out there. But he didn't want him waking the other little boys.

"I'm going to go shut him up."

"Maybe tell him not to wake my children? That might work."

"Yeah," he muttered. "Because the guy is obviously capable of logical thinking."

"I'm sorry about this," she said. "Were you asleep?"

"I was working. It's not that late," he assured her. "Shut the door." He headed back down the walk. Joey had made himself comfortable by leaning against the front tire and opening a can of beer.

"Where'd you get that?"

"Pocket," Joey said, pointing to his jacket. "Want one?"

"No."

"Dude," he said, taking a swig from the can, "it's cold out here."

Sam glanced up at the sky. It was a cold night, though clear. But the wind threatened to freeze him on the spot.

"Feel free to get in your truck," Sam said.

"Gotta go home," he mumbled. "My nothe hurths."

"Your nose isn't your only problem, kid." A large SUV cruised quietly up the street and pulled in behind Joey's truck. A heavy-set man dressed in a fur-trimmed parka, wool pants and knee-high waterproof boots stepped out of the car, but left the headlight shining on the back of the truck.

"What's going on? I got a call from Mrs. Swallow." He looked toward the house, where Lucia and Davey stood in the window next to the colorful lights of a Christmas tree.

"She had an unwanted visitor," Sam said, pointing to the beer-guzzling young man.

"Joey," the sheriff muttered. "You gotta stop falling in love."

"DID HE GO to jail?"

"Davey, it's bedtime." Her son seemed a little too enthralled by the drama, and Lucia wanted to talk to Sam. She beckoned to Davey, who wasn't trying to hide his yawns. "Come on, I'll tuck you in." She looked at Sam before she left the room. "I'll be right back."

Sam, shoes off and feet warming by the woodstove, didn't appear to be going anywhere. A few minutes later, after she'd kissed Davey good-night, reassured him that it would stay quiet, checked on Matty and Tony and brushed her hair, she headed back downstairs.

Sam had moved onto the sofa and taken the spot closest to the heat. He looked as though he was planning to stay, at least until he warmed up enough to walk across the yard to his own house.

"So," she said. "No arrest?"

"The sheriff is driving him home. He's a nephew by marriage, apparently, so he's not going to spend the night in jail."

"What about you?" Lucia said, sitting down a few feet away. She curled her bare feet underneath her and faced Sam. "He hit you."

"I'm not pressing charges. Are you?"

She shook her head. "I just don't want that to happen again."

"It won't," he said.

"I hope not."

"It won't," he repeated. "I'll handle it, man to man."

"Oh, for heaven's sake." She sighed.

"What? You don't want him back here, scaring you and the boys anymore, do you?"

"I can deal with it," she countered, but she heard the doubt in her voice. Darn, it was difficult being alone sometimes, and this had been one of them.

"Maybe," Sam said, but she knew he was fibbing. "But if I'm around and Peckham ever pulls anything like this one more time, he'll be in a world of hurt. I'm not a fighter and I don't go around hitting people, but when a man sees another man hurting a woman, well, all bets are off. And that's what happened tonight."

"You remind me of my husband," she said. "Protective, no matter what."

"Tell me about him." Sam leaned back against the cushions.

"We were on our honeymoon at the beach, in Rhode Island, and we saw a guy yelling at the top of his lungs at his girlfriend or maybe she was his wife. Tony took him aside and put a stop to it."

"How?"

"He must have said something pretty serious, because the guy grabbed his towel and stalked off. The woman called her mother to come get her."

"So it worked out."

"On that particular Sunday afternoon? Yes." Lucia thought back to that week in Narragansett. They had been so young and so thrilled with the excitement of marriage.

Spending every night together in the B and B one block away from the ocean, holding hands over breakfast, splurging on a lobster dinner, walking along the beach at sunset…

"Your husband must have been a pretty tough guy."

"He was a soldier. Special Forces."

"Not someone to mess with."

"No," she said.

"Okay, then, Peckham obviously needs to hear that you're not interested in him, and he needs to get that through his thick head. Sometimes a man has to hear that from another man."

She considered that for a moment. Her husband would have said the same thing. God, how she missed him. Lucia suddenly felt very alone and very vulnerable.

"What's the matter?"

She tried to laugh off her sadness. "I often wonder how I'm going to raise three boys into men the way their father would have."

"Have you thought about marrying again?"

"At times," she admitted. "But my boys come first and always will. How would that work with a husband? And would they accept a stepfather?" She looked at the tree lights. "It's too complicated."

"Do you have any brothers? Anyone to step in and help?"

"No. It's just me and Mama. Two women bustling around three little boys. I hope I don't mess them up."

"Your sons are lucky to have you."

"Thank you for saying that. I know they're missing out—"

"Look at it this way. Your kids got a raw deal losing their father. No doubt he was a good man and he loved his sons, right?"

She swallowed hard. "Right."

"But sometimes having a lousy father is worse than not having one at all. I had one of the worst childhoods a kid could have," Sam said, shifting so he could meet her gaze. "My brother and I practically raised ourselves, and when we were old enough to get out, we left. And we never looked back."

"I'm sorry."

"I'm not telling you this so you'll feel sorry for me," he said, his voice level. "It's not something I usually talk about. I survived. My brother survived. Against all odds, I guess, in retrospect."

"Where are your parents now?"

"They died a few years ago."

"Mine, too. When I was seven."

"Then what?"

"I was raised by my father's mother in Wyoming. My father was half Lakota. He and my mother were high school sweethearts."

"They were happy?"

"I think so, but I don't remember much. My grandmother was everything to me."

He nodded toward the tree. "Wasn't one of the kids supposed to sleep under there tonight?"

"Matty. He did, for a little while. And then he wanted to sleep in his own bed."

"Believe me," he said. "Your kids are going to be fine."

They sat in silence for a few minutes and gazed at the tree. Sam reached over to the only lamp and switched it off, leaving the glow of the tree to light the room.

"You were frightened," he said. "Of that idiot."

She couldn't count the reasons she felt like crying, why her eyes burned and a lump had formed in her throat. "Very."

"Come here," Sam said, stretching out his arm.

That was not a good idea. Vulnerable female snuggling against handsome neighbor? Idiocy.

Sam didn't wait for her to decide. He moved closer and wrapped his arm around her. "Better?"

"Yes." She carefully rested her head on his wide, wool-coated chest. "What about your ribs?"

"Not an issue."

"This is not what I expected," she confessed, looking at the tree blinking opposite them. "I was going to go to bed and read."

"Are you going to cry?"

"Probably. Is *that* an issue?"

His chest rumbled as he laughed. "Yes. It would be pretty bad."

She sniffed. "It just hit me, with Joey pounding on the door, how alone I am. I mean, I've felt that way before, but this time was different. I don't know how to explain it."

She did not want to go there, so she said, "Tell me a scary fish story." It seemed natural to snuggle up to him, to pretend that they were just two people enjoying tree lights on a peaceful winter night.

"How scary?"

"Nothing too bloody."

He took his time thinking over what story to choose, and Lucia closed her eyes and let his warmth seep through her skin. She'd missed this.

"WHY IS SAM sleeping on the couch?"

"Shh."

"Can I watch TV?"

"Shh."

Davey was doing his best to keep his brothers quiet, but it wasn't easy. "He came over to help Mom," he said.

"Why?" This was from Tony.

"Yeah," Matty said. "Why?"

Davey gave that question some thought. He didn't want to scare his younger brothers with the truth: which was that some guy was yelling for Mom like he wanted to be her boyfriend. Like he'd had too much beer. Davey had seen people have too much beer. Like that movie *The Hangover* he wasn't supposed to have seen, but Bobby Gunther had the DVD and they'd sneaked it when

Davey spent the night last summer, right before school started. Davey liked the part with the tiger the best.

"There's a truck out there," Tony whispered, tiptoeing to the window. "Is that Sam's?"

"No."

"Whose truck is it?" Matty joined him at the window. "What's going on? Something's going on, huh?"

"Nothing's going on."

"Yeah, there is." Matty glared at him. "You're lying."

Davey sighed. "There was a drunk guy outside last night and Sam made him go away."

"What's *drunk* mean?" Tony scrunched up his face.

"It's when you act stupid," Matty said. "And burp."

"Oh." He kept staring at Sam, who was just a big lump under Mom's favorite quilt. He was even snoring.

"Shh," Davey said again, trying to get them to leave the room before they woke up Sam. "You want to help me do a Kindness?"

That got their attention.

"IT'S NOT THAT I like lying to my parents," Jerry told Shelly. He perched on his stool, his usual spot, and took a last bite of pancake. "It's just that I'm too busy to go to Vegas for Christmas."

"Just tell them that. It's not like you're a kid. I mean, you're, like, twice my age," she pointed out.

"Not twice," he protested. "I'm thirty-two."

"Old enough to stop lying to your mom," she said.

"I used a snowstorm as an excuse," he admitted. "But it didn't go over well with my mother. She likes having the family together. Lucky for me, my sister and the kids will keep her busy." He sighed. "I hate to miss the cookie decorating party, but politics is a tough business."

"There really is a big storm coming," she said. "You'd probably have a hard time getting there, even if you left right now."

"I could get out of Billings today. If I tried," he mused, pushing his empty plate aside. He sat at the counter, where he could talk to Meg whenever she had a free minute. There were a great many things to discuss, and Meg was distracted by celebrating the holidays with her soon-to-be husband. Getting her to focus on catering for the show was difficult.

"But you don't want to," Shelly said, refilling his coffee. "When are they coming?"

He knew she meant Tracy and the production team, along with the women selected to be on the show. "December thirtieth. Tracy wants to kick off the show on New Year's Eve, with a party at the Dahl. New Year, New Start. Symbolic, she said. She thought she could take advantage of the annual desperation of New Year's Eve, along with some spontaneous kissing footage at midnight."

"Oof." She rubbed her belly. "Baby's kicking."

"Aurora said that was fine with her, believe it or not, and Meg said she'd supply finger food during the party, and a postmidnight breakfast here at the café. I've gone over the contracts for that night, plus the following three weeks of filming."

"I start my third trimester next week."

He ignored that piece of medical trivia. "I've been trying to get the men together for three days to have a meeting about this, but everyone is busy. And I may have to eliminate Joey Peckham from the cast, due to a little stalker problem last night. Tracy was very adamant that the men be mentally stable. So I've set up a mandatory meeting December 27 at the community center. Six o'clock sharp. We're going to have a refresher class, just to review the basics."

"That sounds good." Her gaze drifted to the windows overlooking the parking area. "Here comes Les. With his grandparents."

"They never miss a fundraiser," he said. "Even living that far out of town."

"And Owen just drove up," she said, still staring out the window.

"Great," Jerry moaned. "Now Meg won't think about anything but making MacGregor's breakfast."

He swiveled the stool to watch the incoming customers. To the right of the door was the bake sale table, its surface half-covered with offerings. The supply of stuff was dwindling, meaning a great many baked goods had been purchased since yesterday morning and, hopefully, a great deal of money made. Janet Ferguson sat behind the table and manned the cashbox.

"What do you mean, a stalker problem?" This was from Meg, who had ears like an elephant. The woman could hear a whisper from the next county.

He swiveled to face her. "Never mind. We need to go over the menu."

"We've done that seventeen times, Jerry. I have it memorized, and so does Al." She looked past him and waved. To Owen, Jerry assumed. He liked the guy. He owed him big-time for his help with the Husband School, as folks called it. But he needed Meg's attention.

"I need you to concentrate," he said.

"I need you to lighten up," she said, but she said it nicely. And with a sympathetic smile. "It's all going to be fine, I promise. So…tell me about the stalker."

Owen slid onto the stool next to Jerry. "Oh, yeah. That was bad."

"You know about it?"

"I ran into Murray at the gas station. He had to take Joey home last night."

"Why?"

"He showed up at Lucia's house. Tried to convince her of his love and affection by knocking on her door and singing. According to Murray, Joey was a mess," Owen said.

"Oh, yeah. Big-time," Jerry said. "But Fish Man came to the rescue."

Shelly blinked. "Fish Man?"

"In other words," Owen said, "Sam Hove heard the commotion and headed Joey off. Joey took a swing at him, and Sam punched him in the nose and confiscated his keys."

"You're kidding." This was from Meg, as Shelly attempted to process the information.

"No. Lucia called Murray and he wasn't too far away, so he picked up Joey and drove him home. Got him some ice for his face and put him to bed. That boy is going to have one heck of a headache this morning."

"Good," Meg said. "He deserves it."

"I'm glad Sam was there, but poor Lucia," Shelly said, patting her abdomen again. Jerry thought it had expanded another inch between his first cup of coffee and his third.

"When is that baby due?" he couldn't help asking.

"February 22."

"Two *months* from now?" His gaze drifted to her belly again. Maybe the apron covering made it look like she was hiding a prize-winning watermelon under her shirt.

Owen leaned forward, and Meg met him over the counter to kiss him. "Good morning, sweetheart," he murmured.

"Good morning," she cooed back.

"Save it for the cameras," Jerry said. "The bachelors will need all the inspiration they can get."

"You're a little negative this morning," Meg said, still smiling at her beloved rancher. "That's not like you."

"I'm down a man," he said. "Unless Peckham gets his act together. Do you have any ideas?"

"You're lucky you have the men you have," she said, "considering how much work they've had to do. Dancing, clothes, haircuts, ironing, learning the fine art of conversation? All really difficult things."

"But the payoff is huge."

"They want to be on television," Meg stated. "And they'd like to meet some nice women. And they've put in the work. Give them credit."

"They're a good bunch," Owen added.

"They'll do fine, as long as the women aren't too intimidating."

Jerry put his head in his hands and moaned. "I hope Tracy lives up to her part."

"She's ambitious. And smart. She'll be fine." Meg took another swipe at the counter and picked up Jerry's empty plate. "I have to go call Lucia for all the details."

"Too bad Sam's not on the show," Owen said. "Honey, can I have some coffee? But the guy's not exactly the Montana type Tracy wanted."

"True. But Tracy would have loved to have gotten that nose-punching scene on camera. She told me she's hoping for some testosterone-fueled drama."

"There's plenty of that around here," Meg said. "Always has been, always will be."

"Yeah," Shelly agreed. "That's why I'm glad I'm having a girl."

SAM HEARD THE excited whispers of children and thought, for a millisecond, he was back in the village, one of the many outposts along the Negro River in Brazil. But instead of the smell of brackish water and

spoiled fruit and burning logs, he smelled…
cinnamon?

He opened his eyes when he heard footsteps in the living room. And found he was
in *Lucia's* living room, sprawled out on a
section of her giant couch, covered by a quilt.

And surrounded by three children.

"Are you hungry?" the middle one inquired.

"Do you want coffee?" asked the baby.

The oldest, Davey, stared silently at his
face. Sam wondered if Peckham's gloved fist
had managed to leave a mark after all.

Sam struggled to sit up. At some time in
the night he had slipped into a prone position, a couch cushion under his head, body
turned toward the warmth of the stove. "I'll
get up," he told them. "Just give me a minute."

"Ribs," Matty told the youngest boy. "It's
his ribs again."

"Wow," Tony breathed. "You got to sleep
in your clothes?"

"I did," Sam said proudly, to make them
laugh. "I was going to sleep under the tree,
but I'm too big."

All three boys giggled.

Matty's big eyes stared into his. "I did, too, till I went to bed. I liked the lights."

"So did I," Sam said.

"A lot?"

"Yes," Sam replied, and remembered comforting the woman who'd tried not to cry and the warmth of her body, protected by inches of fluffy blue material. "A lot. Where's your mom?"

"In the shower," Davey informed him.

Well, that was an inappropriate and enjoyable vision. Sam eased himself off the couch and walked over to the stove to retrieve his boots. "I'd better get going."

"We fixed you some breakfast," Tony said. "It was Davey's idea because—"

"Grandma made coffee," Davey said.

"Grandma?"

He nodded solemnly. "Yep."

"That's nice, but I really should go home." He'd never met the famous Mama Marie, but he suspected no grandmother would be happy about finding out the neighbor had spent the night in her daughter-in-law's house. He tucked in his shirt, straightened his sweater and brushed his hair back from his forehead.

"You can't," Davey said. "Not now."

Sam took one longing look at the front door and thought about escaping, but three pairs of eyes pinned him. He was cornered.

"Come on," Tony said. "You gotta be hungry."

"Well, not—"

"Mr. Hove." A plump, dark-haired woman appeared in the doorway. She looked as though she was in her sixties, and she was the spitting image of every Italian mother who had ever appeared in a spaghetti sauce commercial.

She set a baking pan of cinnamon rolls on the table. "Good thing I had these rising last night. I came over the minute the boys called."

"The boys called you?" Had he scared them by sleeping on the couch? He hadn't intended to. Lucia didn't wake him. Or had she tried to and he wouldn't respond?

He stepped closer to the table and inhaled. The rolls were fragrant, round and golden brown, drizzled in white frosting.

"The children wanted to surprise you," she said. She held out a flour-dusted hand. "I'm

Marie, Marie Swallow. But you can call me Mama. Everyone does."

He shook her hand and then she hurried back into the kitchen. Thirty seconds later she returned with coffee, which she poured into a cup for him.

"Sit down," she said. He noticed the table held five place settings. "The eggs will be ready in a minute."

"I should get home," he said.

"Not before you eat."

Sam had no choice but to pull out a chair and sit. Davey took the seat to his right, and the littler boys took places across from them. He was starting to feel claustrophobic and tugged at the collar of his sweater.

Davey leaned over to whisper, "I knew you would like these."

Mrs. Swallow—no way was he calling her Mama—sawed off a large round cinnamon roll, put it on a plate and set it in front of him. She did the same for the three boys, who pounced on the rolls, as hungry as if they'd spent the night shoveling snow on the interstate.

"Tony, pass Mr. Hove the butter."

"Well, this *is* a surprise," he managed to

say as he devoured a portion of his own cinnamon roll. Davey beamed at him.

Lucia, dressed in jeans and a long-sleeved emerald sweater, hurried into the room. Her feet were bare and her long hair was damp. She looked confused by the scene in her dining room. She glanced at her boys, Sam and then her mother-in-law. "What's going on?"

"I really wish you'd woken me up earlier," Sam told her. "Like five or six hours ago."

"Your children asked me if I had anything good for breakfast," the older woman said. "Davey wanted something special for Mr. Hove. So I brought over some rolls. I was making them for—"

"But it's seven-thirty in the morning."

Mrs. Swallow shrugged. "I'm up at five. So?"

"I told Grandma that Sam stayed over," Davey announced. "Because the sheriff came."

"Yes," his grandmother said. "It must have been some exciting evening. Maybe you want to tell me about it in the kitchen?"

Sam saw his chance to escape.

CHAPTER EIGHT

"HE DID A good thing," Mama declared after listening to the story. "You were lucky to have him next door like that, watching out for you."

"He could hardly have ignored the noise," Lucia pointed out. "Joey was wailing and banging on the door."

"Still," Mama said, keeping her voice low so the children couldn't hear them, "you must have been very frightened. You and the children living alone—that's what I worry about. I wish you would move in with me. Safer, that's what it would be," she declared. "Much safer. Less worry."

Lucia hugged her. "Mama, I'm not moving in with you."

"Then I'll move in here."

"And sleep where?" She smiled. "On the living-room couch?"

"I know, I know, we both need our privacy. Two women in the same kitchen is not a good thing," Mama said, then stepped back and frowned. "Your hair is wet. You're gonna catch a cold walking around with a wet head. Go dry it before you get sick."

"I dressed in a hurry." She'd woken up wondering what she'd forgotten. Had heard the boys' voices in the hall and remembered that Sam was around the corner, asleep on her couch. She'd left him there when she'd wakened after falling asleep during a story about a legendary New Zealand eel. At least, she thought the story was about an eel. Something black and wriggly, she recalled. It had been after midnight and she'd been up since five that morning, with a lot of excitement in between those hours, and Sam had a very comfortable chest and a soothing voice. She hadn't had the heart to wake him and send him out into the cold. And she hadn't expected her mother-in-law to show up at this time of the morning.

"What are you telling the boys?"

"Well," she said, moving to the counter to pour herself a cup of coffee. She looked out the window and noticed Sam carrying wood to his back porch. "Davey is the only one who woke up last night and saw what was happening, so I'll tell them that there was a lot of noise last night and Sam came over to make sure we were okay, but he was very tired afterward and fell asleep."

"You can tell them it was because of his ribs," Mama suggested, joining her at the window. "That he didn't feel so good for a while."

"Sounds great."

"But watch out for that man. He's decent, Lucia, but he's not for you. You need a man who's gonna stay."

"I know." She turned away from the window. "But it was nice last night, feeling safe."

Mama patted her on the cheek. "You deserve a good man, Lucia. No one will ever be as good as my Tony, but…"

"I don't think I'll ever marry again, Mama."

"Of course you will, beautiful and young as you are. Tony would want you to be happy, to have a life, to have love." She went over to the oven and opened the door. "Here. I baked a delicious *strata* for us."

"It looks wonderful." Lucia wasn't the least bit hungry. She wanted to go back to bed and hide under the covers. The boys would make a huge mess, destroy the house and fight about action figures, but it would be worth it if she could just lie in bed and feel sorry for herself a few hours. She'd been so busy since Thanksgiving. Her feet hurt.

To top off her woes, Sam had seen her in her old blue robe.

"Go sit with your boys." Her mother-in-law shooed her out of the room.

"Mom," Matty yelled. "Davey said a *stupid drunk* was at our house last night!"

Her oldest shrugged when Lucia frowned at him. "What? You can't argue with the truth."

"Since when did you start talking like a forty-year-old?" She set her coffee cup on the table, sat down and thought of running away.

AT THE SAME TIME, Sam stoked his wood stove and thought of ten different reasons he could give to get out of going to that concert. He could use his sore ribs as an excuse, but that would be cowardly. He could say he had to work. Or he was expecting a conference call. Or there was something really good on television. That his knuckles hurt from punching Peckham. That he was coming down with a cold, the flu, a bout of malaria, strep throat. Or what about an ear infection? Christmas music would burst an eardrum or cause brain damage.

But the truth was that he'd trapped Lucia into inviting him to the concert because he was lonely and she was beautiful.

The truth was that this morning had been a little too cozy. Between the children, whom he liked, and the mother-in-law, who had a right to be suspicious, Sam was definitely out of his element.

Lucia needed a man like Jerry Thompson, a guy with roots. Sam had walked past Jerry's house on his way to buy the flowers. It was an impressive home, easily the grandest in town. Sam shuddered at the thought of stepping into a showplace like that again. He'd spent much of his childhood dreaming of escaping the elegant house with the wide staircase, crystal chandeliers and gleaming floors.

He never talked about his family. Never.

Until last night. And even then he'd omitted the details. Living with two pillars of the community rich enough to be in a constant alcoholic haze was one thing, but living with a mean drunk of a father and an uncaring mother put a different spin on the concept of "family." He doubted Lucia would understand or want to hear.

What would he say if she asked about his brother? Jake had run away at sixteen, taking a duffel bag and his guitar.

And left his younger brother behind. Sam had forgiven him a long time ago—hey, it had been "every man for himself" that awful year—but he'd expected Jake to come back and get him. Or at least call once in a while to make sure the old man hadn't beaten him to a pulp again.

Instead, there'd been nothing. Sam had spent his time playing sports, joining clubs, doing charity work—anything to avoid being home. He spent many weekends with his best friend, Tom Mack, one of six brothers whose parents never noticed how many boys were digging into the macaroni and cheese casserole at dinnertime.

No, Sam's childhood hadn't been anything like the one the little Swallow boys enjoyed. He couldn't imagine those three brothers being separated by years of silence. Their mother, for one thing, wouldn't allow it.

Sam stripped off his clothes and went to shower. With any luck he'd slip and break his leg.

"So," JERRY SAID, plopping himself into the empty space at the end of the pew, "I hear you might still have a thing for younger men."

"That's Sam's seat," Lucia said, "and I don't know what you're talking about."

"Don't look innocent. Murray was in the café this morning complaining about Joey. I'd had three calls before that."

"I know. Meg phoned to see if I was okay."

"And you are, right? I kicked him off the show because of this little escapade."

"That's probably a good idea." Joey needed to grow up, not inflict himself on unsuspecting women looking for love.

"If he promises to behave himself and if Tracy thinks he provides a certain amount of controlled drama, he'll be back in, though. There's no telling what she'll do."

"I suppose."

"You're looking especially nonmatronly tonight." He grinned at her. "Hot date?"

"We're in a church, Jerry." She'd taken time getting dressed tonight in an attempt to overcompensate for the shoddy blue bathrobe. She'd worn her special red sweater, skinny black pants, black suede boots and her grandmother's turquoise and silver necklace. She'd made sure her makeup was perfect and left her hair long and straight, mostly because there wasn't much else she could do with it. She'd inherited her hair from her grandmother, along with some jewelry and a love of baking.

"Your, uh, musical companion paid five hundred dollars for Mama's lasagna."

"I thought he bid three hundred." Which had seemed like a lot of money at the time. Still, it was for charity, which was nice of Sam.

"Owen upped the bid, and Sam upped that. We've made a nice bundle of money for the rescue group and the food bank." He looked over his shoulder as Sam and the three boys came down the aisle. "So I guess he's trying to impress you?"

"Or he's very hungry."

"Yeah, right." Jerry hopped up, shook Sam's hand, greeted the boys and bounced off to the front of the church. Lucia assumed he'd be making public service announcements before the music started.

The boys, Christmas gift bags in their hands, scooted past her and squeezed together on the pew. Their grandmother told them not to eat anything from the bags until they got home. Sam took his seat on the aisle.

"Mission accomplished," he said. "They each got an orange, a candy cane and some kind of ornament."

"Thanks for taking them to do that."

Sam nodded. He glanced around the little church. "Big turnout. Standing room only at the back."

"You know, I thought you'd change your mind about tonight," she said, looking straight ahead as the choir assembled on the altar. She'd been surprised when he'd shown up at the back door at six-thirty. The boys had surrounded him with complaints of having to get dressed up, but they'd been excited over going out to do something at night. Lucia hadn't been able to say much except hello.

"Truthfully?" he asked as she turned to him. He fiddled with the program, rolled it into a tube and then unrolled it. "Yeah, I thought about it."

"This isn't exactly what you're used to, is it."

"Meaning?"

"Meaning I imagine you're used to more g-glamorous evenings," she stammered. "Without three kids tagging along and a whole town observing."

"That's not true. But that's not why I almost changed my mind," he said, still fiddling with the paper.

"Ah." She considered that for a long moment, then lowered her voice to a whisper. "I'm not on the prowl for a husband, Sam. You don't have to worry that I'm going to appear on your doorstep, singing love songs and calling your name."

He chuckled.

"Except I'd let you inside," he said. "That's the problem."

Lucia didn't have a chance to respond to that odd statement because the lights dimmed and the pastor took the microphone to introduce the choir and its director.

"MARTINIS OR ICE CREAM, what will it be?"

Sam found himself facing an attractive older woman with a lot of blond hair and a huge smile. She wore a red-and-green-striped sweater and a necklace made of blinking snowmen.

"I'm Loralee Ripley, Meg's mother." She took his hand and gave it a shake. "I'm actually Loralee Smittle, but I'm in the process of changing my name back. Because really, who wants to go around as a Smittle if they don't have to?"

"Sam Hove," Sam said. "And I agree with you about Smittle."

"It's nice to finally meet you. Meg said you're a good customer, Shelly says you're very polite and Aurora says you haven't been to the Dahl, so I'm assuming you're not much of a drinker."

"That's true."

"Well, this is your lucky night, since Meg's serving root beer floats at the restaurant. We're celebrating the success of the bake sale." She waved to Lucia, who was talking to a couple of women near the front of the church. The boys were gathered around her. "She's already invited Lucia."

"What if I'd picked martinis and not ice cream?"

"I hope you won't take offense, Sam," Loralee said, hooking her arm in his and guiding him toward Lucia's family, "but you don't look like the martini type."

"You do," he said, laughing. "If you don't mind my saying so."

"You got that right," Meg's mother said. "But only on Saturday night, and never more than two."

Somehow he didn't believe her.

He let her lead him to the Swallow family and turn him over to Mrs. Swallow, the grandmother, who gave him an assessing look.

"You should have stayed for the eggs," she said. "I made a *strata* with pesto and mozzarella."

"I'd worn out my welcome," Sam replied. "It was a little awkward, don't you think?"

"Hmm. I've never found a man in my daughter-in-law's house before, but I understand you were protecting her."

"Yes." He'd also been embracing her on the couch, yet he wasn't about to share that detail about his evening.

"I hear you paid five hundred dollars for my lasagna?"

"I had some of your lasagna the first night I came here," Sam said. "Money is no object."

"You helped my daughter-in-law last night," she said. "I would have made you a lasagna for doing that. Meatballs, too."

"Well, I've rented the house until the end of March," he said, aware he had no pride left. He'd never been a cook, probably never would be. A fish on a stick over a campfire was the limit of his culinary skills. And Italian food was his weakness. "If you get the urge to cook."

She nodded. "I'll keep that in mind. You like meatballs?"

"I love them," he replied seriously.

"Mama?" Lucia joined them. "Do you want to go to Meg's with us?"

"She's open this late?"

"No. It's just us." She turned to Sam. "You're invited, of course, or I can drop you off at your house."

"I already asked him, honey," Loralee said, ruffling Davey's hair. "Wasn't that a wonderful concert? I wish I could sing, but I don't have a musical bone in my body. What about you, Davey?"

The boy just grinned, enjoying the attention.

"All right," Sam said, realizing that all things considered, this evening had been a pretty good one. Not that it was a date. He'd conned her into feeling sorry for him and letting him tag along.

Now he was glad he hadn't broken his leg in the shower. "I'll definitely come with you," he said. "Just in case you need a bodyguard."

"It's strange how the man fits right in," Meg said. She handed Lucia a glass of diet soda and ice.

"That's what he does, Meg. Fits in. He's used to making friends in remote villages." She perched on a stool and sipped her drink. "That's us. The natives in the remote village."

"I guess that's one way to look at it."

"Uh-huh."

"The next time he sleeps on your couch, will you take a picture? Just so I can believe it?"

"Very funny."

"I'm serious," Meg insisted. "The whole thing with Mama and the cinnamon rolls? I wish I'd been there."

"The living room was a little crowded." Lucia looked at Sam and sighed. "Last night we sat on the couch and he put his arm around me and told me fish stories."

Meg choked back a laugh. "Fish stories? Did he kiss you afterward?"

Lucia felt her face grow warm. "I would have been mortified."

"He's a handsome man, and a very nice one," Meg stated. "You are single and you are allowed a kiss once in a while."

"Thanks for pointing that out." But could she kiss "once in a while" and not feel horribly strange about it?

They watched Sam and Owen join the three boys at the large center table. All five of them had root beer floats and looked pretty happy. Owen said something that made the rest of them laugh. Loralee and Mama were entertaining Shelly, Les and the Parcells at the table next to the men. Aurora was on her way to join them, having been in charge of scooping ice cream.

"Can I invite him out for Christmas Eve?" Meg and Owen were hosting their first party at the ranch. It would be a simple buffet in the afternoon, so Lucia could get the boys home early to get ready for Santa.

"You don't even know him, Meg."

"He's been in here for breakfast every morning," her friend noted. "And he's very outgoing."

Lucia didn't know why she felt claustrophobic all of a sudden. "Half the men in town are here for breakfast every morning. Are you inviting them, too?"

"I feel sorry for him. No one should be alone over the holidays."

Well, that was certainly true, Lucia thought.

"Besides," Meg said, "it was Owen's idea. He's talking about learning to fly-fish next summer."

Sam wouldn't be here next summer. Or did Owen know something she didn't? "Does he think Sam will give him lessons?"

Meg shrugged. "Who knows? Sam has some great stories. He entertains the old guys every morning. All I can say is, no wonder he's writing a book."

"Who else is coming?"

"Same group you see here. Shelly, Les, the Parcells, Loralee, you, the boys, Mama, Aurora. Plus Jerry."

"And Sam makes thirteen." She could easily picture him at the gathering. He would compliment the cooks, ask questions about the MacGregor history, share details of the Amazon when asked. He would tease the boys and pet the dog. He would make her feel she was part of a couple again, would make her feel what was missing in her life.

She didn't want to feel that at Christmas. She wanted to count her blessings, not be sad. She worked very hard at not being sad.

"Fifteen. You forgot me and Owen."

"Have you picked a wedding date yet?"

"We'll definitely decide soon," she promised. "What's the matter with inviting Sam? If it's awkward, I won't, of course. But I thought you liked him. I'm not trying to find you a husband." She smiled. "I promise, I'm not turning into our mayor. I'd ask him, a guy with no family in town, about to be alone for the holidays, if he was eighty years old and in a walker, you know that."

"I've tried to pretend he's eighty. It hasn't worked."

"What?"

"Last night was bad," Lucia admitted.

"Joey should have been arrested."

"No, it's not about Joey," she said. "Last night I really liked having Sam in the house. We fell asleep looking at the Christmas tree."

"And he spent the night," Meg added, grinning at Lucia.

"In case Joey came back."

"So he has a protective streak. That's nice."

Lucia nodded. "He said he didn't like drunks. He didn't have the greatest childhood," she said. "He didn't say much about it, but that was the drift. He has a brother. His parents are dead."

"So he really is a loner," Meg mused. "Interesting. He seems to like your family."

"The boys are fascinated. Mama is still in awe about the bid on her lasagna and your mother told me he was a man's man, and therefore a 'keeper.'"

"Mom's known a lot of 'keepers,'" Meg said. "Don't listen to a word she says."

"I don't want to make a fool of myself

falling for a man who sends me postcards of giant crocodiles from South America and drops into town once a year."

"Then don't," Meg said. "You could snap your fingers and have any single guy in this town come running. And who knows? Maybe there will be some great guy on the crew of the show who falls in love with blizzards and baked goods and wants to settle down."

Lucia laughed. "Well, that is a possibility."

"Come on," Meg said. "Let's go watch Les moon over Shelly."

"She ignores him. It's sad." They strolled over to the tables.

"Or we could sit with the men. Except that your sons are having a belching contest."

"Matty will win," Lucia said. "He always does."

"This is what I have to look forward to?"

"If you have boys," she said, choosing to sit next to sweet, white-haired Mrs. Parcell. "I don't know what to expect if you have girls."

"I do," Meg said. "They'll try to elope when they're eighteen, like me. I hope I have sons."

"Hurry up and set a wedding date," Lucia said. "And then see what happens."

Owen and Sam pushed the tables together to make one festive gathering while the boys ate their candy canes and asked Les about the horses they'd ridden last month. Owen and Mr. Parcell discussed the price of wheat, Mrs. Parcell and Shelly talked about the baby quilt Mrs. Parcell was making for her, and Les told Sam about the rodeo. They compared injuries, while Mama and Loralee went over the details of Christmas Eve with Meg. Lucia listened, letting the conversations roll around her in the warmth of the room until her boys grew restless, Matty yawned and Tony attempted to crawl into her lap.

"Time to go," she announced, returning Mrs. Parcell's understanding smile.

"Such sweet boys you have, Lucia," the older woman said. "Enjoy them while they're young."

Sam stood, shook hands with Mr. Parcell, clapped Les on the shoulder and lifted Tony into his arms as if he'd been doing it for years. Then Sam, Jerry and Owen helped her load the boys into the van and get their seat belts on. Mama cuddled Tony in the middle seat and Sam climbed into the passenger side for the short and silent ride to Mama's house.

"I'll see you tomorrow," Mama said, making sure she had her handbag. "Unless the weather changes."

"Good night, Mama." Sam walked her to the door of her one-story ranch house, made sure she was safely inside, then hopped back in the van for the short trip across town to Lucia's home. The car smelled like peppermint candy and root beer.

Sam said nothing. And neither did Lucia. It was another night with a clear sky and lots of twinkling stars.

The three boys shuffled sleepily into the house, and Sam followed her to the back door, where she'd left a light on. She hesitated for a moment, heard the boys drop their boots to the floor.

"Go right upstairs," she told them. "I'll be there in a minute. Brush your teeth!"

She closed the door and remained on her porch, as did the still-silent Sam.

"This is a big mistake," he muttered, tugging her into his arms. His mouth found hers, a small quick kiss that stopped, then started again, to become something longer. Something warm, with an undercurrent of passion that made Lucia's legs wobble. She kissed him back, a kiss filled with four years of longing. Her arms went around his neck; he wrapped her body against him. Despite bulky jackets and a porch light, Lucia thought it was the most erotic moment she'd had in years.

When he released her, Sam smoothed her hair, kissed her briefly on the mouth and turned away.

Lucia couldn't say a word.

SUNDAY MORNING AT the café Ben Fargus invited him to his house for Christmas dinner. As did John Ferguson.

Jerry urged him to join the Sunday carolers. "Dress warm and you'll be fine," he'd promised, stabbing a chunk of fried egg with his fork. "Aurora makes an excellent hot toddy."

Sunday afternoon Owen called and asked him out to the ranch for a Christmas Eve gathering. Lucia and the boys were coming, Owen said. He could get a ride with Lucia or Jerry.

Sam politely refused every invitation. He wasn't a fan of Christmas. He didn't have a decorated tree, nor did he want one. His parents were dead; whatever relatives he had were few and distant. He hadn't talked to Jake in three years; somehow there wasn't much to say. His brother's life revolved around his music and the crowds that came with it. Sam's life was quieter, but they were both wanderers, each in his own way.

Their paths rarely crossed, which Sam regretted.

He thought about doing an internet search, finding a phone number, calling to say happy new year, at least. He could at least email the record company in Nashville and ask for the phone number he'd lost sometime in the past years. Not much had been said at their father's funeral, the last time he'd seen his brother. Being together only brought up a lot of memories better left alone.

Remember the time Mom set the Christmas tree on fire and Dad thought I did it? Remember the emergency room and the three little girls with burns? Hey, and what about that time Dad locked us in the base-

ment so we wouldn't interrupt the cocktail party for the governor and you had a fever?

Mama Marie phoned Monday afternoon and invited him for dinner Christmas Day. There would be turkey, she said, along with fish and pasta.

"I appreciate the invitation," he told her. "But I need to stay home and work. Thank you, though, for thinking of me."

"You can change your mind," she said. "There'll be plenty of food on the table, so just come over if you get hungry. Even a writer has to eat!"

It wasn't the writing, he wanted to say. It was Christmas, a holiday better left uncelebrated by members of the Hove family.

So Sam stayed at his makeshift desk, Mrs. Kelly's former dining-room table, and wrote about the Amazon. Killer catfish and mutant piranhas were always good distractions. He tried to ignore the normal little world next door, with its exuberant children making a snow fort in the yard and twinkling tree lights in the front window. He caught glimpses of Lucia coming and going in that old van.

He walked to Thompson's market and

made arrangements with Theo to deliver the food and supplies he'd purchased. Sam's agent called to say he was going to Mexico for two weeks, and his editor emailed to remind him when the manuscript was due.

Russ texted a photo of himself standing knee deep in the ocean with a large-breasted blond woman and a dolphin. The dolphin was smiling.

Sam texted back: You're a long way from Montana.

That's a good thing, Russ replied. Join us?

Sam turned off his cell phone.

His ribs were healing; the pain didn't bother him the way it had the week before. Rest was obviously what he'd needed. He did some stretching; he carried firewood, kept his fire going and lay in the recliner and watched football on television when he was tired of writing. He kept an eye out for Peckham's truck or any signs of disturbance in front of Lucia's house.

On the morning of Christmas Eve he made his own breakfast. He walked to the post office and picked up the box of books he'd ordered online using two-day delivery service. Mrs. Loudermilk wished him a Merry

Christmas and told him her daughter was driving in from Great Falls with the twins; did Sam think the weather would hold?

A crochety voice behind him scoffed. "It will snow or not," she snapped. "What else do you expect? It's winter!"

"Good morning, Mrs. Beckett," the postmistress said flatly. Her expression was less than animated now. "I'll be right with you."

Sam turned to see his other neighbor, the infamous woman who disliked children, noise and Lucia. As he'd expected, she was extremely old and looked pale and fragile. She was bundled in a thick gray coat that smelled of mothballs and she wore an odd orange knit hat over her long white hair.

"I think we're neighbors," he said, trying out a smile on her. "I'm Sam Hove. I'm renting the Kelly house, on the other side of Lucia Swallow's."

"I've seen you walking back and forth." She glared at him. "You caused that commotion the other night."

"No." Sam held his temper. "Someone else did. I put a stop to it."

"All that noise woke me up!"

Mrs. Loudermilk intervened. "Did you need stamps or anything else, Sam?"

"I'll take three of the flat rate priority mail stamps," he replied, turning his back on his nasty neighbor. He paid for the stamps and moved out of the way while he gathered his package and put his money back in his wallet.

"About time," Mrs. Beckett complained. "Getting more and more crowded around here."

"You have a package," the postmistress said, bustling to the shelf that held boxes. She returned and set the box on the counter. "Just in time for Christmas! How about that!"

"Humph."

Sam noticed the box was stamped with the Amazon label, just as his was.

"Mrs. Beckett's quite a reader," Mrs. Loudermilk announced, giving Sam a smile. "Just like you."

Sam wasn't sure he wanted to have anything in common with the old woman, but he nodded politely as Mrs. Beckett glared at them both.

"No one's business what I get in the mail,"

she grumbled, grabbing the box. "No one's business!"

Sam attempted to hold the door open for her, but she brushed him aside and marched to her car.

"She's an odd one," Mrs. Loudermilk said. "Don't pay her any attention. She's like that to everyone."

"I won't," he promised. Lucia certainly hadn't exaggerated her neighbor's cranky personality. "Have a good Christmas."

"You, too," she said, glancing at the wall clock. "I'm shutting down early, at noon. I've got a lot of wrapping to do."

Sam walked the two blocks home and wished Meg hadn't closed today. He would have liked to sit in the warmth of the café and eat an early lunch. But Meg would be at the ranch getting ready for the party he'd politely refused to attend. He'd preferred to be alone and he'd gotten exactly what he wanted.

Like Mrs. Beckett, he headed back to an empty house with a box of books in hand.

He intended to avoid any more holiday celebrations and he intended to avoid Lucia.

Except for one thing: the food kept coming.

He never knew when it would appear, but something would turn up on the woodpile next to the back door, as it had since the day after he'd moved in. Sunday, he'd found chicken breasts simmered in wine and mushrooms, along with a cinnamon roll. Monday, cookies in the shape of candy canes, pink and white and dotted with peppermint sugar. Today's Christmas Eve casserole contained frozen meatballs and sauce.

She had to stop being so nice to him. He didn't deserve it. He didn't want it. He didn't quite know how to react to it.

He also didn't want the food to go to waste, so he ate the chicken, the cookies, the cinnamon roll and the meatballs, feeling guilty all the while. He'd kissed her and she obviously interpreted that impulsive gesture as something more than passion.

Was the widow wooing him?

Sam expected the knock on his back door on Christmas morning. It was late, almost eleven, when he opened the door to see Davey and his brothers standing on the narrow porch.

"Merry Christmas," they trilled.

"Merry Christmas," he replied. "Do you want to come in?"

Davey shook his head. "You're supposed to come over and get a pie. Mom won't let us carry it."

Matty agreed. "She says we'll drop it and break it all up into pieces."

"Lots of pieces," said Tony. "And make a big mess in the snow and then the animals will show up and eat it."

"It's a present." Davey looked up at him, a very serious expression on his face. "'Cuz Mom said you like pie."

"I do," he said. "Am I supposed to come over and get the pie now?"

"Uh-huh. Before we go to Grandma's house. You wanna see our toys?"

He opened the door wider. "Hop inside while I get my boots. So, did Santa arrive last night?"

Tony's head bobbed up and down. "I got a truck. A big yellow one."

"Just like he asked Santa for," Davey said. "We got to see Boo last night at the ranch. Mom made him his own dog cookie."

"I got a bike," Matty told him. "And a bunch of other stuff, but I gotta wait for the snow to melt until I can ride it, and Owen says I can ride it at the ranch and Boo will chase me if I want him to, after I learn how to ride it and not fall off."

"Hold on." Sam sat down to pull his boots on, then lifted his jacket from its hook by the door. He grabbed a mailing box from the counter and tucked it under his arm, then took a shopping bag filled with plastic containers from where it sat on a kitchen chair.

"What's that?"

"Stuff," he said.

"For us? Presents?"

"Tony! You're not s'posed to ask that," his older brother said. "Jeez."

"It's okay," Sam said. "There's stuff in here for you." They stomped across the packed-down snow in the yard. The sky was so blue it hurt his eyes and he had to blink against the glare.

Lucia blushed when he walked into the kitchen. She wore her red sweater and a long swirly skirt that made her seem she was going dancing. Red feathers dangled from her ears.

"Merry Christmas," she said, a little shy.

The last time he'd seen her he'd kissed her, an impetuous, idiotic move.

"Merry Christmas." Well, heck, he wanted to do it again.

"How are you?"

"Just fine." They stared at each other for a few seconds. Lucia looked nervous. Sam felt out of place. The house smelled like cinnamon, apples and turkey gravy.

"I hear you've become a bit of a hermit, refusing Christmas invitations right and left. Mama was disappointed. She wanted to impress you with her homemade pasta."

"I'm not much for Christmas," he confessed.

She eyed the box. "What do you have there?"

He set it on her kitchen table, and the boys gathered around as though it was about to turn into something magical. "These are not exactly Christmas presents."

"Because you're not much of a Christmas kind of guy," she prompted, smiling.

"That's right." He lifted the flaps with a flourish. "We'll call them New Year's presents, just a week early."

"Wow," Davey breathed. "That's something new, huh?"

"Cool."

"Way cool."

"You haven't seen them yet," Sam pointed out. He shared a smile with Lucia. "Weird kids you have here."

"Just show us what's inside, will you?"

So Sam lifted out the books, the best books he could find on birds, fish, reptiles and mammals, mostly books from the Scientists in the Field series. Two for each boy, age appropriate. With colorful photographs and detailed information, they were similar to the kinds of books he'd had access to when he was growing up. The kinds of books that had given him something to look forward to, someplace to run. He'd wanted to show them pictures of the creatures he'd told them about. Reading on a computer screen was different from turning pages and studying the pictures. He hoped Lucia would agree with him, because he'd debated over buying ebooks for the boys and then decided on old-fashioned paper.

"These are for us?" Davey opened a book

titled *The Tapir Scientist.* "This is really cool."

"Here are a couple of DVDs, too. One is about monkeys and the other is about sharks." He handed them to Davey, assuming that as the oldest he'd be in charge of the movies.

"This is very generous of you, Sam." She gazed at the book Matty handed her. *Pink Dolphins of the Amazon?*

"I've seen them," he explained. "They're really something."

The boys thanked him, Tony hugged his leg, Matty jumped up and down and Davey appeared thoughtful.

"I told Mrs. Kramer I'd ask you to come talk to our class," he said, carefully holding the stack of books and DVDs.

"Sure. Have her call me when school starts."

"Really?"

"I'll write down my phone number for you to give to her," Sam assured him, and Davey looked ecstatic.

Matty peered into the box. "There's something else!"

"That's for your mom," Sam said, reaching for the heavy book in the bottom. "The reviewers rated it highly, so I hope you like it," he told Lucia. He handed her a book entitled *Baking,* with a huge photograph of a chocolate cake on the cover.

"Dorie Greenspan? I love her."

"Do you have this one?"

"No." She ran her fingers over the cover. "I've seen it in the bookstore in Billings, though." Lucia seemed ready to cry. "Thank you, Sam. I'll make you something from one of the recipes."

"Can we watch it now?" Davey held up one of the documentaries.

"Sure."

The boys thundered off into the living room, leaving the kitchen suddenly silent.

Lucia finally spoke. "This was awfully nice of you. And all I have for you is a pie."

"I like pie." Which was an understatement, though he hadn't known how much he liked pie until he'd moved to Willing.

"Good thing." She smiled and looked down at the cookbook. "Such a lovely gift."

"I'm glad you like it." Sam remembered the bag filled with Lucia's plastic containers and small casserole dishes. He grabbed it from the floor.

"I brought your dishes," he said. "I washed them, made sure all the lids matched."

"What?" She peeked inside the bag. "Where did all this come from?"

"The food you've sent," he said. "I guess I should have brought this stuff back sooner. I've appreciated it, a lot, but—"

"Food?" Lucia gave him a puzzled look.

"Yeah." The food she'd lavished upon him for two weeks, he wanted to say. Was she going to pretend she hadn't? And why feign surprise? "The food you've been leaving at my back door since I moved in," he stated.

"Since you moved in," she murmured, looking back into the bag of containers. Her cheeks flushed, the red almost matching her sweater. "Are you kidding?"

"Uh—"

"How did the food arrive?" She had an expression in her eyes that made him want to back up a couple of steps.

"You left it on the woodpile by my back door. Under the eaves." Was the sweet widow slightly insane? If so, she'd certainly fooled him into thinking otherwise.

"Tell me, what was your favorite?" Was this a trick question? He watched Lucia set the cookbook on the counter and put her hands on her hips. "You know—the food from the woodpile that you liked the best."

"I know what *favorite* means. Are you all right?"

"Never better," she snapped.

"Okay." He didn't have to think very hard. "The meatballs and spaghetti was great. And the mac and cheese with the bacon? I liked that, too."

"Chicken?"

"Excellent."

"Cookies?"

"Which kind? Never mind. They're all good. You know that. You're *the* baker in the town." Her expression continued to make him nervous. "What's going on here?"

She took a deep breath and exhaled. "Nothing's going on, Sam. I'm glad you enjoyed the...offerings. I hope you didn't think I was coming on to you... You know, trying to seduce the new man in town."

"I thought the gesture was neighborly," Sam fibbed. "Very neighborly."

"You needn't worry." She smiled brightly.

"You don't have to keep hiding in your house for fear the love-starved widow next door is going to pester you."

"Love-starved widow? Lucia, that's not—"

"You are not my type, but maybe I *should* start dating again," she said, cutting off his words of protest. "I don't need drunk kids bothering me or visitors like you thinking I'm lonely and available. Maybe it's time to find someone nice, someone stable." She sighed. "Maybe someone with a dog. Davey? Come out here, right now!"

"I never got the impression you were available. I'm pretty sure you told me a few times you weren't," Sam reminded her. "But lonely? Be honest. We both are. Lonely, that is."

"There won't be any more 'lonely' kisses," she declared. "And there won't be any more little gifts of food. I'll put a stop to it immediately. No matter what you think, I am *not* a desperate woman."

"I don't think you're desperate. And I'm not hiding in my house," Sam said. "I haven't been avoiding you, not really. I hate Christmas. Bah, humbug, and all that. I won't bore you with the family horror stories, but if you'd grown up with Lou and Diane, you wouldn't like Christmas much, either."

That seemed to silence her, at least for a few seconds. He was glad he'd kept his coat and boots on; he could make a quick and dignified exit.

"Thank you for being so good to the boys," Lucia said. "And thank you for the beautiful cookbook. I shouldn't have yelled at you."

"You didn't yell."

"I'm just…embarrassed."

Sam had no idea what she was talking about, but he decided now was a good time to go home. Unfortunately, without his pie.

CHAPTER NINE

"RANDOM ACTS OF KINDNESS," Lucia repeated. She and Meg had shooed Loralee and Marie out of the kitchen after dinner. The older women could relax with coffee while Owen played with the boys. Boo was stretched out in the kitchen in front of the garbage can as Meg and Lucia scraped plates, loaded the dishwasher and washed cooking pots. "It's all about the points the kids earn when they do something nice for someone who doesn't expect it. Davey's been sneaking food out of the freezer and the refrigerator for ten days. I've been too busy to notice anything was missing. I figured I'd counted wrong on the mac and cheese casseroles."

"So Davey must be in the lead."

"If he keeps raiding my freezer, he will be."

"Have you talked to him about it?" Meg looked as though she was trying not to laugh.

"Not yet. I blame Mrs. Kramer. She told them there would be a prize. Davey's competitive, like his father."

"Just tell Sam what really happened," Meg said. "He'll probably think it's funny. Because it is, you know, a little funny."

"He kissed me," Lucia whispered. "The night we came home from the concert. And it wasn't only a little kiss. It was a great big intense kiss."

"A movie kiss?"

"Absolutely a movie kiss."

"He does have a little of that movie star quality to him."

"He thought I was doing it, that's the worst part. When I saw all those plastic containers…"

"At least he returned them."

"I wish he hadn't. I could have gone on thinking—"

"Thinking what?"

"That he thought I was hot."

"You are hot. Look at you. Feathers in your ears, eye makeup, great body. You have, um, flair."

"Flair." Lucia wasn't impressed with that.

"Wearing great earrings isn't the same as being hot."

"I wouldn't know," her friend replied. "I've never been in that league. Loralee was the hot one in the family."

"Maybe she could give me lessons."

Owen entered the kitchen and opened the refrigerator. "Give you lessons for what?"

"What are you hunting for?"

"A Coke. Found one." He shut the door and popped the top of the can. "What are you two plotting?"

"Lessons on how to be hot," Lucia said. "We're having a really ridiculous conversation."

"I don't think you need lessons. Aren't you the woman who had to phone the sheriff Friday?"

"Well, yes," she said, feeling a little comforted.

"And didn't the man who raced to your rescue spend the night?"

"On the couch," Lucia added.

"Get a man's point of view," Meg suggested. "Tell Owen about the Random Acts."

Lucia reached for another grimy saucepan

to scrub. "Shh. I don't want anyone else to hear."

Mama's kitchen was small, tucked in a corner of her two-bedroom, one-story house, so Meg moved Owen to the corner farthest away from the living room.

"Does this have anything to do with Sam Hove?"

"Why?"

Owen shrugged. "Just a wild guess."

Lucia narrowed her eyes and stopped scrubbing. "Wild guess?"

"He's around a lot," was the rancher's explanation. "You seem to like him. Why didn't he come for dinner today?"

"He doesn't like Christmas," Meg said.

"How can you not like Christmas?" Owen took another swig from the Coke can. "Though I like Thanksgiving better. No gifts to wrap. Lots of football on TV. Pumpkin pie."

"He's been avoiding me," Lucia added. "He didn't go to the caroling or your house yesterday because *he* thinks I've been bringing him all sorts of gifts from my kitchen in order to get his attention and make him fall madly in love with me."

Owen's eyebrows rose. "He told you that?"

"Not in so many words."

"We need a male perspective," Meg said. She explained Davey's school project and the bag of plastic containers, and how Sam brought flowers last week and Christmas presents for the boys this morning. Owen leaned against the wall and listened to the whole story, minus the part about the kiss on Saturday night.

"Yeah. I remember the flowers. All right," he said. "Forget the whole food thing."

"Really?"

"Yeah. Food's important, but it doesn't have much to do with sexual chemistry. Cooking is a bonus, but it's not a deal breaker. Has Sam asked you out?"

"Well, yes, but I said no, that I don't date."

"But he went to the concert with you," Owen pointed out.

"He invited himself."

"Right. Who kissed who? Whom," he corrected. "He has kissed you, right?"

"How do you know that?"

"Another wild guess." Owen smirked and Meg elbowed him in the ribs. "Answer the question. I'd rather stay in here than go back in the living room and listen to Loralee and Marie argue over the baby shower. They're also discussing whether or not it was a good idea for Shelly to spend Christmas with Les."

"I think it's sweet," Lucia said, hoping that Shelly and her baby would find a family of their own. Les was young, but clearly in love.

Owen shrugged. "I'm staying out of it. The boys are watching a DVD about sharks again. I've seen enough blood in the water for a while."

"Be nice," Meg said. "Or we'll kick you out of here."

"I just asked a question," he protested. "For informational purposes."

"He kissed me," Lucia told Owen. "It was a pretty good kiss. But he started it." She felt her cheeks grow hot.

"Well, there you go."

"What's that supposed to mean?"

"He's asked you out, he wanted to go to the concert with three kids and your mother-in-law and he made a move on you. He's interested." Owen tossed his empty soda can into the trash as if it were a basketball. Boo flinched and jumped to his feet. "He seems like a decent guy. You either go out with him or you don't. Ball's in your court."

"Thank you for the analysis," Meg said. "I especially liked the sports references."

"You're welcome," Owen said. "I'm just getting warmed up for the Husband School Refresher Course Friday night. And after the women arrive, I'll bet guys will be lining up for my wisdom."

"And mine," Meg reminded him. "I'm still on the education committee, as well as the caterer."

"And I'm historic sites," he said. "Plus the location committee. We're going to be busy. When are we getting married?"

"Soon," Meg promised. "You'll be the first to know."

"Hurry up," he said. "Boo and I are lonely out there on the ranch." The dog heard his name, jumped up and focused on Owen. "I'm going to take the boys and Boo for a walk before it gets dark," Owen said, giving Meg a quick kiss on the mouth. "Since my job here is done."

He left the kitchen, and they heard him tell the boys to turn off the television and get their coats and boots on.

"A month ago I was calling him Ranch King," Lucia said. "Now all of a sudden he's Dr. Drew."

"He's improved a lot since we've been engaged." Meg reached for a dish towel. "I agree with him. I think Sam is genuinely attracted to you. And you are to him. That doesn't mean you have to do anything about it."

"That's true." And she'd spend the rest of her life reliving one heck of a great kiss. How sad.

"Tell him the truth about Davey and the food. You'll both laugh about it and that will be that."

"He forgot his pie, the one I made him for Christmas."

"Take it to him," Meg said as three boys and a dog stampeded through the kitchen. "Thank him again for the cookbook and wish him a Merry Christmas. It's that simple."

"No, it's not." She couldn't help smiling as she reached for the turkey roaster, though. "But I'll do it. And Davey has to find another way to earn points."

"You forgot this," Lucia said when Sam opened the door. It was dark, after eight o'clock, on Christmas night. He'd spent the day working, reliving the weeks in search of a giant catfish in India. Given the diets of giant catfish, those memories always made him lose his appetite.

She handed him his pie. It was wrapped in plastic, tied with a big red bow and sitting in a basket.

"Wow. Thank you."

"Can I come in?" she asked as though she hoped he'd say no.

"Sure." He stepped back to let her enter the kitchen. The only light on was over the sink, which made the room seem gloomy. "Come into the living room. I've got the fire going."

She hesitated. "I can't stay long. The boys are alone. Tony's asleep and Matt and Davey are watching that shark movie you gave them. For the third time."

"A friend of mine directed it. It's pretty accurate and they did a good job with the editing." He put the pie on the counter. Apple, he thought. He'd try to make it last more than two days.

She stayed rooted to the rug. "I put your phone number on speed dial. They're supposed to call me immediately if something happens."

"If we go in the living room we can keep an eye on your house." That didn't sound good. "I mean, not to sound like a stalker, but at least from the living room you can see that your lights are on and the house isn't on fire."

"All right." Lucia kicked off her boots and set them neatly by the door. "I'm really embarrassed about something and I need to get this over with."

"The last time a beautiful woman told me she needed to 'get this over with,' she told me she'd wrecked my boat."

"If you have another boat, it's safe from me," Lucia muttered. She shrugged off her coat and he noticed she still wore the red sweater and the long skirt she'd had on this morning. He liked the earrings. Sam wanted to reach out and tickle those feathers along her neck. Did she know how tempting that was?

"So," he prompted. "Get *what* over with?"

"My apology. For my behavior this morning."

He led her into the dining area, past Mrs.

Kelly's table piled with papers and maps. His laptop sat at the far end, a cup of cold coffee next to it. There was nothing in the room that looked like Christmas except the tree lights visible in Lucia's window.

"Sorry about the mess." Neither he nor the living room were particularly tidy. He wore the thickest fleece sweat pants he could find online and a black wool sweater, along with socks thick enough for hunters to wear in Alaska during the winter. He'd showered but not shaved and he figured his hair was sticking up all over. He made an attempt to smooth it down.

She crossed the room and went over to the side window, stared at her brightly lit house for a long moment and then turned to face him.

"Just so you know, I haven't been bringing food to your house," she announced. "Davey has. As part of a school project."

"You're kidding." Sam choked back a laugh. All this time he'd thought Lucia was trying to impress him, and instead an eight-year-old kid was doing his homework. "I thought you were the world's kindest neighbor."

"Uh, no. As embarrassing as this is, I'm not kidding. When I saw the bag of empty containers, I realized you must have thought I'd been sending them to you."

"And it was Davey's idea?" That was disappointing. He was distracted again by the long earrings, by the way she slid her hair back behind her shoulders.... She seemed nervous, and he couldn't understand why. Sam stepped a little closer to her so they were both near the woodstove and able to see out the window. The street was dark, no car headlights in sight. Her house appeared perfectly fine. "Do you want to sit down?"

She glanced at the window. "No. I'm not staying long. Random Acts of Kindness," she said. "That's what he was doing. Sneaking food over here for points. Without my knowing anything about it."

"I thought you were flirting with me," he admitted.

"No wonder you've been so...nice."

"Hey," he said, running his hand through his hair again. "Are you angry with me about something?"

"No, of course not. I'm embarrassed."

It seemed natural to put his hands on her

shoulders and gaze into those serious hazel eyes. "Then we're good," he said, daring a smile. "And I'll make sure to thank Davey for his kind deeds. The meatballs were spectacular."

She smiled back, just a little. "I'm not a lonely, desperate housewife."

"I never thought you were," he fibbed.

"Yes, you did. I know it."

He leaned down and brushed his lips across hers. "That was not a 'lonely kiss.'"

"What?"

He brushed her mouth again, tasting a bit of sweetness. Sugar cookies, maybe. "You said, 'There won't be any more lonely kisses' this morning. I'm following orders."

She reached up and cupped his neck. "What kind of kiss was it?"

"An 'I love pie' kiss?"

She shook her head. "You have to stop fixating on food."

"You're right," he murmured, bringing his hands up to frame her face. "This is much better."

"This isn't better," she whispered. "This is a mistake."

"Probably." He kissed her anyway, this

time the way he wanted to. Lucia pulled him closer, her lips soft and pliant against his. After a long, sweet moment, Sam drew away. He lifted a feather with the tip of his index finger. "Would you wear these every time you come over here to apologize for something?"

"I wasn't really apologizing."

"You said you were."

"It was more of an explanation. I overreacted when I saw all that Tupperware."

"And the school project?"

"Just a misunderstanding," she said, wriggling out of his embrace. "I absolutely cannot keep doing this."

"Doing what?"

"You know, kissing you. I don't do things like this."

"You could have fooled me," he teased, but she moved away from him.

He followed her back into the kitchen and lifted her coat from the hook while she jammed her feet into her boots.

"I'm a mother."

"I'm aware of that. I caught on the first day I met you."

"We're too different," she said with a sigh.

"There's no sense in continuing this, no matter how much— Never mind. I like you."

"I like you, too." He liked her so much he wanted to take her into his arms again. "So is that it?"

"We are neighbors and friends," she declared, raising her chin a bit defiantly. "But you *are* a good kisser. Merry Christmas."

Sam didn't know what to say to that. Before he could think of anything she was out the door. He flicked on the porch light and watched her disappear around the corner, heading home.

He walked into the warmth of the living room and, ignoring the work waiting for him, eased himself into the recliner. His ribs were healing so nicely that now he only had infrequent aches when he'd overdone it. Willing had been good for him, but it was time to start getting back into shape. There was a new trip to plan—Russ had emailed him info on mysterious drownings in Colombia and promised to follow up with newspaper clippings via snail mail.

But he would be in Willing for at least two and a half more months, more than enough time to finish writing the book and get his body ready for another rigorous trip.

Sam noticed Lucia's lights had been turned off. The boys would have to watch the shark video another day. But the tree lights were still on, and Sam pictured Lucia curled up on her couch and enjoying them. He wished he were over there with her.

And that was dangerous. If he were any other kind of man, he would be over there right now, explaining the difference between bull sharks and great whites to the boys. He would be taking Lucia to dinner and bringing her roses when he could find them at the market, and he would make promises he intended to keep. Such as till death do us part and for better or for worse.

But he wasn't that kind of man. He'd been on his own since he was eighteen. The day he walked out of the family home had been the day he'd finally taken a deep breath and felt free. His abusive, alcoholic mother had delighted in beating his brother and him. And his fiery, alcoholic father had done nothing to stop her. There'd been no grandparents. His mother's aunt had intervened twice, the second time succeeding in convincing Diane that the boys were needed to work on her Pennsylvania farm. They'd fished the Delaware River instead. They'd hiked and climbed and laughed.

Like Lucia's boys. A reminder that it was okay to be a child. He thought those summers had saved his life.

But as an adult Sam didn't like staying in one place. He'd get claustrophobic, restless, short-tempered. He'd go to bed thinking about maps and rivers and what he and the crew could find next. He wasn't husband material, and he certainly never wanted to be a father. Especially not a stepfather.

So Lucia, as much as he was attracted to her, would remain a sweet and dangerous temptation. Because she deserved better.

THAT HADN'T GONE the way she'd planned. Lucia turned off the shark movie, herded her sleepy boys to their beds and then put on her warmest flannel nightgown before fixing herself a cup of herbal tea. She curled up on her couch in the dark and admired her twinkling Christmas tree.

There was a man in her life, whether she wanted one or not. He was right next door, big as life, handsome and funny and vital. He seemed to like her boys and he certainly seemed to like her.

She hadn't been kissed in years. And she had no doubts that she'd enjoyed every second of every kiss, whether a brush of lips on her cheek or a real embrace.

Sam was very good at kissing. Was he one of those men who had a woman in every port in South America? She doubted it. There was something lonely about him. She knew he'd been telling the truth about an awful childhood. It explained his being so remote, so private, yet pleased when people were kind to him.

She didn't think he expected kindness.

And although he enjoyed meeting people and being around them, and he was free with stories about his adventures, which he told with self-deprecating humor, this big, surprisingly gentle man was more comfortable asking people questions than answering them.

Lucia sipped her tea and thought a little more about those kisses. She was falling in love with him. Maybe. Since she'd picked him up from the snow, she'd been aware of the attraction.

Those kinds of feelings didn't arise often, she knew. And admittedly he was a decent and intriguing man. But if she was falling in love with him, she was the only one who had to know. She didn't intend to make a fool of herself over a man who couldn't stay in one place and be a husband and a father.

She needed a man who would stick around this time. She'd loved her husband, supported his job, respected his commitment to the army and his dedication to his career. But if—if—she ever married again, she wanted a husband who came home for dinner every night.

"Hɪ, Sᴀᴍ."

"Hey, Davey, how's it going?"

Davey watched Sam carry split wood from a pile and stack it neatly on his back porch.

"Not so good," Davey admitted. He didn't think he was supposed to say he was sorry for the Kindnesses. Mom had said it was okay. But she'd looked like it wasn't. Davey couldn't figure out what he'd done wrong, except for not telling Mom. Maybe the points were supposed to be sort of secret. Like that was the most important part.

"What's wrong?"

"Mom said I have to do Kindness stuff for lots of people, not just you."

"Well, I enjoyed the attention," Sam said. "The food was greatly appreciated. Thank-you."

Davey sighed. "Now I gotta think of something else."

"What are other kids doing?"

"I don't know." The girls in the class did things for each other, like give stupid presents, but Davey didn't think that should count. Mrs. Kramer had told them to expand their horizons. "What are you doing?

"Taking a break from work," Sam said. "I needed some fresh air and Hip delivered another load of wood. Figure it's going to snow?"

"I hope so."

"So, what's up?" Sam stomped his feet in the snow and rubbed his gloved hands together.

The boy shrugged. "Not much."

"Same here."

"I like The Quiet."

"Yeah, I know what you mean."

"You do?"

"Sure. It helps me concentrate when I'm working on my book. Other times I really like hearing people talk, though. People think the jungles are quiet, but they're not. It's a different kind of noise, but I like that, too."

Davey moved over to the woodpile, picked up two pieces of wood and handed them to Sam, who placed them neatly in the stack. "This isn't a Kindness," he told him. "I'm just doing it."

"Well, thanks. I could use the help."

"Mom said your ribs are better."

"Definitely improving," Sam said, stretching his arms overhead as if to prove it. "Where are your brothers?"

"Cleaning their room. I'm done. I have my own room and I don't mess it up too much." He grabbed two more pieces of wood and handed them to Sam. It felt good to be outdoors working. "Mom said I could go outside as long as I stayed in the yard."

"What exactly is a Kindness?" Sam placed one piece of wood kitty-corner to the other piece to keep it dry. He was really neat about it.

"You do something nice for someone who doesn't expect it," Davey recited.

"What about your other neighbors? Could anyone else use some help?"

"Just Mrs. Beckett and she's mean. She lives in the white house but we can never ever go in her yard or she gets mad. She's really old and she gets mad about everything."

"Thanks for the warning," Sam said. "I met her at the post office and she wasn't exactly cheerful."

"She's not gonna like a Kindness."

"No, it doesn't sound like it."

They stacked the rest of the wood in companionable silence. Davey liked being around someone who didn't talk about stupid stuff.

"Do you have kids?" he asked when the work was done.

"No."

"Why not?"

"I never got married."

Davey thought about that for a moment as they stood under the porch overhang and looked at the finished stack. Shelly wasn't married and she was having a baby, but he was glad that Sam didn't have any kids who missed him the way he missed his dad.

The stack of wood was higher than Davey's head. "We did a good job," he said.

"We did," Sam agreed.

"BACHELORS TO THE RIGHT, everyone else to the left."

What seemed a simple instruction caused chaos. Jerry's temples throbbed. He hoped he wasn't getting a migraine.

"*Husband School* bachelors to the right," he clarified. "All other single men who are not going to be part of the show and all volunteers and interested spectators please take a seat to the left of the aisle."

The crowd eventually did as they were instructed, which Jerry decided was nothing short of a miracle. He surveyed his group of twenty-four bachelors with great pride and satisfaction. There should only have been twenty-three, but naturally Joey Peckham hadn't taken rejection easily. The swollen nose and the purple circle under one eye did not add to the kid's appeal, but there he sat, oblivious to his own idiocy.

Well, he'd leave Joey for Tracy to sort

out. She'd hinted she wouldn't mind a little drama, and if she kept Joey in the show, she'd likely get it.

"Okay, okay, settle down," he told the crowd. He had a good showing tonight. Some of the bachelors twitched nervously, but the rest of the crowd looked pumped, as though they were about to watch a championship basketball game. Excitement was in the air, all right.

"Okay, everyone. The big night is almost here."

Applause broke out, which immediately vanquished Jerry's migraine. In fact, he almost felt a little emotional.

"Less than a year from now, Willing could be the dating capital of America."

More applause.

"Everyone who sees the show will want to live here," he assured the crowd. "People will want to visit the town with an abundance of single, Western men. Hopefully," he said, giving the bachelors a warning look, "our single men will impress our visitors and the television audience. Viewers all over America will fall in love with you, too."

Jerry believed it, as well. There was someone for everyone, that was his motto, and since no one understood women anyway, who knew what—and who—they would find attractive?

"When's the show going to be on?" This was from Mike. Though he was sitting on the bachelor side of the aisle, he had his notebook and pen with him. He intended to document the entire experience and hopefully get a blogging gig on the E! website. Jerry figured him for one of the front-runners this season. He was shy, but he'd recently remodeled his house. Women appreciated carpentry skills.

"This summer, we hope."

Another hand went up. It was Pete, a decent enough guy with some acreage outside of town. The woman who married Pete could have her own horse, a definite plus for the outdoorsy type of female. "Do we get to pick who we date?"

"No," Jerry said. "That's up to the producers and, I guess, the women selected to be on the show."

"How many are coming?" This was from a nondescript fortysomething-year-old who happened to own seven snowmobiles, Jerry had no idea why. But if Tracy wanted to film a snowy date to the middle of nowhere, he knew the man to call.

"Twelve," Jerry said. "Tracy will explain the show's concept when she gets here. It's a competition, but it's also about a town looking to save itself from extinction. The town is part of the show. We're more than the background," he explained, which was exactly what he'd told Tracy at their last meeting.

"How long are they gonna be here?" This was from Ben Fargus, a man who insisted on knowing every detail of everything that went on in the town. He was a politician's nightmare.

"At least four, maybe five, weeks. Depending on how the filming goes. Again, Tracy will spell out how it's going to work when she gets here. She will be doing a lot of filming, then crafting the story later out of the footage."

Les raised his hand. "What does that mean?"

"She won't know the story until after it's told," Jerry said. "Next summer some of you could be television stars." He himself hoped for an article in *People* magazine, maybe a photo spread of the town. He would pose by his house, ask Owen to stand next to the marble bull statue in the park. He'd had two calls already from a reporter at *US* magazine; she'd used the word *cowboy* a lot, which she seemed very excited about. Jerry had made a note to buy some pearl-snapped shirts and a new pair of boots.

"What's the name of the show?" someone called out, but Jerry didn't see who had asked the question.

"You're gonna love this," he said, looking at the expectant crowd. "It's pure genius."

"Well?" Aurora, right in the front row where she could annoy him, spoke up loud and clear. "What is it?"

"Willing to Wed," he announced. "Perfect, isn't it?"

The applause was deafening.

CHAPTER TEN

AURORA TURNED TO Meg and Lucia after Jerry finished listing details about the New Year's Eve party and the filming of the show's first episode.

"Trust me," she said. "Something's going to get screwed up."

Sam, seated behind Owen, whispered, "I had no idea that life in Montana would be so interesting."

Owen nodded. "Man, neither did I."

"But you grew up here." Sam had heard the stories of the MacGregors founding the town and a cattle empire. He'd seen the statue and the plaque in the park. Now he and Owen watched as the three women stood and moved toward the crowd gathered around the mayor.

Sam had arrived a few minutes before the meeting started and found an empty seat in the second row. He hadn't seen Lucia since

Christmas night and, despite his noble intentions to stay away, discovered that a town meeting gave him the perfect excuse to see her.

He didn't think she'd noticed him yet.

"I went to college and for a lot of reasons didn't return until last summer, after my great uncle died. I didn't know what I wanted to do with my life. I had the successful business, the degrees, the city...but something happened when I came home," Owen remembered.

"Let me guess. Meg?"

"I walked into the café and there she was, still the same beautiful woman I'd fallen in love with when I was just a college kid. And Jerry was talking about a television show and how the town was in trouble of fading away, and there was Meg, looking like she wished I'd go away and stay away."

"And you didn't."

"She tried to get rid of me," Owen said, "but I wouldn't leave. I carried her engagement ring around in my pocket hoping for another chance. What about you?"

"I've never felt that way," Sam confessed. "I've met some women who might have been special, but before it could get serious—or even before that—I'd be off for three months, six months, whatever. My work has always been more important."

"Yeah. I get it. But I signed you up for the catering committee anyway," Owen said, not bothering to hide his smile.

"The catering committee," Sam slowly repeated. "Now, why would you do that?"

"I figured you needed some help getting a date for New Year's Eve."

"I think she's ignoring me," Sam said, watching Meg and Lucia huddle over a clipboard.

"Cheer up." Owen stood and looked toward the other side of the room. "At least you're not waiting for a bus of women to show up."

"You put me on the catering committee? Really?"

"Yep. Follow me. We'll get our assignments. You can thank me later."

"I'll thank you now," Sam told him, as Lucia glanced over and smiled at him.

"Watch yourself," Owen said from behind him. "Or you may never see the Amazon again."

"The what?"

Owen laughed, which caused Meg to glance up and bestow an especially tender look on her fiancé. Sam envied the couple. From what he'd seen, they were obviously a good match, despite whatever they'd been through to finally become engaged.

"When are you getting married?"

"Soon," Owen said. "As soon as Meg makes up her mind about the date. But it will be before summer. I'm tired of driving back and forth to town."

"You won't live in Willing?"

"We're trying to figure that out," he said as they approached the women. "Meg has the restaurant and I have the ranch. And there's ninety miles in between."

Aurora poked Sam in the chest. "New Year's Eve, Fish Man. I need you behind the bar."

"I thought I was on the food—"

"You are," she said. "You're going to help

Lucia with the appetizers and snacks, then me with the bar, and then we'll move the party to the café for the breakfast." She checked her notes. "Yeah, that just about covers it. Lucia? You want to give Sam any instructions before we leave?"

"Are you sure you're up for bartending?" she asked.

"I am."

She appeared dubious. "I didn't think you'd be involved in all this."

"I'm calling it a Random Act of Kindness."

"Very funny," she said.

"Can I walk you home?"

"How do you know I didn't drive?"

"Your van was in your driveway when I passed your house. What'd you do with the boys?"

"Mama is babysitting."

"Then we can walk very, very slowly."

She laughed, which he assumed meant yes. They retrieved their jackets, bundled up against the cold and headed back to Janet Street. She tucked her arm in his and held on.

"Tell me about your next job," she said. "Where will you go when you leave here?"

"Colombia, I think."

"What's in Colombia?"

For the life of him, Sam didn't have an answer.

"WE HAVE TO make snow sexy," Tracy stated, leaning against the bar. "How do we do that?"

Lucia didn't dare look at Aurora for fear of bursting into laughter. She concentrated on refilling the cheese tray while the producer rattled off a series of questions to anyone within hearing.

"Making snow sexy," Sam murmured as he filled glasses with the beer from the tap. He actually sounded as though he was considering the problem. "Snowball fights, sledding, snowmobiles, a bonfire?"

"Bonfire? I love it! Jerry? Where are you? I want to ask you about a bonfire!" She took off after Jerry, who'd been waylaid by one of the crew as he headed toward the stuffed grizzly Owen's grandfather had shot after being attacked.

Willing had been invaded as of 11:20 last night. The twelve contestants, young women whose looks ranged from beauty-contest contender to cute girl next door, had been housed in Meg's cabins and Iris's bed and breakfast. Tracy and the crew camped out in Jerry's enormous house, which also served as the production center. The cast and crew had wandered into the café for breakfast this morning, as there was nothing scheduled except getting some rest for most of the day. Unlike other dating shows, Jerry explained, the female contestants were allowed to explore the town, provided they had a small film crew with them to record anything interesting.

After the meet and greet New Year's Eve party, one-on-one and group dates would be arranged and filmed. There would be group dates and private dates until the women voted to keep twelve men out of the original twenty-four, leaving six remaining couples.

Tracy was a little murky about the rest of the details, but as far as Lucia understood, there were "stay" and "go" options, such as the women asking the men, "Are you willing to wed?" and the men answering yes or no.

There would be a "twist" near the end of the show, Tracy assured them, when the men would have the chance to ask the question of the women they'd hopefully fallen in love with. The point was to keep the audience guessing who would be "Willing to Wed" and stay in Montana.

Lucia thought the idea was insane, but Meg liked it. "It's a crazy way to meet a husband," she said, "but it sounds more interesting than signing up on those internet dating sites."

The rest of the single women in town agreed with Meg. They were also hoping that the men on the film crew were single and straight. Those who had met Sam saw the way he looked at Lucia, and those who cared for her took a step back from flirting with the new man in town and privately wished her all the luck in the world.

"Romance is all around us," Meg said. "This is a little surreal."

"I like this place," Sam said, and set another filled beer glass on the counter.

"I can't imagine why," Lucia drawled, her cheese tray finished. "Twelve beautiful women, here for love and romance and a few hours of fame, not to mention furthering their acting or modeling careers."

"And twenty-four Montana bachelors looking as though they're going to pass out or run like hell," Sam added. He grinned. "The bear adds a nice touch."

Owen was being filmed in front of the grizzly. He'd been answering questions about the town's history for the past hour, since before the party began. He'd dressed for the part of town historian, too, wearing a checked Western shirt with pearl snaps, dark slacks and polished pointed-toe boots. The women had been shooting admiring glances his way ever since they'd arrived.

"The bear's been here forever," Meg said.

"I heard." Sam grinned. "So, aren't you two supposed to mingle and help the guys with conversation?" Sam inquired.

Meg picked up the two appetizer platters. "I'm heading out now. Les looks like he needs help with that little redhead with the silver miniskirt."

Two well-toned young brunettes, also in miniskirts and obviously contestants, stepped up to the bar and asked for ice water. "We have to pace ourselves," one of them told Sam.

Lucia perched on a bar stool and felt about

sixty years old in her vintage black lace dress and cowboy boots.

"Where's Shelly tonight? I thought she and Les were a couple."

"Not as far as she's concerned," Lucia said. "But he's been a good friend to her since she arrived in town."

"She looks as if she needs more than a friend. The baby's due soon?"

"In six or seven weeks. She'll be here eventually. I know she doesn't want to miss the excitement."

"You could come mingle with me as soon as Aurora gets back," Lucia said, eyeing the sea of people with some trepidation. It seemed most of the town was here. Free food and free drinks would attract people who normally stayed at home and went to bed before the new year arrived. And then there was the opportunity to be on television. Aurora had gone to ask the band to turn down the volume so the sound didn't interfere with recording conversations.

Sam shook his head. "The mayor told me to stay behind the bar and appear unavailable. If anyone asks I'm to say I'm married and my wife and I are expecting our fourth child."

"Please tell me you're joking."

"I am not," Sam assured her. "Aurora has been assigned to scare off any women who think I'm part of the show."

"She's your pretend wife?"

"Uh, no," he said. "You are. We needed someone with kids to make it look real."

"None of this is real," Lucia reminded him. "It's a television show."

"Play along," he said. "Be the domestic goddess you are already and order me around a lot."

"Because that's what wives do?"

"I'm joking." He grinned at her. "But go on, boss me around."

"That's easy enough."

"Well?"

"I'm thinking of something."

"I can make you a drink," he said. "You look beautiful tonight. Have I told you that already?"

"No, but thank you."

It hadn't entered her mind that any of these women might think Sam was part

298 THE HUSBAND PROJECT

of the show, part of the town. They were all attractive, and in cute outfits, heels and full makeup, they were nothing short of gorgeous. Twenty-four stunned and anxious men crowded around them, as a country-rock-bluegrass band played against the back wall and cameramen wove through the crowd.

The contestants were being taken, one at a time, to be filmed in front of the bear as they answered questions from Tracy and her assistant.

"What are they doing?"

"Private interviews," Sam explained. "Otherwise known as a PI. The more footage they have, the more they'll be able to shape the story they want to tell and the more interesting they can make it to viewers."

"What are they asking them?"

"Go listen," Sam said. "I'd like to know, too." He leaned forward. "But give me a kiss before you leave."

"What?"

"For the sake of the show," he said, laughing down at her. "You know, to make our relationship look real."

"None of this is real," she grumbled, but she stood on tiptoe, leaned over the bar and kissed him on the cheek.

"Thanks," he said. "That was very domestic."

She was good at domestic.

Since Christmas night Lucia had managed to treat Sam as an amiable friend, someone with whom she enjoyed spending time, in a neighborly way, of course. So who would ever know that deep down she wanted to pretend that he was staying here, that he would be part of her life and her children's lives, if he was the kind of guy who was going to open a hardware store or an insurance office. If he wanted babies?

She wanted more babies.

She'd walked home with Sam the other night and felt safe and, better yet, part of a couple again. Once again she acknowledged that being alone wasn't easy. She'd known when she'd married an army man that she would be alone a lot, but she hadn't expected to be alone permanently. God, how she missed Tony.

So here she was, secretly in love after just

a few weeks. She was a sensible woman, a woman with responsibilities, a woman who followed directions and played by all the rules.

Sam looked at home in the midst of this crazy chaos. She'd never seen so many people in the Dahl, except for that one rainy Fourth of July right before a local character sold the place to Aurora and moved away.

The scraps of conversation swirled around her as she headed to the front corner of the room.

"And then I moved to Santa Monica…"

"My folks bought the place back in the sixties…"

"Favorite color? Huh. Blue? Or brown?"

"Broke it in three places."

"The traffic is awful."

"…a farm in Nebraska. We raised corn, then milo."

"Three sisters," one of the women said. "I'm the only one who left New Jersey."

"I have a pair of socks you can borrow," Lucia heard Mike Breen offer. He was talking to a pretty woman with a square face and big blue eyes. Her light brown hair was tousled, but not in a purposeful way. She looked casual, despite the black cocktail dress and five-inch heels. Too short to be an aspiring model, she was definitely one of the less sophisticated women in the group.

"I can't take your socks."

"I live right down the street," he insisted. "I'll be right back."

Lucia introduced herself as Mike hurried toward the door. "I'm Lucia Swallow, one of the caterers," she said. "Welcome to town."

"Thanks. I'm Cora," she said, pointing to her name tag. "Cora Crewes. And my feet are killing me. I don't wear heels very often."

"And your feet are cold?"

"I brought my running shoes with me, but I forgot socks." She laughed, a cheery sound. "And that very nice man offered to loan me a pair of his."

"He *is* a nice man," Lucia said.

"Is he doing this to be famous? He said he's a writer."

"He owns the newspaper. And he's a good guy." She looked around at the men in the crowd. The excitement level had risen and so had the volume of the conversation. "Most of the bachelors take this very seriously."

"I wish I could say the same for the women,"

Cora said. "I'm not sure if everyone is here for the right reasons."

"And you?"

She smiled, revealing twin dimples. "I'm lonely," she admitted. "And I don't want to be lonely anymore. I want to find a good man, fall in love, have a couple of kids and make a life together. It's as simple as that."

"Cora!"

Tracy took her arm. "Time for your PI. Put some lipstick on and fix your hair."

Lucia watched the women weave through the crowd. Tracy could be obnoxious and overbearing, but she knew how to get things done. Lucia didn't understand why Jerry was so crazy about her, but assumed he was one of those men who loved bitchy women. She herself didn't get the appeal.

She looked back at the bar, where Sam continued to serve beer. Aurora was next to him, opening a wine bottle and laughing with him about something. Lucia hoped Cora was right, that Cora could find a good man and fall in love, that it would be a simple process.

Falling in love with Sam was complicated.

But pretending he was nothing more than a good friend was simple, as long as she kept reminding herself there were worse things in life than a broken heart.

"If you see me kill the banjo player, don't say a word. Just look the other way."

"I like the banjo guy. He's a little on the elderly side, but he still plays with gusto," Sam said. "If you need an alibi, though, just say the word."

"I need an aspirin," Aurora muttered. "Between the banjo—which is always out of tune, by the way—the band, Tracy and the romantic intensity in the room, my head is throbbing."

"Not a fan of emotional intensity?"

"Haven't been for years," she said, reaching under the counter. She popped the lid on an aspirin bottle and shook two pills into her palm. "Want some?"

"No, thanks."

"I'm surprised you haven't staggered home by now. This is getting insane. But everyone seems to be having a good time." She poured a glass of water, swallowed her aspirin and glanced at the clock. "Fifteen minutes until midnight. Then we'll see who kisses whom and which of our bachelors has charmed the woman of his dreams."

"I think Tracy will make sure she gets it all on film, even if she has to do several takes."

"No doubt. The woman is relentless." Aurora leaned on the counter of the bar. "Thanks for the help tonight. You did good."

"You're welcome. The get-together is like a college frat party, except in Montana. And with older people."

"Well," she said, considering the partying crowd, "I went to a school without fraternities or sororities, so I wouldn't know." She glanced at the clock again. "We'd better get the champagne ready."

"Where is it?"

"Outside on the back porch. I'll call Jerry to help you carry it in."

"Not a problem. I can handle four bottles at a time," he said. Then he remembered the doctor's warning about lifting heavy things. Carrying a couple of cases of champagne was probably a stupid idea.

"I'll send him to help you as soon as I can

pry him away from the cameras," she said. "You'd think he was running for governor already."

Sam hadn't been to this part of the bar before. The long hallway that led to the back room was lined with photographs, awards, sports memorabilia and a shelf with trophies. He stopped to look at the high school football team photos and noticed Owen in the back row of one of them. There were military photos, too, of men Sam assumed had been from Willing and had served in the armed forces.

He stopped in front of one in particular, a familiar face with serious dark eyes and a fierce expression. The man wore an army uniform decorated with patches and medals. His name was Anthony Swallow, Master Sergeant.

And he was the man on the plane in Nicaragua, the same man who'd said that Willing, Montana, was home.

Of course. Sam should have recognized him. Matty, the middle child, had his eyes. And Davey had the same serious expression. The littlest boy resembled his mother, but could grow into a sturdy version of his father, who looked like he was pure muscle.

This was the man who told him where home was.

And now Sam understood. He had come here to heal and to write, to lick his wounds and feel sorry for himself.

In doing so, he'd found another man's family. Another man's wife and children, who were now alone and missing him terribly.

Sam stood in front of the photo, the champagne forgotten and the noise from the other room unheard. What kind of weird coincidence had brought him into this little town with its big dreams and friendly people?

In less than three weeks he'd become addicted to Meg's breakfasts, volunteered to work on a community project, befriended a little boy who wanted nothing more than to win a school prize and fallen in love with the little boy's mother, his neighbor.

He was on his way to becoming part of another man's family—

All of a sudden Sam remembered the champagne. He was supposed to be retrieving bottles for the midnight celebration. Sure enough, the cases sat outside in the cold, chilling nicely in the freezing Montana night.

Jerry hurried up to join him.

"Got it," he said, lifting one of the cases. "Don't mess up your ribs. I'm going to need you for karaoke night."

"Karaoke night? I can't sing."

"Doesn't matter. You want to shut that door behind me?" Jerry staggered down the hall, Sam following with four bottles in his arms. They made their way past the band, now performing a curious blend of rock and roll and bluegrass, to the bar, where Aurora waited with trays of champagne flutes.

"You've gone all-out," Jerry noted, checking out the glasses. "Real glass."

"Nothing is too good for you," she said drily. "I got them on Craigslist."

"Are they clean?" He picked one up and peered at it while Tracy leaped up on the bar, presumably to check out the action.

"Bite me."

Sam paid no attention to any of them. He looked for Lucia in the dancing crowd. And everyone was dancing. Everyone. Even Lucia, now being twirled by a handsome young man who was tall and tanned and smiling with good humor.

Not a pleasant sight. Sam's gut tightened.

"Get off my bar," he heard Aurora snap.

"I took off my shoes," Tracy protested. "I want to see the full effect of this."

"Get off my bar *immediately*," the bartender said. "Then take a paper towel and spray cleaner and wipe off your footprints. No one dances on the bar or the pool table or any tables at all."

"I don't—"

"Come on down, babe," Jerry said, reaching for her. "The camera guys seem to have it under control."

"Jerry," Sam said. "Who is that guy dancing with Lucia?"

Jerry set Tracy on her feet and Aurora banged cleaning supplies on the bar. "Where?"

He pointed toward the bear, which now wore a beaded necklace and a L.A. Raiders football cap. "There."

"Oh, that's Jack. Former town council member, until he took off to California last month."

"But he's back?"

"He's working for Tracy now. He's on the crew. Good guy. We'd wanted him for the show, but he got a paying gig."

And he was dancing with Lucia, who was definitely enjoying herself. Her black hair swirled around her shoulders and Jack's hands were on her waist as he led her through the steps. Sam wasn't much of a dancer, but suddenly he decided he needed to take lessons.

"Whoa," Jerry said, checking his watch. "Three minutes until midnight. I have to tell the band to get ready."

Three minutes? Sam waded through the crowd to find her before time ran out. Dancing Jack was not going to take advantage of her by stealing a New Year's kiss at midnight. Sam heard the band finish their song, heard Jerry's voice announcing the approaching countdown as the guitarist played "Midnight Rider."

"Midnight Rider?" he heard someone say. "How cool is that!"

Sam found Lucia, breathless, laughing and panting in the crowd of sweating bachelors and gyrating young women in glittery dresses. He planted himself right in front of

Lucia and effectively blocked Jack, whose attention had fortunately been diverted by two young women in silver sequins.

"Hey, Sam," Lucia said. "Are you having fun?"

He didn't know how to answer that. He couldn't say he detested Dancing Jack, a guy he'd never been introduced to. He couldn't say *I met your husband on a plane and he told me about this town, his home, and I never forgot it and that's why I came here and met you.*

He couldn't tell her he was falling in love with her, because he didn't know what that would mean. Sam couldn't speak.

She lifted her hair off the back of her neck. "Jerry should be pleased. This has turned into a good party."

The countdown began. Lucia's face was flushed, her eyes sparkling. Jack had had quite an effect. Sam didn't like the way he felt. Possessive had never been something he'd felt before.

Maybe it was because of all this darn snow.

"Sam?"

"Eight—seven—six," the crowd chanted.

Sam tugged Lucia to him as the numbers continued. Her face tilted up, her eyes shining as she met his gaze.

"Three—two—one. Happy New Year!"

"Happy New Year, Sam," she whispered, and then he kissed her. Her lips were warm, and he held her face within his hands and kissed her, for the future, for the new year, whatever it would bring.

She returned the kiss. He doubted anyone noticed them, because there was kissing and hugging and general hooting and hollering all around them. The band played "Auld Lang Syne" and someone threw confetti.

He couldn't take his mouth from hers, didn't want to stop touching her and holding her. This was new territory, these feelings and this woman.

"Happy New Year," he said finally against her lips. "I'm not good at this," he confessed.

She seemed to grasp what he meant. "I think you're doing fine."

"We haven't known each other very long," he began.

"We have time."

"I can't say how this is going to work,"

Sam said, touching his forehead to hers. "You and me."

"I understand," she whispered. "All we can do is try not to hurt each other too much."

CHAPTER ELEVEN

"WE HAVE TO KEEP the women happy."

"Duh," someone said.

Everyone laughed but Jerry. Last night had been awesome, a party that would go down in Willing's history as one of the best events ever. At some point after midnight Tracy's crew dissolved into the dancing crowd and partied hearty with the locals and the contestants.

"What happened last night?" Shelly, now pouring Jerry's coffee, had gone home early after watching all the activity from a safe spot behind the bar.

"What *didn't* happen, you mean," Pete Lyons said, wincing and rubbing his forehead.

"For starters," Jerry said, "after midnight Loralee and the rest of them partied until Aurora kicked everyone out and sent them to the café for eggs."

"She didn't come home until after four," Shelly said. She and Loralee were roommates, which somehow seemed to work for them.

Jerry hoped there was film of the line dance, but he doubted it. He vaguely remembered a couple of the cameramen lifting Loralee in the air. He didn't know why they'd felt the need to carry the woman around, but they'd all looked like they were having a good time doing it.

"I heard Tracy fired everyone," Shelly said, pulling up a chair to join the meeting. Since the café was empty of customers except for their table, she didn't have anything else to do.

"Nobody paid any attention to that." Jerry assumed they'd been fired before, and who else was Tracy going to hire to come to Montana in January?

No one, that was who. Their jobs were safe. Everyone was sleeping the party off this morning, even Tracy. She'd donned her sleeping mask and taken a pill. He'd given her his bedroom and he'd camped out on the leather couch in his office.

He'd called an emergency meeting of the

town council, planning on getting their attention after they woke up and before the football games started. It was eleven o'clock on New Year's Day. Meg intended to close at noon. She was doing the cooking herself, as Al required time off to watch college football.

This morning Jerry's mind was on women. The men were as ready as they would ever be, but that was only step one.

Step two? Make the women enjoy Willing and enjoy the Montana lifestyle. He and Tracy would be meeting later to go over details of the dates she'd planned to film.

Karaoke night.

Trivial Pursuit contest.

Snow sculpture.

Ranch excursion, if the weather held up.

"Uh, none of this sounds very interesting," someone pointed out after looking at the short list of ideas.

"We're going to *make* it interesting," Jerry snapped.

Duh.

THE PARTY WAS at Lucia's house this year. But this time it included Owen, Les, Shelly, Loralee and Sam.

"Who'd have thought?" Meg remarked, looking at the crowd gathered in the living room to watch football. "This is a different group from last year."

"Where's Aurora?"

"The bar opened at one. She ordered a bunch of food from Chili Dawgs and the games will be on the big-screen television. Big day and night at the Dahl. The cameras will be rolling, just in case anything interesting happens. I heard the women planned to sleep late and rest up for tomorrow."

The three boys sat bunched together on the couch between Owen and Sam. Davey was reading something to Sam, and Owen held the remote control and either cheered or groaned, depending on what was happening on television. Les sat next to Shelly, who looked content with a pillow behind her back as she absently rubbed her belly. Les kept giving her nervous glances.

"I don't think Les had a good time last night," Lucia said. "He spent a lot of time by the food, and then he sneaked out before midnight."

"I saw a couple of women trying to talk

to him, but he didn't dance. Do you think anyone noticed he left?"

"I doubt it. And Jerry would be the only one who would care."

"The question is," Lucia said, "does Shelly notice?"

Loralee stepped over to the dining room table with her now-empty paper plate in her hand. "Are you talking about poor Les? Shelly notices," she said. "But she's not saying anything to me about what she's thinking."

"I thought she told you everything."

"Look, sweeties," Loralee drawled, "people don't have to *tell* me anything. I just *know.*" She helped herself to a handful of Wheat Thins. "For instance, Lucia can't take her eyes off Mr. South America over there. Good for you, honey. Go get him."

"What great advice," her daughter murmured. *"Go get him?"*

"And he can't take his eyes off Lucia. You don't have to tell me anything," she said. "It's none of my business. But poor Marie is freaking out."

And that was another issue, Lucia realized. How to have Sam in her life without breaking her mother-in-law's heart. Mama had told her she would find someone good to share her life with. But Mama would worry that no one was good enough for her daughter-in-law and her grandsons. And any man in Lucia's life would be a painful reminder that her own son was gone.

"Is that why she's not here today?"

"She said she was tired from last night."

"She's worried you'll move to Brazil or Belize or Costa Rica and the boys will grow up in some awful village along a dirty river."

"Wow," said Meg. "That's thinking ahead."

"We're barely dating," Lucia said. "And I'm not planning to live on the banks of a dirty river." But Loralee had brought up a good point. It was one thing to kiss the man in Montana. It was another to enter his world and live in a hot, strange village in the middle of the Amazon.

"She watches those shows on the Discovery Channel," Loralee explained. "You see a lot of sad-looking villages on those shows. All those huts. Snakes. Bugs." She shivered. "Giant crocodiles."

"Shh," Meg said. "He'll hear you."

Loralee ignored the comment. "Why

would he care if we talked about crocodiles? I saw this show about a town in the Philippines that caught a twenty-foot crocodile, put him on a cart and tied him up."

"Oh, I saw that, too," Lucia said. "Davey and I watched it. They dragged the crocodile to a refuge, but it wasn't the same crocodile that had killed people, so they're still looking."

"Does Sam hunt for crocodiles?"

"Not that I know of." Now that was a frightening thought—Sam in the Philippines looking for the thirty-foot croc that had a taste for humans who fell out of their canoes.

"I hope not," Loralee said. "He should stay here, not go off risking his life to see giant reptiles and fish and whatever else he looks for. He's good with the boys. Like Owen. He'll make a good father."

"Speaking of which." Lucia was more than happy to change the subject of Sam and parenthood and dangerous reptiles. "Have you and Owen set a date yet?"

The subject was not about to be changed, at least not by Loralee.

"I don't think it's a good idea to move somewhere like that. I agree with Marie.

It's something to consider very carefully, Lucia," Loralee said. "I once followed a man to Alaska."

"Let me guess," her daughter said. "It didn't work out."

Many hours later, when all but one of her guests had gone home and the last college football game was in the third quarter, when her children had been tucked into bed and the lights and the volume of the television had been turned down, Lucia joined Sam on the couch.

"This was a really nice day," he said, putting his arm around her and holding her against him.

"Am I hurting your ribs?"

"No." He kissed the top of her head. "And even if you were, it wouldn't matter."

"What would you be doing right now if you were in Brazil or Colombia or somewhere like that?"

He took his time answering. "I would be in my tent—a really small tent—with mosquito netting. I'd be trying to get some sleep, but I'd be worrying about the next day's shoot and whether Russ—he's my partner in most of these shows—would catch anything big enough to make things interesting."

"It's dangerous."

"Yes, it can be dangerous. But I don't go out of my way to take foolish chances. We do everything we can to minimize that. The locals are a big help and we listen to their advice."

"But no matter what, you love it."

"Yeah," he said. "I do. Remember I said I couldn't say how this is going to work? With us?" She nodded. "Well, I was being honest. I don't know what to do about the two of us."

"I don't, either," she replied. "I didn't expect to like you so much."

He took her hand and rested their clasped fingers against his thigh. "I was done for the minute you untied my boots," he said. "I've never met anyone like you and I'm overwhelmed."

She thought about that for a long moment. "I'm a practical woman," she said. "I have to be realistic and sensible, not just for my sake but for the boys. I don't have any romantic illusions about falling in love, no matter how good a kisser you are."

He shifted to face her, smiled a little as he

met her gaze. "I have a feeling you're going to break my heart."

"You're a survivor," she said, laughing to hide the effect he had on her. "And *I* have a feeling you're going to be just fine."

SAM DIDN'T THINK he was going to be "just fine." He knew he could survive just about anything—sinking boats, raging rapids and malaria, for instance—but he'd never been in love before. Not like this.

He could easily escape. Packing up his bags, arranging for a ride to Billings, a phone call to Jerry... All were fairly simple matters and could be dealt with. He'd healed faster than he'd thought; he could fly to Nicaragua and finish the book in a hotel overlooking the water.

Instead, he sat next to Lucia at a small table in front of the Dahl's stage while Jerry sang "From Now On All My Friends Are Gonna Be Strangers" into the microphone. The place was packed with the television crew, the cast, the bachelors and assorted locals. Thursday, he'd been told, was Karaoke Night in Willing and had been a tradition for over sixteen years at the bar, drawing a crowd from Lewistown when the roads were decent.

Oh, if that grizzly could talk.

Jerry finished channeling his inner Garth Brooks to a round of applause.

"Welcome to the *Willing to Wed* talent contest!" Jerry rubbed his hands together in anticipation of an exciting night. "Our twelve beautiful ladies have the opportunity to perform for you tonight. Then everyone, meaning all our lovely guests and all twenty-four lonely bachelors, will vote for the winners. The top three finalists will get to choose who they'd like to take on a one-on-one date!"

"I've been to some wild and strange events," Sam whispered to Lucia. "But a talent contest for a reality TV show?"

"This is what's called being in the right place at the right time." She took a sip of her wine while Jerry repeated his speech because he'd goofed on the introduction and the director wanted to make sure the lighting was right.

"Maybe." Sam nursed a cup of black coffee and considered how long it would take twelve people to sing twelve songs. "How long is a song? Three or four minutes?"

"Yes." They watched as the tallest blonde in the group, introduced as Heather, took the stage. Aurora punched buttons on the machine and the introduction to "God Bless America" roared out of the speakers.

"Thirty-six minutes, then," he said, noting that Heather had a fine, patriotic voice and wore a very tight red-and-blue striped sweater. Her skinny jeans sparkled and her high heels were red. "With five minutes between singers, that's approximately ninety-one minutes, about an hour and a half."

"Shh."

"Sorry."

Heather sang her heart out and received an enthusiastic round of applause. Jack Dugan adjusted the microphone and waved to Lucia, who waved back. Tracy put her hand on his arm and pointed him toward the speaker. The woman was a relentless perfectionist, Sam decided. He had no doubt the show would be a success, because women like Tracy didn't handle failure well.

"Heather doesn't seem like the cowgirl

type," Lucia murmured. "I think it's the eye-lashes."

"I don't know about that. She has a lot of energy. The crowd loves her."

"The crowd," Lucia said, "is desperate for entertainment. And they are drinking alcohol."

"Well, there is that," he agreed.

"I noticed you don't drink," she said. "Is there a reason?"

"I'm not an alcoholic," Sam said. "Recovered or otherwise. But my parents were. The idea of drinking to have a good time lost its appeal when I was a kid."

"Which makes sense."

"I like this bar, though. It has more of a pub feel than bar." Now was the time to tell her about Tony, to lead into it with the photos in the hall. Instead, he fidgeted with his coffee cup. "Aren't Meg and Owen coming?"

"Maybe later. I wish I knew how to do that."

"What? Sing?"

"No. Apply false eyelashes."

"Why?"

She shrugged. "It's a good look."

He glanced at his watch. "Davey told me you got the new superhero movie."

"Yes. The boys are watching it with Kim tonight," she said, eyeing him with pity. "Would you like to come home with me and see it?"

"And now," Jerry shouted, "I bring you one of my favorite performers, Joey Peckham!"

"He always does 'Folsom Prison,'" Lucia said. "Want to go home?"

She didn't have to ask him again.

Home. Now that was an interesting concept.

"WELL, WHAT DO you think?"

"I think," Meg said, "we're making a lot of money." She tapped at her laptop's keyboard and studied the numbers. "Jerry was right. This has been a great business opportunity. Hurray for Hollywood."

Lucia agreed. Supplying twenty people with three meals a day, plus a generous portion of round-the-clock snacks, meant a lot of work but a fat addition to her savings account. "Do these people ever sleep?"

"I don't think so. They've filmed everything from sunrise to snow fights, indoors and outside. They take forever to film one little portion of a date. I don't think I could kiss on demand. On camera."

"Me, either," Lucia admitted. "It's awkward. And what if you don't really like the person, but you don't want to hurt his feelings?"

"I think I'd go ahead and hurt his feelings," Meg said.

"Do sharks have feelings? I like sharks," Tony said. "Do you?"

"I'm not sure," Meg answered, rolling her eyes at Lucia. They were meeting in the café, at a back table on a frigid Saturday afternoon. Tony was eating a hamburger and fries with great gusto while watching Tracy direct Pete Lyons's lunch date with Heather, the karaoke prize winner of ten days ago. "What about your mom? Does she like sharks?"

"Nope."

"Hmm."

"Don't say a word," Lucia begged. "He'll repeat every darn thing you say at the dinner table tonight."

"And who is coming for dinner?"

"You know."

"I can make a wild guess."

"He checks Davey's homework and he's teaching Matty how to read. He's helpful." She made him sound like a nanny, for heaven's sake.

"He's made himself at home here," Meg said. "Everyone likes him."

"I know."

Tony piped up again. "Are you talkin' about Sam?"

"Yes," Lucia said. "We are."

"I like him," the little boy said, sticking a French fry in his mouth. "We're goin' fishin'."

"So, I guess he's staying for fishing season?"

"He hasn't said one way or the other." She gathered up her papers and tucked them into her purse. "I can't picture him staying here for any length of time." Lucia looked at her son, knowing full well he was listening to every word. "But we'll see."

"Meanwhile, you and Tony are becoming experts on sharks?"

"I love sharks," Tony said. "Mommy said maybe we'll see some in Sea World."

"The vacation fund is getting fat," Lucia explained.

"Sam caught a bull shark," the boy announced. "But he let it go."

Lucia raised her eyebrows. "A bull shark. How can Willing compete with that?"

"I don't know," Meg said. "But we have Jerry."

"I'M TRYING TO put a positive spin on this," Jerry told Sam, who seemed more interested in Meg's chili special than the filming of tonight's dating drama. The man spent more time in the café than he did himself, especially lately. "I knew it was coming, but I've been too busy to prepare some comforting remarks to those men not chosen."

"How many of them get the axe tonight?" Sam buttered a thick slab of homemade wheat bread and looked as though he didn't have a care in the world. Jerry envied him.

"Twelve," he replied, checking his notes again. He appreciated Sam's interest, but this was going to be a tough afternoon. "After the snowmobile races. Owen's barn has been staged for the ceremony."

"Ceremony?" This question was from

Shelly, who had managed to ease her frighteningly large abdomen close enough to the counter to refill their coffee cups.

"The 'Are you Willing to Wed?' ceremony." Jerry sighed. "I'm getting real tired of that phrase."

"At least it mentions the name of the town," Shelly offered.

"Which is, of course, what I live for," Jerry declared, rubbing his temples. "Tracy said to expect some drama. She's really excited about it."

Sam frowned. "It's been two weeks, right?"

"Thirteen days."

"Are some of these guys taking it seriously?"

"They've all taken it seriously," Jerry said. "They've worked their tails off since October getting ready for this. The whole town has."

"I noticed."

Jerry slid his phone in his pocket. "Do me a favor?"

"If I can."

"Come out there with me. I could use the moral support and I may need some help consoling the losers." He winced. "Losers. Jeez, that's a bad way to phrase it."

"Can I come, too?" Shelly was already untying her red-checked apron. "My shift ended five minutes ago."

"Out to the Triple M? That's a long drive. And it'll take hours. What if you go into labor?"

"I won't."

"B-but you don't know that," he sputtered, turning to Sam for help. "Tell her."

Sam obliged. "You, ah, do look really pregnant, Shelly."

"I'm not due for weeks, not until February twenty-second." She glared at both of them. "And I want to be there for Les."

"Les," Jerry repeated, knowing full well that the young rancher had zero interest in anyone but Shelly. Yet some of the younger women, and a couple of the older ones, found the kid's awkward charm appealing. "He has a good chance of making it into the next round of dates. I wouldn't worry too—"

"Please?" Shelly's blue eyes filled with tears. "I don't want him to feel bad. And Hip's on duty at the filming. He goes everywhere with the crew in case there's a problem."

Sam cleared his throat. "Having a baby is a very big problem, especially if you're, what, ninety miles from town?"

Shelly affectionately patted her bump. "She's kicking. She's fine."

Jerry tried one more time. "You can buckle a seat belt around that?" He nodded toward her belly.

"Yes."

"Sam?"

"It's your call, mayor," he said, turning to look out the large window. "I've had four people tell me that it won't snow until tomorrow."

"Okay. But no jumping up and down." Jerry grabbed his coat and watched Shelly hurry off to get her things. "She thinks Les is going to get his heart broken by some out-of-town woman?"

Sam sighed. "From what I've seen, I think she's the only one with the power to do that."

"The boy's got it bad," Jerry muttered. "And she doesn't seem to notice."

"I don't know," Sam said as they watched

Shelly waddle across the room. "Women usually notice but pretend they don't."

"Until they decide what they're going to do about us," Jerry added. "Which is what's going to happen this evening."

IT CAME DOWN to the final pick, Sam noted. He stood in a far corner of the barn with Owen and Jerry and watched as six-foot Heather, the one who sang karaoke, asked Pete Lyons if he was "Willing to Wed." Since she had come in last during the snowmobile race, she was the last one to select a bachelor to continue on the "journey." The word, as Sam had learned, was a euphemism for "TV show."

Pete gulped and managed to say yes after three takes. And as easy as that, Les was off the hook. He stood on the stage with eleven others who hadn't been chosen and a big grin broke out across his face. He looked over at Owen and gave him a thumbs-up.

"I don't think the boy is heartbroken," Sam pointed out.

"They'll have to cut out that part," Jerry said. "We can't have the guys looking relieved. Tracy wants heartbreak, maybe a few tears, for the exit interviews."

"I don't believe Les is that good an actor."

Shelly, perched on a bale of hay next to them, agreed. "I guess I didn't have to worry about him."

"No," Sam said. "But I'm sure he appreciated the thought."

They watched Tracy herd the rejected bachelors toward the camera set up for the private interviews.

"Now they get to look pathetic," Jerry said. "I'm not sure that's the image we wanted to portray."

"Can you use them again next season?" Sam felt the guys had been good sports during the past weeks.

"Next season," Jerry mused. "Next season?" He slapped Sam on the back. "I like how you think, Sam. You're an optimist, like me."

Sam had never considered himself an optimist, but maybe Jerry's enthusiasm was contagious.

SAM'S DAYS RETURNED to his former routine: He had breakfast at the café, where he picked up the news of the day, heard about various dates and filming, often talked with Owen, enjoyed watching Joey avoid him and then walked home. Sometimes it snowed. He wrote, piling up pages for the book and enjoying reliving some of the best times in his life. So far, he reminded himself. He read most afternoons, or kept Tony company while Lucia baked. When the older boys came home from school he joined them for a snack in Lucia's kitchen.

Most of the time he stayed for dinner, which Lucia insisted upon; he always washed the dishes, though. And he continued to order books for the boys whenever they expressed interest in a subject of any kind.

"You're spoiling them," Lucia said, but she didn't seem at all upset about it. She'd hugged him and returned to kneading bread dough.

He questioned Jerry about the library and what it would take to reopen it, even once a week. The frazzled mayor promised to look into it in February, after the show had finished filming.

Sam had seen some of the dates between the pretty women and the increasingly confident men. How anyone fell in love or developed a relationship under the scrutiny of the crew and with cameras filming their every move was a mystery, but several couples actually appeared to be making progress. Mike Breen was spending less time writing in his notebook and more time attempting to win dates with a sweet contestant named Cora.

The dating couples made it look easy.

And maybe it was.

Lucia continued to entrance him.

And the photo of her late husband continued to haunt him. He'd tried not to go over that conversation on the plane, but it was impossible not to wonder what Lucia would think about the coincidence of the meeting. He didn't want to cause her pain.

He didn't know what he was going to do in six weeks, but he knew he didn't want to leave. Not yet. Not now.

He couldn't imagine taking a woman— any woman—into the Amazon to live his crazy life. And he didn't want to leave her for months at a time while he worked. She deserved more than that.

But could he be content living in Willing for the rest of his life?

And would she have him if he decided to stay? Well, Sam decided, there was only one way to find out.

"I'VE BEEN KEEPING TRACK, of course," Jerry announced, tapping his iPad and studying the data on the screen. Four days from now, on Sunday evening, Willing would celebrate the end of filming with a bonfire. And of course that would be filmed as the grand finale. Couples would be reunited in Los Angeles in a month and tracked for six weeks after that. "Would anyone like an update?"

"Yes. Immediately." Aurora, who would never be called a "morning person," set her coffee cup down on the table. Jerry didn't know why she was in the café in the first place; he'd never seen her eat so much as a hard-boiled egg.

She pulled a large floral notebook out of her purse.

"What's that?"

"My notes."

"I'll get mine," Meg said, scurrying off to the cash register. She retrieved a yellow legal pad and hurried back to the table. "Okay, start."

"Mike Breen and Cora Crewes," he announced.

"That's obvious," Meg said. "I saw that from the first night."

"Obvious," Aurora echoed. "She is definitely 'Willing to Wed' to stay in Willing."

"Don't be cute," Jerry said. "It doesn't fit your personality."

Meg intervened. "Joey and Heather?"

"No," Aurora said. "I think she's smarter than that. But the redhead from Oregon—what's her name?"

Jerry checked his notes. "Sylvia?"

"That's it. I think she likes the young bad-boy image. The black eye that Sam gave him didn't seem to bother her."

"Darn. I thought she liked Pete."

"Pete didn't like her."

"Danielle, that's the one," Jerry said, tapping the screen. "She and Pete went on a picnic in Owen's barn. Tracy said it was romantic and authentic, in a *Little House on the Prairie* way."

"Meaning what?"

"I have no idea," he admitted. About 80 percent of what Tracy had said these past weeks had been unintelligible. Between trying to please her and making sure the town was shown in the most flattering ways, Jerry hadn't had much sleep. Last night he'd dozed off during the romantic candlelight dinner set up in his own dining room. "Pam from Idaho Falls wants to move here and open an antiques shop."

"Cora was talking about selling vintage clothing and Western art. She thinks that when the show airs this summer we'll become a tourist stop."

"I guess Hip's carved animals inspired her," Jerry said. "She'll need quite a bit of space to display his work, so maybe she'd lease the space next to the clinic."

"Iris is having *Willing to Wed* T-shirts printed, with the B&B logo on the back," Meg announced.

"I like 'Welcome to Willing' better," Shelly stated. "That would be cute for babies and little kids."

"You're right." Jerry typed in that idea. If romance was here, then weddings and babies would be right behind. "We need to hype the church."

"Hype the church?" Meg seemed confused.

"For weddings," he explained. "We could

become a destination spot for weddings for people all over the country. You could put together wedding menus, wedding picnics, ranch weddings, church basement receptions—always nostalgic and popular—and we could build an arch in the park. Photographs next to the cow!"

"Bull," Aurora snapped.

"It's a g-good idea," Jerry sputtered. "Keep an open mind."

"You are so easily offended. It's not a cow," she said, giving him that haughty look that made him want to put a bag over her platinum head. "It's a bull. The bull that started the MacGregor cattle empire."

"Someone's been doing her homework," Jerry answered. "Bull, cow, whatever. Cora and Mike will love it. And the rest of them?" He smiled so hard his ears hurt. "We'll make all their dreams come true."

"I think you're the one with the dreams coming true," Meg teased.

"This is only the beginning," he said. "We're just getting started."

THE FIRST SUNDAY night in February was billed as the most romantic event in the history of Willing, Montana.

Posters hung in the windows of every storefront, whether it was occupied or not. Valentine's Day was coming, so the colorful posters featured a drawing of a bonfire with red hearts shooting up out of the flames like fireworks.

Light Her Fire! it said. Bonfire in the Park!

"It's not going to be huge," Jerry warned some of the members of the council Monday morning. "It's the atmosphere that counts."

"I like it," Hank Doughtery said. "I can set up the grill to roast marshmallows."

Sam sat at the table next to the mayor and eavesdropped shamelessly.

"Chili Dawgs will stay open late, maybe even do a food stand," Jerry informed them. "Meg will serve hot chocolate. Lucia will provide cookies. The show is picking up the tab, so it doesn't come out of the town budget."

Mike, in his position as town treasurer, verified that. "I'm looking forward to this," he confessed. "I might even, well…"

"Propose?" This came from Jerry, who spoke the word with reverence.

"Well, yeah. Sounds crazy, huh?" Mike blushed. "It's just that, well, I'm not getting any younger and we want the same things."

"Congratulations," Sam said. "And good luck."

"You are talking about Cora." This was from Pete Lyons, rumored to have found love with either Heather or Danielle.

"Well, who else?" Mike sounded shocked at the question.

Les half smiled. "I can think of eleven others," he said. "Boy, I'm glad I got cut after the first part. Those women made me nervous."

"Your heart wasn't into it," Hank said kindly. He gazed past Les to the pregnant waitress fiddling with the cash register. "Shelly looks a lot healthier now than when she got here. She gave up on finding the baby's father, didn't she?"

"Yeah." Les didn't appear happy talking about it. "He didn't deserve her. Or the baby, when it gets here."

Mike clapped him on the shoulder. "Maybe I'm not the only one who should be proposing on Sunday."

Les turned white and fled to the men's room.

Love was in the air, Sam realized. And he was in the same boat as these other guys. He wasn't going to ask Lucia to marry him, at least not in front of the cameras, but he intended to state his intentions. Maybe they could compromise, make Florida their home base. Or Costa Rica. He could teach the boys to swim and fish. They would travel; he would show them the world.

If Lucia said yes.

"I'M NOT SURE about this." Lucia and Sam walked downtown with the boys, but the sky was growing dark and the snow had started to fall. Snow wasn't unusual, but the forecast was a blizzard. Maybe two, back to back, according to the Weather Channel. "We really have to hold on to them."

"I can do that." Sam assured it. "You take Tony, and I'll make sure Davey and Matt stay right next to me."

"Don't let them get too close to the fire," she warned. "There will be sparks."

Davey looked up at Sam and rolled his eyes, which made Sam laugh.

"I'm serious," Lucia protested. "There *could* be sparks."

"Jerry said it won't be a big bonfire, especially not in the park in the middle of town.

It's more symbolic," Sam explained to her. "It's supposed to be romantic and look good on TV for the big finale."

"I'll be sorry to see everyone go. They've made things pretty exciting around here."

"You'll always have Karaoke Night," he reminded her. "And Meg said the Trivial Pursuit contest starts the first Saturday night in March."

She made a face. "I never make it past the first round."

"I've been known to rule the science category. We could be a team."

"The tournament goes into April," she said. "Aren't you leaving in the middle of March?"

"Well, I—" This was the opening he'd been waiting for, something he could use to start the conversation, if only he wasn't walking into a park crowded with people while nearby speakers blasted "Baby Won't You Light My Fire."

"The Doors," Lucia said, smiling. "That must have been Gary's idea. He's only in his fifties, but he has a thing for classic rock."

"Can we have hot chocolate?" This was from Matty, who tugged on Sam's hand and looked up at him with pleading eyes. "And cookies?"

"Stay close," Sam said. "Here, keep hold of my hand."

"I'm too old to hold hands," Davey declared.

"Hold on to my coat, then. So your mother doesn't have to worry about you getting lost." Sam followed Lucia and Tony along the edge of the crowd to a folding table where Meg, Loralee and Shelly served hot chocolate in paper cups and laughed together about something. Les hovered nearby. The bonfire roared in the center of the park, but away from the monument. As Jerry had promised, the fire was small but dramatic. The cameramen darted in and out of the crowd and several volunteers helped with lighting the area where couples would give their interviews.

To no one's surprise, Mike was prepared with an engagement ring. When he asked the woman he'd fallen in love with if she was "Willing to Wed," Cora cried, along with Shelly. So did Jerry. The cameras were rolling and Tracy high-fived every member of crew she could reach.

Mama Marie made a toast in Italian, and

Loralee hugged everyone within a ten-foot radius.

Tracy presented the twenty-four bachelors with T-shirts that read, Ready, Willing and Able printed over an outline of Montana, and declared the filming a great success, with more romance to come in the future. The crowd cheered. Jerry high-fived the members of the crew. Sam herded the three boys and stayed close to Lucia's side, just in case Jack Dugan or Joey Peckham got any ideas. He talked to Owen, who had taken Shelly's place at the beverage table. He congratulated Mike, chatted with Cora about her future plans and kept Matty from eating an entire platter of heart-shaped sugar cookies.

"This is so much fun," Lucia said, tucking her gloved hand in the crook of his arm. "I didn't think I'd get caught up in the excitement and the romance of it all, but I did."

"Do you think it's possible to fall in love in such a short time?" Sam gestured toward Hank. "He's in the process of convincing Heather to move here."

"Really?"

"And look at Les," he said. The young man had his arm around Shelly, which was progress, considering she spent a lot of time pretending he was only a friend and he spent a lot of time pretending to be only a friend. "He's just a kid, and he's in love with— How old is she?"

"Nineteen, but—"

"Do you think that will—" He stopped as Shelly doubled over and clutched her belly. "Luce?"

"Watch the boys." She took off along the edge of the crowd, which was now dispersing as the fire died down. Sam grabbed Tony's hand, Davey grabbed Matty's and the four of them followed Lucia to where Meg and Les surrounded Shelly. Owen already had his cell phone out, presumably to call for help.

"I felt kind of funny today," the girl said, wincing. "But nothing really hurt."

Les guided her into a folding chair. "You're having the baby?"

"I guess," she said and then groaned.

Meg leaned over her and waited for her to stop panting. "Shelly, have you been having contractions?"

"I didn't know that's what they were," she

whimpered. "It really didn't hurt, not like this. This is sort of, you know, *sudden*."

Lucia turned to Sam. "Maybe you'd better get the boys home. Would you mind?"

"Of course not," he said. "But is there anything I can do here now? Should we carry her inside?"

"Take her into my house," Jerry said, appearing from behind Owen. "It's the closest place to get warm."

"I just called Hip," Owen said, pocketing his phone. He put his hand on Shelly's shoulder. "Everything is going to be fine."

Les knelt in the snow in front of her. "Yeah, Shell. It's going to be okay," he said, his voice soft and reassuring. She gazed at Les with an expression of such trust that Sam felt a lump form in his throat as he watched the two of them clasp hands.

Sam figured the young man just aged ten years.

"Come on," he told the boys. "Let's go see the fire die out and then we'll head home."

"But what about Mom?"

"Your mom's going to help Shelly, because she's going to have her baby."

"I don't get it," Davey said, turning to

look over his shoulder at the crowd forming around Shelly. "What's the big deal?"

"What do you mean?"

"Why's everybody so surprised? She's been having a baby for a long time."

"You're right," Sam said, trying not to laugh. "These things are exciting, though. It's part of nature, but it never stops being something special."

"Even when it's fish?"

"Even then." He took Tony by one hand, Matty by the other, and kept Davey in front of him as they watched the fire burn down to embers. They even helped kick snow over the coals.

"Okay," Sam said. "It's a school night so I'd better get you guys home and ready for bed."

"Will you read us a story?" This was from Tony, who Sam knew really loved to be read to.

"Cool." Davey grinned at him. "You can tell us about stingrays."

"Sure," he promised. "And I'll show you a map of Costa Rica. Have you ever heard of it?"

"No Costa Rica," Mama Marie said, appearing next to him. "And no stingrays, either. I'll take them home."

"Grandma!" Davey gave her a hug. "But we *like* stingray stories. Stingrays have *venom* in their tails."

"That's nice," she said. "Nice for them. But not so nice for people who step on them, remember." She looked at Sam. "I told Lucia I'd take care of them."

"All right." He was not about to argue with a grandmother. "I'll walk you home."

"You're a nice man," she said. "But I don't want my grandsons messing around with wild animals."

CHAPTER TWELVE

LAURA MARGARET JONES was born thirty-four minutes after her mother was carried into the mayor's first-floor guest room. Fortunately the two cameramen who slept there had already packed up to leave. There was no filming of the birth, since they had followed several loving couples to the Dahl to celebrate a job well done.

Lucia spent most of those thirty-four minutes keeping Loralee from drinking Jerry's single malt Scotch.

"I'm not good at medical things," she kept saying. "I don't even know how I managed to give birth to Meg. It was a horrible experience," she said. "I think I fainted. Twice."

Tracy sat on the couch, drank tequila shots and never stopped texting.

Jerry ran around looking for clean towels, but by the time he found some in the clothes dryer, Laura had made her entrance into the world at five pounds, six ounces, and three weeks early. Lucia had caught a glimpse of little Laura before she was whisked away by the emergency team.

Hip had delivered her himself, and the volunteer medics from Lewistown had arrived in the ambulance three minutes after the birth. Now everyone was on their way to the Lewistown clinic. Les and Loralee were following the ambulance in Les's truck, but mother and baby were doing just fine.

"Les never let go of her hand," Meg said, wiping her eyes. Owen hugged her to his chest. "Not once."

"I think he's been in love with her since the day she got off the bus," Owen said, rubbing Meg's back.

Lucia remembered Sam's question about believing that someone could fall in love so quickly. Did she believe that?

Yes, because when she'd met Tony Swallow she'd lost the ability to form sentences. He'd been charming and so handsome that she'd been more than a little overwhelmed. And then she'd learned what kind of man he was and she'd fallen in love so hard she should have had bruises.

Meg sniffed. "Do you believe love can happen that fast?"

Owen handed Meg a handkerchief and considered the question. "Yes," he said. "It happened to me. Sometimes a man just knows."

DAVEY KNEW HE was in trouble.

A three-way tie for first place? No way were two girls going to beat him to a twenty-five dollar gift certificate to Thompson's Market. Davey knew exactly what he'd buy, too. The Valentine's candy had been on display for three weeks.

So he needed points. A bunch of them, because he knew the girls would cheat and paint each other's fingernails or trade glitter glue or something, even though Mrs. Kramer had warned them that the Kindnesses had to be real.

Real, he fumed. What could he do?

Mom picked him and Matty up after school. Today she picked them up in the car because she'd been to Lewistown to visit Shelly. Shelly had a baby girl and was coming home tomorrow, unless the storm was bad.

Everyone at school was talking about the storm, even the teachers. A blizzard, they'd said. *A bad one.* The snow had already started. It was coming down thick and heavy when they got home. Tony wanted to play outside, but Mom said no, it would be dark soon.

The lights were on in Sam's and Mrs. Beckett's living rooms when they pulled into the driveway.

"Is Sam coming over?"

"I don't know," his mother said. "I'll ask him."

"I'll do it," Davey said. "I have something to show him. From school." He hefted his backpack to prove it.

Points, he thought. It was all about the points. Who knew kindness was such hard work?

"Hey, Sam," he said, when his friend opened the door.

"Hey, Davey." Sam looked happy to see him. "Come on in."

"I'm here to invite you for dinner," he said. *Point.*

"Thanks," Sam yawned. "I'd like that.

Seems we're going to get a real blizzard to-night."

"You're happy about that?"

"It's something new for me," he confided. "I'm looking forward to it."

Davey nodded. "We could build a snow fort tomorrow."

"Deal."

He unzipped his backpack and pulled out the package he'd wrapped carefully in paper towels. "I made this. For you."

"Really?" Sam took it but didn't unwrap it. "Are you sure?"

"Yeah." He watched as Sam opened it to reveal the ceramic fish Davey had crafted from a slab of clay. "It's a fish. Probably a bass."

"It sure resembles a bass," Sam agreed, holding it very carefully. "Thank-you, Davey. It's a very good-looking fish."

"You could keep pennies in it," he said. "Or paper clips, you know, when you're writing your books."

"I will. I'll take good care of it. Thank you."

Davey had to be honest. "Do you think it

counts as a Kindness? I mean, I made it for you. I didn't just *pretend* to make it for you."

Sam considered the question, gazing at the fish in his palm and then back at Davey. "It's definitely a Kindness," he said. "It has to be worth at least three points."

"I can only get one at a time," he said. "That stinks."

"Are you winning?"

"Not yet," Davey said. "But almost. I have a couple more good ideas."

LUCIA DIDN'T WORRY when Davey didn't return home right away. He liked to carry wood for Sam, and Lucia had realized it was something they both seemed to enjoy doing together. She kept checking out the window while she put together the chicken casserole, expecting to see the two of them trudging across the yard. Sam's back porch light was on, as was just about every light in his house, and smoke puffed from his chimney.

Tony and Matt were fixated on a documentary about lions and their cubs, so they barely paid any attention when she told them she had to go outside for a few minutes. They were accustomed to her carrying wood in the evenings. When they were little she'd make them stand in the door and wave to her so she'd know they were okay.

"Hey," Sam said, pulling open the door for her. "I was on the phone. Am I late?"

"Not really."

He kissed her, held her in a long hug, sighed against her neck. "I heard it's a girl."

"Yes. And she's beautiful."

"I know. Les was showing off pictures of her at the café this morning." He drew back to smile. "How are you?"

"I'm good."

"Come on in for a minute?"

"Sure." She assumed her son was in the living room, absorbed in Sam's stacks of research books. The living room looked as though a tornado had hit it. Papers were stacked everywhere, maps lay spread out on the furniture, empty coffee cups sprouted from every surface.

"I finally finished my book today," Sam announced. "I emailed the entire manuscript to my agent two hours ago. There are some rough bits, but the stories are cut into chapters and I'm pretty sure the book holds together."

"Congratulations." She wondered if that meant he would leave town now.

"You'll have to excuse me. I stayed up all night," he said, running a hand through his hair. "I need a shower and an hour to clean this place up."

"Where's Davey?"

"I thought it would take me at least until March, but— What do you mean?"

"Davey," she said. "He was here, right?"

"Yeah. He brought me a gift." Sam showed her a green ceramic dish on the mantel. "And then he left."

"He left," she repeated, feeling the first twinges of worry. "But he didn't come home. It's snowing really hard now. Why didn't he come home?"

Sam seemed confused. "Maybe he's getting wood. He said he was trying to get more points."

"What would he be doing for points?"

"He didn't tell me," Sam said, grabbing his boots from the hearth. "Come on, maybe he's back home by now."

"I would have seen him," she insisted, feeling panic rising in her chest. "I would have heard him come in the house."

"We'll find him," Sam reassured, looking determined and grim. "I promise, we'll find him."

But they didn't.

They searched Lucia's house from the cellar to the crawl space above the bedrooms. They called his name over and over. Matty and Tony thought Lucia and Sam were playing hide and seek, but Davey couldn't be found.

Then Sam walked the neighbors' back yards, shining his flashlight at woodsheds, along the sides of the houses, in front yards, even under porches. The boy might have crawled under a house to get out of the storm, he thought. The visibility was terrible, but Sam called for the boy so many times he grew hoarse. He hiked through the snow to Mrs. Beckett's front door, since the living room was lit up as if she were home. She didn't answer, which was no surprise. Lucia had said she was a hermit, didn't like people in her yard and rarely answered her door.

He shone the flashlight around Mrs. Beckett's house, not caring if the light scared the old woman. He trudged back and forth in her yard as the snow came down relentlessly in sheets of white wind. Sam had never been so scared in his life. Breathing became difficult, not only because the cold air blew back in his face, but also because he was fighting not to panic.

Lucia, pale and weeping, waited at her kitchen door for him. Sam shook his head. He didn't want to tell her how difficult it was to see anything out there, how his heart stopped when he spotted a snow-coated bush that could have been a frozen child.

He'd grown dizzy with relief when he'd confirmed it was just a bush, then sick with dread. The boy was out there somewhere, hurt or lost. What else could explain his disappearance? Terror, cold and unyielding, wound itself around Sam's heart.

"Where?" she gasped. "Where could he be?"

"I've walked a grid behind all three houses," he said. "He's not there."

"He's lost in the snow," Lucia sobbed. "Why didn't he come home?"

"Call Owen," Sam said. "He's staying in town tonight. Call Meg. Call Jerry and Theo and Hip. Call the sheriff, too. I'm going back to search my house. I don't know why he would go there, but it's worth a shot."

Lucia was already on her cell phone. The little boys started to cry.

HE'D BROUGHT HER a Valentine. Davey had made it for his grandmother, had glued red hearts on the front and written Happy Valentine's Day in neat letters inside, but he could make another one if there was school tomorrow.

No one liked Mrs. Beckett. He'd seen her twice and she'd had an angry face both times. He thought she looked like a mean old cat, though he knew it wasn't nice to think things like that about an old lady.

So he knocked on her front door intending to hand her the card and then run home as fast as he could. Before she could yell at him. Before she could scare him with her mean face. She didn't answer the door, and he couldn't leave the card on the porch because it would get wet.

So Davey walked around the house to the back porch, which looked just like the one at his house and Sam's house, except Mrs. Beckett's porch looked like it was going to fall down soon. He knocked again, louder this time in case she wore a hearing aid.

"Mrs. Beckett?" Davey searched for a place to leave the card. He was going to count his gift to Mrs. Beckett as a Kindness and go home for dinner. His feet were cold and the snow was really coming down hard. He knocked one more time.

He heard a voice from inside, someone calling. Davey froze. Was she going to phone the sheriff? He hurried to shove the Valentine card in the doorjamb, but the back door swung open.

Just like in a scary movie.

And just like in a scary movie, a wobbly, high-pitched voice called out, *"Help me."*

BOO LED SAM and Owen to Mrs. Beckett's back porch. Sam wondered later if the little dog actually understood he was on a rescue mission or if he simply wanted to find his best playmate for a romp in the snow.

"Pray that dog is right," Owen said, when Boo began to bark and whine at the back door. The men hurried up the steps, shining their flashlights along the porch. Sam saw the red construction paper first.

"He's here!"

"The door's unlocked."

Boo kept barking, his tail wagging furiously.

"Davey!" Sam stepped into the kitchen, the dog rushing past him into the silent house. "Davey! Are you here?"

"Sam?" The familiar little voice sounded in the darkness. "Boo!"

Owen fumbled for the light switch, but nothing happened when he flicked it on. "Must be a fuse."

"Are you okay?" Sam shone the light on the floor and followed the wet imprints of small boots to the back bedroom. Stacks of books lined the hallway, making it barely wide enough to walk. "Davey, say something! Are you okay?"

"Yeah."

Sam shone the light in the room Davey's voice had come from. The little boy sat there on the floor, holding an elderly woman's hand.

"I think she fell," the boy said.

Sam thought she was dead, but when he touched her neck he felt a faint pulse. "How did you get in here?"

"She called me to help her," Davey said. "And then she held my hand and fell asleep. I was trying to figure out what to do."

Owen followed him into the dark room. "Hip's on his way. We'll take her to Lewistown in Theo's truck. It's going to be quite a ride."

"Tell Lucia," Sam said, gathering Davey into his arms with an overwhelming, fierce protectiveness. Boo yipped with canine joy. "You have to tell Lucia."

"I already did." He held up his cell phone. "She's waiting for you."

Sam carried the child home in his arms, though Davey insisted he could walk. Sam wasn't about to let him go, wasn't going to risk anything happening to the boy between one house and the other. He left poor Mrs. Beckett in Hip's care.

He didn't allow Lucia to see how shaken he was.

Davey shared his story with his horrified mother, wide-eyed brothers and his weeping grandmother and let Meg warm his cold toes with a hot water bottle. Jerry, who'd arrived at Lucia's at the same time they'd carried Davey home, promised that a Good

Samaritan Award would be in Davey's future and the boy asked, "How many points do I get for that?"

Matty and Tony kept hugging their older brother as if he'd been gone for weeks. Brothers, Sam realized, always had a bond. No matter what.

Sam escaped, certain no one noticed. He staggered home with the snow stinging his face, the wind blowing his breath back into his mouth. His book was finished, he acknowledged, standing in the shower underneath the hot spray until his skin was red.

His book was finished and he could leave if he wanted to. And he wanted to.

He didn't think he was capable of love and loss and the terrifying aspects of being a father. And if he married Lucia, no matter where they lived, he *would* be a father. He would be a husband.

He just didn't think he was that courageous.

LUCIA WAITED THIRTY-SIX HOURS. She waited for the blizzard to end, for the sun to come out, for Hip to shovel a path from her driveway to her kitchen door. She waited for a phone call; she waited for Sam's knock on the door.

When she grew tired of waiting, she baked him a pie. She asked Mama, who had stayed at the house during the blizzard, to watch the boys while she delivered her thanks to Sam for rescuing her son.

He answered her knock and accepted the pie from her outstretched hands, but she noticed he didn't meet her gaze or offer to take her coat.

"I wanted to make sure you were all right, after the storm and…everything."

"I was coming over today," he said. "To say goodbye."

"Goodbye?" She said the word as if she didn't know what it meant. As if she couldn't quite process what Sam meant.

"I'm heading out," he said.

"Out," she echoed. She knew *that* word. He was walking *out* of her life. She was *out* of time. He was ripping her heart *out*. Ah.

She struggled to stick a bright smile on her face and deliberately kept her voice light and teasing. "One little blizzard and you're running back to the Amazon?"

He didn't smile. "It wouldn't have worked."

She didn't know what to say. It wasn't as if she hadn't thought the same thing.

"Us," he explained. "Wouldn't have worked."

"I get it," Lucia said. "Of course. In the long run, it just wasn't practical."

"Right."

"Well, then." She struggled for something to say. "When are you leaving?"

"Tomorrow."

"Tomorrow," she repeated, trying to absorb the fact that he was leaving, that she'd fallen in love with someone so totally wrong for her and she had been a fool to think otherwise, that he would stay and be a husband, a father, a lover.

"I wanted to say goodbye to the boys. If that's okay."

"Of course it is." *Of course it's okay to break their hearts, so go ahead, tell them that you're leaving, say goodbye.* "They'll miss you."

"I'll miss them."

"Hard to stay in one place, huh?"

He winced. "Something like that."

Lucia removed the pie from his hands. "I guess you won't have time to eat this, so I'll just take it back."

"Lucia," he said, but she turned toward the door and kept walking. "I'm sorry. I really am."

"I am, too. But I'm sure you wouldn't have been happy here," she said. She didn't care how sorry he was. He had let her suppose he was going to stay, he'd let her fall in love with him, he'd behaved like a man who loved *her*.

She'd actually believed it was possible to love again. She'd never forgive him for that.

FOR FOURTEEN DAYS Sam rented a room in a coastal motel, stared at the Gulf of Mexico and dreamed of snow. He tracked down his brother and left a message with a sultry female who promised to make sure he received it. Brothers, he'd learned from the Swallow boys, shared a special bond. Good or bad, they grew up in the same family. They had a history that no one else shared. Davey and his brothers would tell the blizzard story for many years to come, embellishing it perhaps, but entertaining their families with the frightening details.

He phoned Jerry and had a long conversation with him, then a shorter one with Owen.

He learned that Mrs. Beckett had died, leaving her considerable estate to the Willing Library fund. Her funeral service was respectfully attended by members of the town council, the Swallow family and a handful of curious neighbors.

He also learned that Davey had come in second in the Random Acts of Kindness contest. He'd donated his five dollar prize to the county animal shelter.

Sam lasted exactly two weeks before packing his bags.

"I WANT ONE," Lucia declared, snuggling a sleepy baby in her arms.

"Me, too." Meg gazed blissfully at little Laura as the infant struggled to keep her eyes open and failed. Her mother, having been up all night, was asleep on Lucia's couch.

"You know how to get one," Loralee said. "All you have to do is pick a date for the wedding."

"You took the words right out of my mouth," Mama said. "Look at us, four grown women cooing over that child."

"We do need more babies," Meg said,

touching Laura's tiny fingers. "Okay, I've picked a wedding month. April," she declared. "When there's little chance of snow."

"Really?" This was from Loralee, who pulled a pocket calendar out of her purse, flipped the pages and waved the month of April at her daughter. "Pick a day, any day, go ahead."

Meg turned to Lucia. "You're the matron of honor. Do you have any plans for April?"

"Not a thing," she replied. "I'm free."

Loralee shook her head. "I can't believe that handsome neighbor of yours went back to the jungle."

"And the dirty rivers," Mama clucked.

"With crocodiles!" This came from Tony, playing on the floor with his dinosaur truck and about a thousand plastic soldiers.

"I'm sorry," Meg said. "I didn't mean to bring it up."

"That's okay," Lucia said, dropping her voice so her youngest son wouldn't hear. "I'll get over it. I had my little fantasy there for a while, but it didn't work out. Heather is now renting the house next door and Sam is most likely on some expedition in South America, catching a giant fish."

"No, he's not," Shelly said, yawning. "He's standing right there at your front door."

Lucia whirled to see for herself at the same time as she heard the knock. Sure enough, Sam stood behind the glass panel. He wasn't smiling.

"Aren't you going to let him in?" Loralee didn't believe in leaving men standing out in the cold.

"Sam's back," Tony told his dinosaur. "Sam's back!"

"Hear what he has to say," said her mother-in-law. "Men can surprise you."

"Amen to that." Loralee handed Meg the calendar. "Go ahead. Circle something and we'll get to work while Lucia talks to the Fish Man."

Lucia handed the baby to Meg, who immediately dropped the calendar and cuddled Laura to her chest. Lucia rose from the couch and took her time walking to the door, all the while hoping she wouldn't let him know how hurt she was.

She needn't have worried, because Sam looked pretty bad himself. He stepped into the living room, opened his arms and pulled her against his chest. She heard him sigh, felt the tickle of his whiskers against her neck, and then she drew back so Tony could get his own hug.

"Come here," Mama said to the child. "Come sit on Grandma's lap for a minute."

"What are you doing here?"

Sam peered past her to the women gathered on the U-shaped couch. "Good morning. I'm sorry for interrupting. Congratulations, Shelly."

"Thanks."

"Maybe we should go," Meg suggested, but Mama and Loralee didn't budge. They might as well have been stapled to the sofa cushions.

"We're planning a wedding," Meg's mother stated. "You've got to strike while the iron is hot. Right, Marie?"

"Right." She eyed Sam sternly. "Take him into the kitchen, Lucia. Hear what he has to say."

"He can say it right here." Lucia watched Sam unzip his jacket. He unwound the striped scarf from around his neck and kicked off his boots. He tucked his gloves into his jacket pockets and draped it over the back of a dining-room chair. He seemed prepared to stay awhile, but she'd made that mistake before and it had cost her two weeks of heartache, embarrassment and pain, not to mention her children's sorrow at losing a man they'd grown to love.

"Could we, uh, do this somewhere else?"

"Heather's renting your house," Lucia told him. "You're out of luck if you think you can waltz back and—"

"I'm all set," he said, tugging her toward the kitchen. "Will you let me explain?"

"Let him explain, for heaven's sake," Meg urged. "He looks like he hasn't slept in a week."

"Thanks." He actually smiled, which was the last thing Lucia needed to see. She loved his smile.

"Come on," she said. "But this better be good."

"I hope so," he murmured. "Because after this I'm out of ideas."

"After what? And why are you back here?" He took her to the alcove by the back door.

"First thing," he said. "I'm sorry. I left because I was scared. Losing Davey that night was the worst thing that ever happened to me. All I wanted to do was get out of here so I never had to go through that again."

"Okay. I get that." She waited. "I don't want to ever go through that again, either."

"Second thing? I am in love with you. Totally, completely, hook, line and sinker." He smiled. "That's fish talk."

"Go on."

"I'd thought about you and the boys moving to Florida with me. Or to Costa Rica, as a family, you know?"

She knew. And moving away from her friends and Marie and her business made her stomach do a flip. But not in a good way.

"Third thing. The most important one." He looped his arms around her waist, held her in place while he spoke. "About five years ago I met a man on a plane. We were leaving Nicaragua one morning and he had the seat next to mine. He asked me where my home was, which I didn't answer, because I haven't stayed in one place since I was eighteen." Sam took a deep breath. "This is hard, Lucia."

"Go on." But she wasn't sure she wanted to hear this. Something warned her that this wasn't the same story he'd recounted last

December about how he happened to come to town.

"Someone told me his home was Willing, remember? I think I told you I never forgot that."

"But you never saw him here, did you?"

"I did." His hands tightened at her waist. "I saw his picture on the wall at the Dahl. In his uniform."

"Oh, my God. Tony."

"I didn't tell you before because I thought it would hurt you. And, I suppose, I didn't know what to make of it." He pulled her close again, and she went into his arms, rested her cheek against his chest while he stroked her hair.

"He loved coming home," Lucia said, swallowing tears.

"And I do, too," he whispered. "If you'll let me."

"But your work—"

"I've made enough money—and saved enough money—to do what I want."

"And how do I know you'll stay, that you won't get tired of us and leave?"

"Because we'll get married. I take that seriously, having never done it before. And I bought Paula Beckett's house. So even if you say no today, I'll be right next door, eating pie. I'll adopt a dog so the boys will have to visit every day. I'll buy lasagna from Marie and steal casseroles from your freezer."

"Seriously, Sam. What will you do here?"

"I've thought of writing a series of children's books," he said. "And we can take the boys on some incredible summer vacations." He looked into her eyes. "My heart is in your hands."

"Then it's safe," Lucia said, reaching to draw his head closer for a kiss. "And it's home."

* * * * *

LARGER-PRINT BOOKS!

GET 2 FREE LARGER-PRINT NOVELS PLUS 2 FREE MYSTERY GIFTS

Love Inspired

Larger-print novels are now available...

YES! Please send me 2 FREE LARGER-PRINT Love Inspired® novels and my 2 FREE mystery gifts (gifts are worth about $10). After receiving them, if I don't wish to receive any more books, I can return the shipping statement marked "cancel." If I don't cancel, I will receive 6 brand-new novels every month and be billed just $5.24 per book in the U.S. or $5.74 per book in Canada. That's a savings of at least 23% off the cover price. It's quite a bargain! Shipping and handling is just 50¢ per book in the U.S. and 75¢ per book in Canada.* I understand that accepting the 2 free books and gifts places me under no obligation to buy anything. I can always return a shipment and cancel at any time. Even if I never buy another book, the two free books and gifts are mine to keep forever.

122/322 IDN F49Y

Name	(PLEASE PRINT)	
Address		Apt. #
City	State/Prov.	Zip/Postal Code

Signature (if under 18, a parent or guardian must sign)

Mail to the Harlequin® Reader Service:
IN U.S.A.: P.O. Box 1867, Buffalo, NY 14240-1867
IN CANADA: P.O. Box 609, Fort Erie, Ontario L2A 5X3

**Are you a current subscriber to Love Inspired books and want to receive the larger-print edition?
Call 1-800-873-8635 or visit www.ReaderService.com.**

* Terms and prices subject to change without notice. Prices do not include applicable taxes. Sales tax applicable in N.Y. Canadian residents will be charged applicable taxes. Offer not valid in Quebec. This offer is limited to one order per household. Not valid for current subscribers to Love Inspired Larger-Print books. All orders subject to credit approval. Credit or debit balances in a customer's account(s) may be offset by any other outstanding balance owed by or to the customer. Please allow 4 to 6 weeks for delivery. Offer available while quantities last.

Your Privacy—The Harlequin® Reader Service is committed to protecting your privacy. Our Privacy Policy is available online at www.ReaderService.com or upon request from the Harlequin Reader Service.

We make a portion of our mailing list available to reputable third parties that offer products we believe may interest you. If you prefer that we not exchange your name with third parties, or if you wish to clarify or modify your communication preferences, please visit us at www.ReaderService.com/consumerschoice or write to us at Harlequin Reader Service Preference Service, P.O. Box 9062, Buffalo, NY 14269. Include your complete name and address.

LILPDIR13R

ReaderService.com

Manage your account online!

- Review your order history
- Manage your payments
- Update your address

> ### *We've designed the Harlequin® Reader Service website just for you.*

Enjoy all the features!

- Reader excerpts from any series
- Respond to mailings and special monthly offers
- Discover new series available to you
- Browse the Bonus Bucks catalog
- Share your feedback

Visit us at:
ReaderService.com

RS13